THE HONEYWOOD FILE

The Honeywood File

An Adventure in Building

H.B. Creswell

 ACADEMY CHICAGO PUBLISHERS

© 2000 Academy Chicago Publishers

Published in 2000 by
Academy Chicago Publishers
363 West Erie Street
Chicago, Illinois 60610

First published in 1929

Printed and bound in the U.S.A.

Library of Congress Cataloging-in-Publication Data

Creswell, H. B.
    The Honeywood File : an adventure in building / by H.B.
    Creswell.
        p.   cm.
    ISBN 0-89733-473-6
    1. Architectural practice—England—Fiction. I. Title.
PR6005.R55H66   2000
823'.912—dc21   99-10243
                                                 CIP

CONTENTS

To
C.B.
Q.A.G.
W.

PREFACE

Although *The Honeywood File* is designed to engage aspirants to architectural practice with lively presentment of the adventures that await them, a picture in which men and women rather than architects and builders occupy the canvas, and which is more concerned with the fabric of life than with the fabric of houses, will perhaps amuse those who have fallen under the spell of bricks and mortar or who are curious of the unexplored.

H.B.C.

THE FILE IS OPENED

The Honeywood File is to be read as an architect's correspondence file. It consists of a folder endorsed "Honeywood". Within it letters received and carbon copies of those sent out are clipped together in order of date. An actual file taken from an architect's office would, of course, convey little: it would be prolix; raise questions it did not answer and answer those it did not raise; give no clear impression of events and shadowy presentments, only, of persons; and it would be loaded with superfluities: in a word, it would be tedious and unintelligible.

Any file, therefore, which is to present to the reader such a clear picture of characters and events as it would awaken in the memory of the architect who conducted the correspondence, if he is imagined as perusing it months or years after it was closed, must be stripped of redundancies; subjected to selection and arrangement; given order and proportion and, in addition, the letters themselves must have a colour brighter than reality.

The Honeywood File is put forward as representing an actual file that has been reorganized in this way; but such reorganization does not necessarily involve a departure from verisimilitude. It may enhance verisimilitude, and this has been the author's endeavour; and as the whole value of, and much of the interest in *The Honeywood File* depends upon acceptance of the picture as a true one, he wishes to state that his chief concern has been to make it so.

He also wishes to state that before setting pen to paper he engaged with himself that all characters should be imaginary and all incidents fictitious. There was no virtue in keeping this engagement, for in no single instance was he impeded by the restriction, and only once or twice, when invented incidents awakened memories, was he reminded of it. Now that all is done he can affirm that, though some incidents are paralleled in his experience, none of the events are so; and that no character in the book is associated in his mind with any person alive or dead he has ever known or, for that matter, heard of or read about.

The Honeywood File was first opened when the author sat down before a blank sheet of paper, and James Spinlove, a complete stranger, announced himself at the point of the pen. Sir Leslie Brash, who was apparently standing next in queue in the unknown, then inked himself down; and his temperament and social level were settled at once and forever by a facile—and apparently meaningless—alliteration which fell on the paper to close a sentence. That fine fellow Grigblay, the graceless Potch, the humble Bloggs and the rest, all happened in the same way; and why they should be themselves and not others, or, being themselves, should think, act, and speak as they do, is beyond the author's comprehension. Where, he asks, have they all come from? The only answer to this question seems to be—the inkpot.

As with the characters, so, very much, with the events: the author has not generally known from one page to another, and often from one sentence to the next, what was going to happen nor how the cat would jump or an entanglement unravel. From week to week, keeping pace with serial publication in *The Architect's Journal*, the broken end of the last number was usually his sole incentive to the next.

Thus, no author ever posed as editor of his own lucubrations with a much better claim to indulgence than here. The detachment of this "editor's" commentary; his quickness to pounce upon and claw out on the carpet and publicly dismember everything that attracts his attention, and his eagerness to reprove or commend, are no elaborate affectations, but the reactions of an imperfect nature to personalities and events with whose creation he has had nothing to do.

To him, as has been said—and now to the reader—enters James Spinlove, the architect from whose hypothetical office *The Honeywood File* is supposed to derive. He proves to be an Associate of the Royal Institute of British Architects, which marks him as decently educated and technically well-equipped; and the indications are that he has been in practice half a decade, so that his years do not count much more nor much less than thirty. He has probably built various small houses, a village hall, and so forth. He employs an assistant and a boy clerk.

We open the file at the back—for each succeeding letter is, properly, filed on the top of the preceding one—and we find the following:

THE COMMISSION

FREDERICK DALBET TO JAMES SPINLOVE

Dear Jim,   15.1.24.

I accidentally ran into an old friend of my father's the other day.
He told me he had bought land in Kent with the idea of building
himself a house and was looking about for an architect. I told him
what an incompetent ass you are and of that house of yours which
is getting ready to fall down at Ightham, so he may write to you.
The name is Sir Leslie Brash (Knt. Bac.). He and my father were
lifelong friends, so take care of him. He is an expert economist and
financier; you can read of his crimes in *Who's Who*: recreations—
conger fishing and cursing; however, though peppery, he is a real
good sort, but you must mind your "p's" and "q's" with "dear Maude",
as my mother calls her. I have not seen her since she became her
ladyship, and shall be amused to see how she wears it. When are
we two going to meet?

Yours,

SIR LESLIE BRASH TO JAMES SPINLOVE

Dear Sir,   17.1.24.

I write on the introduction of Mr. Frederick Dalbet, from whom
you have, I anticipate, received intimation. I have purchased property at Thaddington, near Marlford, and am contemplating erect-
ing a residence upon it. The location to be occupied by the mansion I should request your advice upon. The fall of the ground I
apprehend to suggest a south-east aspect, but Lady Brash desires
the edifice to face in the opposite direction as there is a chimney—
a pumping station, if I am correctly informed—some two miles
distant on the S.W. which interferes with the prospect. These mat-

ters, however, Lady Brash and myself desire to discuss with you. I should be glad to be advised whether you would be prepared to act for me in the capacity of architect if we decide to proceed, or perhaps you will consider it advisable for me to get rid of the property and purchase another as I entirely failed to observe the chimney when I acquired it. In the event of your expressing willingness to act for me I will suggest an appropriate date when we may meet on the property.

Yours faithfully,

SPINLOVE TO BRASH

Dear Sir, 18.1.24.

I beg to thank you for your esteemed favour of the 17th inst., and it will give me great pleasure acting for your good self and meeting you on site as per your letter. I am free Tuesday and Thursday and every day the following week as advised at present if suitable to your convenience and will thank you to let me know *re* same.

Thanking you in anticipation,
Yours faithfully,
JAS. SPINLOVE.

This is terrible! Is it possible that Spinlove would sign himself "Jas.", and beg to thank and be ungrammatical and guilty of solecisms and prostrate himself like a shopkeeper? It is not likely, but it is in some degree possible and that is why I have, for this one occasion only, played off a practical joke on the reader.

This letter is not on the file but has been substituted by me in order to pillory a style of letter-writing which, because it is adopted in certain business circles, is supposed by some to be businesslike and to give an impression of efficiency. Needless to say, no diction is businesslike which is not lucid; and faulty grammar and the use of such expressions as "as per" and "re same", implies ignorance and not efficiency. An architect has to correspond with many different kinds of persons under a great variety of circumstances, and no letters are of greater importance than those addressed to his clients, where not only are lucidity, firmness, and self-control called for, but frankness, sincerity, tact, and—if he possesses that gift of the gods—charm. Spinlove will be likely enough to make mis-

takes: but he is a decently educated man and socially, if not in rank, Brash's equal. What Spinlove did, in fact, write, as recorded on his file, is as follows:

SPINLOVE TO BRASH

Dear Sir,   18.1.24.

I have to thank you for your letter of yesterday and to say that I shall be most glad to act for you in the matter you speak of. I can go with you to the site on any day next week, except Tuesday and Thursday; or on any day during the following week except Saturday if you will be so good as to name day and hour and place of meeting. From your description the site seems to be most attractive. I think that the chimney of which you speak may not prove such a serious annoyance as you now suppose.

Yours faithfully,

This is all right, but if the last three words had been "is now supposed", it would be happier. In formal correspondence it is well to avoid the personal "you". Spinlove, however, ought not to have referred to the chimney. I myself know nothing of what lies ahead—I had no idea of any chimney till Brash referred to it—but Spinlove ought to have divined that he will hear quite enough about this chimney without introducing the subject himself. The indications are that Spinlove is not socially astute. It is Lady Brash who objects to the chimney—and did not Spinlove's friend Dalbet, warn him of "dear Maude"? Spinlove will get into the lady's bad books if he does not take care. The arrangements seem to have been completed by telephone and Spinlove does not record and file telephone messages as he would do if his office organization was more thorough, for we next read:

SKETCHES AND ESTIMATES

SPINLOVE TO BRASH

Dear Sir Leslie Brash (*sic*),   25.1.24.

I have roughly worked out the dimensions of the house for the purpose of giving you an idea of the probable cost, as you asked. I enclose on a separate sheet a list of the rooms with approximate sizes following the instructions you gave me. Assuming that the house is built of brick with tiled roof, iron casements in oak frames, the stairs in oak, and reception rooms panelled in oak and with oak floors, and the whole house well, but not extravagantly, fitted and decorated, I think the figure you should have in mind is from twenty to thirty thousand pounds. This does not include entrance road, fencing, terrace, if any; nor, of course, laying out of garden, nor the cottages you spoke of. It does, however, include—as you will see— garage, stable, and kennels.

As I told you, I think the site an excellent one in every way. If you keep the house well up on the N.W. side, with entrance from the upper road and through the wood, you will be close to the highway, though screened from it. You will have an almost level approach, and the fall of the ground towards the S.W. will admit of readily forming a terrace and give the house a most attractive set- ting. The wood upon the N. and curving towards the East, will shelter the house and, as I pointed out to Lady Brash, will prevent the chimney being seen from any of the windows. I hope Lady Brash will be reconciled to the chimney as there are insuperable objections to placing the house in any other position, or setting it at any other angle than that fixed by the fall of the ground which, also, is the ideal for aspect and for prospect. The view is truly wonderful and I should not, I may say, have noticed the chimney if Lady Brash had not called my attention to it.

I will not take any further action until I hear from you.

Yours sincerely,

It would have been perhaps wiser if Spinlove had opened his letter "Dear Sir". We may assume that he was cordially greeted by the Brashes, that the common friendship with the Dalbet family thawed the ice and that the interview was intimate and not formal; but even had his client not been his senior in years and his superior in rank, Spinlove ought to have waited for him to initiate the more familiar address. Spinlove is also too garrulous: he is, of course, naturally enthusiastic at the splendour of the opportunity before him and is anxious to do himself justice and perhaps to make sure that Brash shall perceive what a discerning architect he has got; but a great part of his letter is clearly a repetition of what he has already said in conversation, and he ought to have more gumption than again to drag in the wretched chimney. He is in danger of taking a side in a matrimonial squabble, and, be it said, if he knew how his bread was buttered, probably the wrong one. It is to be hoped that his appearance and address will please. His letters certainly will not.

BRASH TO SPINLOVE

Dear Sir (*sic*),   30.1.24.

I am in receipt of your communication and am astounded at your estimated valuation. It is desirable I should finally intimate at once my conclusive inability to contemplate such a monstrously outrageous figure. May I be permitted to mention that though a matter of ten thousand pounds—the difference between the two estimated valuations you give—appears to you to be of no importance, such a sum is of considerable importance to me. My anticipated conception of the cost of the house is ten or twelve thousand pounds. If I consented to expend fourteen thousand on the mansion and garage, etc., that would be an outside maximum figure. I have, as you remind me, to provide for laying out garden, fencing, roads, etc. Then there is water supply, drainage, and electric light to be included in the anticipated total of cost. Have you considered these? Your suggestion that I should expend in all nearly forty thousand pounds is, if you will permit me to say so, preposterous. I must request you to reduce your prices very considerably, for I cannot consent to entertain proposals of such dimensions as those you formulate. I apprehend it is not necessary for me to indite a reply to other matters communicated in your letter, but I may mention that Lady Brash, who is temporarily residing in the neighbourhood, yesterday observed black smoke issuing from the chimney.

Yours faithfully,

We may feel sorry for Spinlove. He is not to blame and he did not deserve to be taken so heavily to task. Such things, however, frequently happen. Brash is disappointed; he is old enough to be Spinlove's father, and although he does not suppose, as many do, that an architect is a superior kind of builder who submits estimates and then builds, his ideas of the duties of an architect are evidently confused. Spinlove made a mistake in not asking Brash what he meant to spend, and he will not be likely to make that mistake again.

It will, however, be a long time before he has to ask the question, for it is usual for a private owner to bring forward, at the outset, a point so much on his mind as the cost of his project, and it is strange that Brash did not do so. No harm has, however, been done, for Brash has no intention of being unfair, and if Spinlove handles the matter wisely he will rise in Brash's confidence and esteem.

SPINLOVE TO BRASH

Dear Sir,   2.2.24.

I am sorry my letter caused you disappointment. That would not have happened had I known the sum you wished to spend, for I should then have cut the coat according to the cloth, as the saying is.

May I explain that, given certain materials and a style of building, the cost of a house is in the main determined by its size—by the measure of its cubic contents. On the enclosed sheet I give, approximately, the number and dimensions of the rooms of such a house as might be built for the fourteen thousand pounds you are prepared to lay out. You will see that the house is smaller and more plainly finished than was indicated in the original proposal. Central heating, drainage, water, and electric light services are, of course, included as before. I should mention that until a complete design has been worked out it is impossible to give you a close idea of cost; but if you will let me know what you want to spend I can scheme accordingly.

The round alternative figures I gave you were intended to cover uncertainty of the value of the decorations, fittings, and finishing you intended, which is a matter for you to decide and not for me. I need hardly say that I have no wish to persuade you to spend more than you want to spend. My hope is that I may be able to help you to lay out your money to the best advantage.

Yours faithfully,

Spinlove piqued and on the defensive is a more impressive person than Spinlove ecstatic and full of himself. He has answered Brash effectively. He has put him in the wrong and he has done it neatly, and with politeness and dignity.

BRASH TO SPINLOVE

Dear Sir,   6.2.24.

I am obliged for your letter of February 2nd. The dimensions of the apartments you indicate impress me as much too restricted. I am particularly disappointed in the dimensions of the reception rooms, and I desire at least three more bedrooms. You have included for only two bathrooms: a third is most imperative. I appreciate your theory of the dimensions of the house influencing the cost, but apprehend there must be an erroneous misconception and that a residence of the character you indicate could not possibly involve an expenditure of £14,000. If this is so I shall either have to disburse a larger sum or relinquish the ambition of building altogether. Lady Brash yesterday inspected a mansion that might, with suitable alterations, she thinks, accommodate us. Before arriving at a definite decision, however, I enclose a sketch depicting exactly the residence we anticipate we shall require. The arrangement will suit us admirably and if you will draw proper plans following my sketch we shall have something definitely depicted before us. I have not delineated the bedrooms; I leave that to you. I will also desire you to prepare some sort of a picture depicting the exterior view of the house; just a slight sketch will suffice—but Lady Brash par-

ticularly desires a *pretty* house. When the plans are drawn I comprehend that it will be admissible for you to indicate a more exactly
accurate estimate. You will perceive that the dimensions I have al-
located to the various apartments are in excess of those in your last
communication but less than was originally desired.

Believe me,

Yours truly,

P.S.—A friend of ours has recently purchased a charming bungalow on the South Coast, the walls of which are composed of
Brikko and the room covered with Slabbo. I have not viewed the
edifice myself, but Lady Brash informs me that it is extremely pretty
and that residences can be erected with these materials much more
inexpensively than with bricks and slates. It occurs to us that you
could considerably reduce your price by availing yourself of these
substances, and I also understand that their use makes it possible
for walls and roofs to exactly match in colour.

*It is to be noticed that Brash has climbed down. He evidently regrets
his previous asperity, and asks Spinlove to believe that he is his truly.
These sensitive tokens of the set of the wind are not to be ignored. It is a
frank and cordial letter; the lofty diction which prefers "recently purchased" to "just bought", and so forth, is the result of success supervening
on defective education, and has no significance.*

SPINLOVE TO BRASH

Dear Sir,   8.2.24.

Thank you for your letter enclosing sketch. I note your wishes,
but there are difficulties which will, I fear, prevent my giving effect
to them. For instance, it will scarcely be possible to attempt to make
any plan until the position of the house on the site, or at least its
aspect, is settled. I am also sorry to say that when your plan is drawn
out to scale—that is, when the various walls are arranged in the
positions fixed by the dimensions you give—the house will not
take the form you indicate, nor, indeed, any practicable form. For
example, the front is nearly one-third as long again as the back, so
that the gun-room, kitchens, etc., would form an inaccessible wing
and the passage marked "private corridor" would be outside the

building altogether. It is necessary, too, that all habitable rooms should have windows opening on to the outer air, and even w.c.s and larders must conform to this rule, which is enforceable by law and takes no account of the private tastes of the owner, so that the arrangements, adjoining the room marked "Den", will have to be completely remodelled. Also, I am afraid, it will be impossible to enter the house from the front door, except, of course, by going up the front stairs and down the back, which cannot be your intention. Up the back stairs and down the front is also the only way the servants can get to the door to answer the bell; moreover, the front stairs could be used to reach the bedrooms only by going out by the back door, or by one of the windows, and in at the front door. I mention these matters in order to make clear why it is impossible for me to adopt your plan, but I will make sketch designs for a house with a S.W. aspect which will give you the accommodation you show and provide, as nearly as may be, the areas you have fixed for the chief rooms.

I do not know either of the building materials you mention. There are a good many new patent materials which may be suitable for cheaply-built bungalows, but which could not be used in such a house as you intend. A uniform colour in walls and roof is a thing to be avoided rather than sought, and I think that the coincidence you refer to is accidental and due to callousness on the part of the builder. I shall hope to send you sketches in the course of the next ten days.

Believe me,

Yours truly,

This letter is a serious error of judgment. One might think that it was facetious and ironical, but the true explanation is, no doubt, that Mr. James Spinlove, A.R.I.B.A., has no sense of humour. He has regarded Brash's plan as a serious proposal; finds it a hopeless obstacle to all solutions of the problem and with enormous earnestness, sits down to explain why he cannot make use of it. Unfortunately, Brash's sense of humour—if he ever had any—is squashed flat under the dead weight of that self-importance which gained and supports his knighthood, so that the fat is probably in the fire. Spinlove is starting badly. I feel almost ashamed of him, for he is in a sense my protégé, and I had no idea he could be so foolish. All he had to do was to thank Brash for his plan in a cheery note and take it for what it was worth—namely, for the information it may give of Brash's needs and prejudices. Spinlove's design need not follow the other: he will have conclusive explanations for his deviations, but probably no questions will be asked. A client's plan expresses only nebulous ideas, and the vivid actuality of the architect's design usually drives it out of remembrance. Spinlove might have made things quite safe for himself by telling Brash, when thanking him for his plan, that he proposed to prepare one himself so that the two might be compared and the best points of each combined in the final scheme. Spinlove, however, did nothing so tactful.

BRASH TO SPINLOVE

Dear Sir,   9.2.24.

I apprehend that it is surely not necessary for me to elucidate that the very rough sketch I transmitted to you to inform you of the mansion I desire was not intended as a maturely conceived proposition. I comprehend very little of "prospect" and "aspect", and of what is "possible" and "impossible" for an architect, but I know the kind of residence I desire, and I consider that I have in various ways indicated my wishes with sufficiently lucid clearness.

The appropriate relative colours of the walls and roof of an edifice are, I consider, a matter of opinion and not of fact. I have not weighed the proposition and am amenable to guidance by your judgment, but I fail to comprehend why you should be so decisive in condemning buildings materials of which you admit you know nothing.

I await your sketches with interest,

Yours faithfully,

It will be noticed how much more dignified and effective Brash is when his native pepper rules. This letter shows him to be, as Dalbet described him, a real good sort. Spinlove ought to congratulate himself on getting off so lightly, and feel heartened to know the ingenuous nature of the man he has to deal with. I say ought to feel; but unawareness of his own stupidity and his lack of knowledge of men and affairs, have apparently caused this letter to throw him into consternation.

SPINLOVE TO BRASH

Dear Sir,   12.2.24.

You have, I entirely agree, given me the fullest particulars of your requirements, and my last letter was intended only to explain why the plans I am shortly sending you cannot follow the lines of the sketch you were so obliging as to give me, although they will, I trust and believe, fulfil its intentions. I very much regret that unfortunately I do not appear to have made this clear to you.

I ought also to have explained in commenting on "Brikko" and "Slabbo" that it is important, as I am sure you will agree, that the materials of which your house is built should be strong and that they should last. For this reason it is advisable to use in your house only materials which are known by experience to endure. Cheaply-built bungalows are in quite a different category, as I need, I think, scarcely point out.

The traditional association of bricks and tiles with the architecture of houses also makes it necessary to use bricks and tiles to give architectural character to your house. The substitution of unusual materials for such a purpose would create great difficulties in design, and the result would be certain to disappoint you greatly.

Yours faithfully,

It was not necessary for Spinlove to prostrate himself so completely, but the fault, if any, is on the right side. There is a respect due to years, and if Brash had any suspicion that Spinlove's offending letter was facetious he is now disabused. Brash does not appear to have replied, for we next find:

SPINLOVE TO BRASH

Dear Sir,   19.2.24.

I send you to-day under separate cover sketch plans and perspective view of the proposed house. The sizes of the rooms are figured, and I hope the arrangements will be clear to you. The small scale block-plan shows the position on the site. These drawings are intended only as preliminary sketches, but they will at least serve to reduce the problem to practical issues. To the best of my judgment the building shown will cost £19,500. I do not think that the cost need be higher, but I do not think it will be much less.

Yours faithfully,

These preliminary sketches, it is to be noticed, show a smaller house than Brash wants, do not follow his pet ideas of plan arrangement, and the estimate is 40 per cent more than he wants to spend. Brash also has in mind to give up the idea of building altogether and adapt an existing house. Spinlove, therefore, for whom this commission is a big opportunity, must feel considerable anxiety. Such positions frequently occur, anything may happen and no one could foretell what. A rise in stocks or a badly-cooked breakfast may settle the question one way or another. Apparently there was a rise in stocks.

BRASH TO SPINLOVE

Dear Mr. Spinlove,   21.2.24.

Lady Brash and myself are delighted with the plans of the house and with the charming picture delineating a view of the exterior. We are filled with admiration for the skilful ingenuity with which you have fitted everything in, and with the appropriate completeness of the arrangements. Lady Brash is particularly delighted with the cupboard in the recess in the kitchen passage and with the door shutting off the domestics' domain. There are certain insignificant matters which we desire altered: for instance, the entrance hall and staircase to be transferred farther along so as to leave an expanse of blank wall for the wisteria Lady Brash desires to plant in that situation, but these alterations I can elucidate when we meet.

The estimate of cost, is, I regret to intimate, a disappointment; I anticipated you would be able to reduce it after the plans were drawn out. I apprehend it will be requisite to minimize the expenditure, but we are so greatly enamoured with the design that I trust it may not be necessary to have recourse to material alterations. Would it be possible to omit the morning room and the two projecting bays for the present so that they could be eventually added at a later date?

Can you call at Zimmon Gardens at six on Wednesday to discuss matters? Lady Brash will be disengaged at that hour. Perhaps you would be so good as to telephone to the house.

Yours faithfully,

Spinlove is clearly competent, but he is no less clearly lucky. It was quite on the cards that his design might outrage some prejudice of his client of which he could know nothing, or that in exercising his discretion, he might seriously have missed the mark, or that the plans might have been misread. If any of these things had chanced, Brash's pepper might have made him impatient and, with the added discouragement of the estimate, led him to abandon the whole project, or to consult another architect. As it happens, Spinlove has made a complete conquest. His preliminary sketches have been swallowed whole, the design is practically settled, discrepancy of cost is in a fair way to being adjusted and, from being captious and critical, Brash has become enthusiastic and appreciative. The interview evidently took place, for the next letter is dated a fortnight later.

SPINLOVE TO BRASH

Dear Sir Leslie Brash,   9.3.24.

I enclose revised sketch plans which you will see embody the whole of the alternatives except the shifting of the entrance hall and staircase, which, as I expected, cannot be moved without entirely remodelling the plan and designing the house on altogether different lines. It is unfortunate that the position of the front door and the window do not give an opportunity of training a wisteria in that particular position, but all planning is a balance of advantages, and I am afraid this one will have to go.

By comparing the dimensions on the revised plan with those shown on the original sketches, which I also enclose, you will see the reductions I have been able to make, and that I have also saved what space could be spared in bathrooms, passages, and so on; but nothing has been unduly pinched. I have also reduced the heights of floors as arranged, and taking everything into consideration I think the cost will be reduced from £19,500 to £17,300. To this has to be added the cost of the terrace, £1,200, which it was agreed should be included with the house, making the new estimate £18,500.

Will you please tell Lady Brash that things are so arranged that the chimney will be visible from no windows except those of the kitchen offices, gun-room, and servants' bedrooms. If you will let me know that you approve I will prepare contract drawings and documents for the purpose of securing tenders.

Yours faithfully,

BRASH TO SPINLOVE

Dear Mr. Spinlove,   14.3.24.

We appreciate the plans extremely, although we are disappointed you cannot transfer the entrance hall and staircase. I am somewhat apprehensive at the reduction in the dimensions, and anticipate we may be spoiling the ship to save a pennyworth of tar. I have therefore augmented some of them. Also I desire you will not take any chance of risks of bathrooms and passages being restricted, or the rooms too low in height. In order to meet the cost of expenditure I have decided not to erect a garage, kennels, etc., at present. I shall perhaps make a temporary wooden structure suffice to begin with, particularly as it may be desirable to first build cottages for the male outdoor staff. The terrace should be included. Will you therefore proceed with the contract and inform me immediately when the operations will commence and how long a period they will take to complete.

Yours sincerely,

SPINLOVE TO BRASH

Dear Sir Leslie Brash,   17.3.24.

Thank you for your letter. I will get on with the contract drawings at once.

In reply to your question, all well, the building will start in about four months' time, and take about two years to complete.

I enclose list of seven builders I propose to invite to tender. Five, as you will see, are of London; the other two are provincial firms operating in the district. All are of good standing and known to me. If there is anyone else you would like included will you please let me know.

In order to save the cost of the builder finding his own water, I propose to have the well sunk at once. As we know we shall get plenty of water at about 130 ft. it will not be actually necessary to employ a consulting engineer, but I propose nevertheless to do so both on the ground of economy and efficiency. I suggest the name of Mr. P. F. Toodlewipe, A.M.I.C.E., who is known to me.

Yours sincerely,

BRASH TO SPINLOVE

Dear Mr. Spinlove,   22.3.24.

I was dumbfounded at your communication intimating an anticipated delay of four months. I am at a loss to comprehend why this should occur. Surely now that everything is settled arrangements can be agreed with a suitable builder? Also the length of time the work will take. Two years! We are completing arrangements to take up residence next summer. Surely the operations will be terminated in fifteen months from now! Can nothing be done to expedite progress?

Certainly do as you propose as regards the well.

There is a builder at Marlford—Nibnose & Rasper—whom you might append to your list, and also a most respectable man, Mr. John Reaker, at Thaddington, who did work for a considerable period on Lord Imagwire's estate, whom I desire should tender. I fancy his son carries on the business now in partnership with a person named Mr. Smith.

Yours sincerely,

SPINLOVE TO BRASH

Dear Sir Leslie Brash,   24.3.24.

I am afraid that four months from now is as soon as you can expect to see the builder at work. It will take me seven or eight weeks to work out the design in detail and prepare the necessary drawings and contract documents. The preparation of bills of quantities to enable builders to tender will probably take four weeks, the builder ought to have at least ten days in which to arrive at the figure of his tender, and a fortnight would be a short time in which to settle and sign the contract and for the builder to get his plant on to the site. It is true that the house might be built even in one year only, if a special point were made of it; but it would invite disaster to scramble through work of this kind, and it is doubtful if a really good builder would enter on such an undertaking. I will do all I can to expedite matters.

Thank you for names of builders. I will inquire about these firms.

Yours sincerely,

CATASTROPHE OF
THE TRIAL HOLES

SPINLOVE TO MESSRS. REAKER & SMITH, BUILDERS, THADDINGTON, KENT

Dear Sirs, 28.3.24.

I understand that you have done work for many years on Lord Imagwire's estate. I want some trial holes dug in the meadow south of Honeywood Spinney on the top of Honeywood Hill. The enclosed plan shows the ground and the position of the holes, which should be 8 ft. deep. If you can undertake this work I will ask you to put it in hand at once and give me notice so that I may go down and see the ground.

If you are accustomed to building large private houses will you tell me of some you have built and give me the names of two or three architects under whose direction you have worked?

Yours faithfully,

Spinlove seems to have forgotten that he is an agent of Sir Leslie Brash. In ordering this work without making clear that he acts as agent, he assumes responsibility and could, in fact, be made to pay for it.

The following letter seems to have found its way into the file instead of the wastepaper basket. It is a circular, with the name of addressee and subject added, printed by a firm which claims that its output is indistinguishable from autographs, and that it "brings business". The sort of work done by firms who depend upon this means of getting it, would not suit Spinlove, as no doubt he perfectly understands.

DOMO IDEALO LTD. TO
JAMES SPINLOVE, ESQ., A.R.I.B.A.

New House for Sir Leslie Brash

Dear Sir,   2.2.24.

As a practising Architect of eminence you will be aware that, however dainty and refined the architectural design of a domestic habitation may be, the two things which will count with your client are COMFORT and EFFICIENCY, and these we are prepared to absolutely guarantee with the minimum of trouble to yourself, as our large staff of experts are always at your valued disposal.

We understand that you are the architect for the above house, and shall be glad to prepare estimates at the shortest notice for Electric Light, Heating, Water Supply, Lifts, Sanitary Work, &c., also for Carving in any material, Ornamental Plaster, Lead, Iron, and Decorative Art-craft Guild Handiwork of all descriptions.

May we call your attention to our Ultra-Violet Ozone and Water-Softening installations, without which no daintily appointed modern gentleman's house can be considered complete. On receipt of a card or telephone message we will immediately arrange for one of our expert representatives to wait on you. Awaiting your esteemed favours.

We are dear Sir,

Yours faithfully

for DOMO IDEALO LTD.,

B. PIDGE,

Manager.

SPINLOVE TO NIBNOSE & RASPER, BUILDERS, MARLFORD, KENT

Dear Sirs,   28.3.24.

Your name has been given me as builders of large country houses. If you are willing to tender for such work in the neighbourhood of Marlford I should be glad to know of buildings carried out by you and to receive the names, as references, of architects under whose directions you have worked.

Yours faithfully,

SPINLOVE TO GEORGE BULLJOHN, ESQ., J.P.
THE HAVEN, BUXFORD, NR. MARLFORD

Dear Mr. Bulljohn,   28.3.24.

Do you know anything of Nibnose & Rasper, and of Reaker and Smith, Thaddington, builders, and can you tell me what sort of standing and reputation they have? I have not seen you at the club for ages, but I hear you are sometimes there.

Kindest regards,

Yours sincerely,

REAKER & SMITH TO SPINLOVE

Sir,   29.3.24.

Your esteemed favour of the 28th inst. to hand and shall have attention. Our man up Honeywood way will be through with his present job Tuesday and will get on with it. We are used to working along with an architect and have just completed additions to Wheatsheaf (Public) in Main Street under Mr. Pintail, F.A.I., of Station Yard, Marlford. Mr. Reaker is away from business at present so am shorthanded.

Awaiting further esteemed favours,

Yours to oblige,

NIBNOSE & RASPIER TO SPINLOVE

Dear Sir,   31.3.24.

We are obliged for your letter and enclose list of some works executed by us with the names of the architects concerned. Mr. Claude Lambwad, F.R.I.B.A., of South Moulton Street, W.1, knows us, as we have done work for him for many years. We shall be glad to tender for the work you mention and hope to receive particulars in due course.

Yours faithfully,

BULLJOHN TO SPINLOVE

Dear Spinlove,   2.4.24.

I would not recommend you to have dealings with Reaker and Smith. Old John Reaker was widely esteemed, but the son is of a very different stamp. I may tell you that he is at this time in prison for being drunk while in charge of a motor-car. Smith has only lately come on the scenes. I hear of him as a bookmaker. Nibnose & Rasper is a most respectable firm. Whether they are up to the standard you want is not for me to say. Hope to see you again soon.

Yours sincerely,

SPINLOVE TO REAKER & SMITH

Dear Sirs,   12.4.24.

I have been expecting to hear from you. Are the trial holes ready for me to see?

Yours faithfully,

SPINLOVE TO THE SAME

Dear Sirs,   16.4.24.

I wired to you this morning. "Have holes been dug, wire Spinlove", but have received no reply. I wrote to you on the 12th asking for this information. I must expect your immediate response by wire or telephone.

Yours faithfully,

BRASH TO SPINLOVE

Dear Mr. Spinlove,   16.4.24.

I enclose a communication I have received to-night from the farmer who is in charge of my daughter's mare, which is out at grass at Honeywood. My daughter is greatly distressed and I am also excessively annoyed and disappointed. I had no idea pits were being dug, but in any eventuality it was culpable negligence on someone's part that they were not protectively fenced. One can only be thankful that worse misfortune has not resulted. Immediate attention is necessary. I have wired to Bramble to employ a man to warn children.

Yours faithfully,

(ENCLOSURE) GEORGE BRAMBLE, COWKEEPER, TO BRASH

Sir,   15.4.24.

Your mare had an assidence up on Honeywood going on three legs near fore all tucked up and carried back very bad I never saw one that way and thorough crocked up and off feed I got her into float with rails under her and had to put on a twitch and a nice job she was a bit chafed under belly by rails but no harm and I got her slung comfortable now in cow stall and vet blistered her and tied up leg bad rench and sprained shoulder he says and dont quite know what to make there is a lot of narrow holes dug top of Honeywood I dont doubt she blundered and no wonder I did very near and deep water standing and children come in after cow slop flowers I druv off but you know what kids is and something had ought to be done or there might be a worser assidence awaiting your orders.

Yours obediently,

REAKER & SMITH TO SPINLOVE

Sir,   16.4.24.

Re wire duly to hand you did not prepay reply so write informing you same all finished twelve days ago as promised.

Awaiting further esteemed favours,

Yours to oblige,

SPINLOVE TO NIBNOSE & RASPER

Dear Sirs,   17.4.24.

I write to confirm arrangements made with Mr. Rasper on telephone this morning that you will secure stout covers over trial holes dug South of Honeywood Spinney and to thank you for your message this afternoon telling me this work has been completed. I am much obliged for the particular attention you have been so good as to give to this matter.

Yours faithfully,

SPINLOVE TO BRASH

Dear Sir Leslie Brash,   17.4.24.

I need not tell you how concerned I was at the contents of your letter. The holes were securely covered to-day. I telephoned a message to this effect both to your Office and to Zimmon Gardens. I ordered the holes to be dug for the purpose of determining what draining and foundations would be necessary, but the person I employed did not keep me informed, as I asked him, of what he was doing. He should of course have covered the holes. I am more sorry than I can say at this unfortunate accident. I sincerely hope the mare will completely recover.

Believe me,
Yours sincerely,

Spinlove has been "unlucky"; but if he had had the foresight to order the holes to be covered he would have escaped this "ill-luck". As matters stand, he has not only made himself responsible for paying the cost of the work, but also for vet.'s fees and, perhaps, for the value of an expensive horse. These sorts of dangers, anxieties, and miseries always attend on the employment of builders who are not competent and conscientious; and it is scarcely possible for any architect under the strictest contract conditions to get any kind of work rightly done unless the persons he employs possess those qualities, which, it may be added, are readily found among builders scattered over the length and breadth of the land. Spinlove asks for further trouble by writing the letter which is next on the file.

SPINLOVE TO REAKER & SMITH

Sirs,   17.4.24.

Your letter telling me the trial holes had been finished nearly a fortnight ago reached me only after I had learnt that a valuable horse belonging to the owner of the land had blundered on to one of them and been very badly injured. This as you will realize may be a serious matter for you. My instructions, which you acknowledged, were that I was to be informed directly the holes had been dug, but you neither did this nor replied to subsequent letters and telegram asking for information. Your omission to protect the holes is almost criminal. Children have been seen in the field and the pits are now half filled with water which will have to be pumped out before the bottoms can be seen. Your conduct of this matter in not completing the work and leaving me in ignorance of what was being done is inexcusable.

Yours faithfully,

The probable explanation of this tactless letter is that Spinlove feels he is in some degree responsible and seeks to defend himself by making clear to Reaker and Smith that he holds them liable. What he has, in fact, done is to warn those gentlemen and arm them against him: he has told them his side of the case. If he had merely complained that the holes were left uncovered and that he had not been notified, the ingenious Smith, always hoping for further esteemed favours, would probably have expressed regret for the omission and pleaded a misunderstanding and thus have admitted liability.

BRASH TO SPINLOVE

Dear Mr. Spinlove,   17.4.24.

I note that the holes have now been rendered secure. I apprehend, however, that it is due to myself for me to say that your extreme promptness in getting the covers fitted leaves me at a loss to comprehend why they have been supplied only after the harm is done, instead of previously. I do not consider that it was incumbent on me to direct your attention to this matter in anticipation. I extremely regret to intimate that I have a very bad account of the mare from the veterinary surgeon who is attending her.

Yours truly,

SPINLOVE TO BRASH

Dear Sir Leslie Brash,   19.4.24.

I am very sorry you have so bad an account of your mare. It was of course the clear duty of the builder who dug the holes to protect them, and in employing for this work a firm, Messrs. Reaker and Smith, which had been especially recommended by you as reliable people, I felt that they might be trusted and that your interests would be protected. I did not know that the mare was in the field when the holes were dug so that the need for covering them was perhaps not obvious.

Yours sincerely,

Spinlove appears to be losing his head.

REAKER & SMITH TO SPINLOVE

Sir,   19.4.24.

Yours to hand and *re* same beg to state no instructions to cover holes were given and we do work we are asked and not work we are not asked and not paid for doing or where would we be, and a nice thing to be told by an architect I must say. I am about attending to my work and no time to waste writing letters and telegrams. I said I would do the job as soon as ever the man cleared up and I done what I said and no one has any cause to complain, and if anyone goes and does a silly thing like putting a horse in a field with a lot of pit-falls to catch him well thats no fault of mine but the fault of them that ordered the pit-falls and put the horse in on top of them and if you are not satisfied I respectfully ask you to settle my account (enclo.) and we will say no more about it.

Soliciting your further esteemed favours,

Yours to oblige,

Spinlove probably considers this letter extremely rude, and is much annoyed; but in point of fact the writer has no intention of being offensive or even disrespectful. He feels, reasonably enough, that he is being got at: he has no arts to hide his indignation and simply states his views. Spinlove invited such a letter and also an inflated bill. It is wise, particularly in dealing with a firm such as Reaker and Smith, to avoid rupture until the account has been delivered. Spinlove shows himself altogether too stiff in the neck in his reply. The bald address "Sirs" instead of "Dear Sirs", is inappropriate unless used in formal official correspondence on which the applicable subscription is "I am, Sir, your obedient Servant", or where, as in Smith's case, the writer feels that "Dear Sir" trespasses on familiarity. Twenty years ago things were perhaps different, but broadly speaking, no British subject has any right to address another in the tone of frigid, contemptuous resentment Spinlove adopts; and if he does so he will rightly suffer.

SPINLOVE TO REAKER & SMITH

Sirs,   22.4.24.

I have received your letter and need only say in reply that your view of the facts is untenable.

The amount of your account, returned herewith, is excessive and out of all reason. When the total has been substantially reduced and is supported by a detailed measured or day-work statement with vouchers I will consider it. The account is to be made out to Sir Leslie Brash, Zimmon Gardens, S.W.3, and not to me.

Yours faithfully,

BRASH TO SPINLOVE

Dear Mr. Spinlove,   22.4.24.

In view of the trend of your communication, and although I am of opinion that your organization should have prevented the accident, I consider it desirable that I should intimate to you that as I have not hitherto put the blame for the damage to my daughter's mare upon you it was not necessary for you to seek to defend yourself by fixing the responsibility on my shoulders. If, however, it had been necessary, permit me to indicate that in one sentence you asseverate it was the clear duty of the builder to cover the holes, and in the next but one that the obligation to do so did not eventuate.

I suggest to you that this subject should now be permitted to terminate, but I feel it desirable to remind you that I was not previously informed that pits were being dug and that no instructions were given to protectively cover them until after the neglect to do so had involved me—as I regret to fear—in the loss of a valuable hunter; and also to elucidate to you that I regard the proper carrying out of instructions—and not merely the appropriate issuing of them—as the duty of all persons I employ whether as architects or in other capacities. I shall be obliged if you will intimate to me that you accept this interpretation of your obligations.

Believe me,

Yours sincerely,

The stately creature! It is a devastating but not an unfriendly letter. On the contrary, it is evident that Brash likes Spinlove and respects his

capacities. Such a letter could only be written, and tolerated, when ad-
dressed to a man young in years and experience by one mature in both.
We may also imagine that Spinlove's personality is frank and boyish,
and that this and his youth perhaps serve him well at this juncture; for
Brash has ample grounds for feeling extremely annoyed and dissatisfied
with his architect, and if that architect were not amenable to this kind of
discipline, his employer might well decide to be quit of him before worse
disasters overtake his house-building adventure. Spinlove ought to have
let Brash know that the pits were being dug; he ought to have employed
a builder whom he knew to be of good standing, and he ought to have
ordered the holes to be covered. If he had taken one only of these proper
precautions all might have been well.

SPINLOVE TO BRASH

Dear Sir Leslie Brash,   24.4.24.

I can only thank you for your letter and say that I accept your
view of my obligations, fully and without reserve. Permit me, however, in justification of myself to say that I had no intention of
"putting the responsibility on your shoulders", but wished only to
explain how it was that I did not take the necessary precautions.

Yours sincerely,

This justification of himself by Spinlove is a lame business. He has
already said: (1) that it was the clear duty of the builder to protect the
holes; (2) that the obligation to do so scarcely arose; (3) that responsibil-
ity lies with Brash, since the builder was employed on his recommenda-
tion; and now (4) he acknowledges that he himself did not take the pre-
cautions which he admits to have been "necessary". Spinlove's "case"—as
the lawyers call it— would not have been a bad one had he held his
tongue, but he has gone far to make it hopeless. However, there is not,
apparently, going to be any "case" unless Reaker and Smith take action.
Spinlove would, this time, be right in deeming the letter which follows
to be a rude one. Mr. Smith intends to be saucy and mildly sarcastic.
Spinlove could only expect some such reply to his letter from such a man,
and deserves no sympathy.

REAKER & SMITH TO SPINLOVE

Sir,   24.4.24.

Yours to hand, but unfortunately we have your letters to prove it so I am afraid it will come a bit thin for Mr. James Spinlove, Esq., P.R.I.B.A., R.A., K.C.B. The account must be made out to Sir Leslie Brash, must it? Well it's not, nor yet to Dempsey nor Madame Tussaud. It is going to be made out the same as it is made out to the fellow who ordered the work and has got to pay for it.

No my lord; we humbly regret account (enclo.) is not going to be substantially reduced nor yet reduced at all and have not got clerks to waste time copying out the men's day sheets, so will thank you to send cheque per return as work has now been completed four weeks.

Yours to oblige,

SPINLOVE TO SNARTY BOLT & CO.

Dear Sirs,   25.4.24.

I should be glad if you would make an appointment for your representative to call and see me here on the subject of a heating lay-out.

Yours faithfully,

There are letters of a similar kind to various other contracting specialists from which we may deduce that Spinlove is up to his chin in the contract drawings.

SPINLOVE TO BRASH

Dear Sir Leslie Brash,   28.4.24.

Reaker and Smith have sent me their account for digging trial holes, £37 2s. 6d. This, in my opinion, is nearly twice as much as the work is worth. They also ask for immediate payment, have refused to make any reduction, and refused also to give details showing how the charge is arrived at. I think they feel they have put themselves in our black books and have nothing more to lose, and that they mean to make the most of the claim. They have written in such terms that I cannot continue negotiations. I should mention that after I had entrusted them with this work I made confidential inquiries, and had a very bad account of both Mr. Reaker and Mr. Smith. I am afraid it will be necessary to let your solicitors take charge of the matter. I know of no circumstances that could justify any such claim.

I enclose Messrs. Nibnose & Rasper's account for covering the holes and pumping out water so that the bottoms could be seen. I think £4 5s. a moderate charge for this work.

Yours sincerely,

It is most unfortunate that Spinlove should bring solicitors on the scenes at this early stage and in such a trivial matter. With his enormous advantage in education and social standing, he should have no difficulty in coming to terms with Smith if he swallowed his humiliation, taught himself to be amused at Smith's letter, and realized that he should not have written that to which it is a reply. It is, however, a failing of our friend Spinlove to be inordinately stiff in the neck, and, as we have already observed, his sense of humour is far to seek. If he approached Smith with diplomatic overtures designed to save his own bacon he might well fail; but if he sincerely tried to do the man justice by putting himself in his place and regarding him as a human being reacting to vanity and self-preservation in the same way as himself, the thing would probably be settled in ten minutes, leaving good feeling instead of bitterness on both sides. Whether such action is in this case worthwhile is, however, another matter. It would probably best fit Spinlove's idea and serve his ends if he sent Smith say, £25, with a gesture signifying he could go to the devil, and later on charged Brash fifteen or twenty as a disbursement. That, however, is not Spinlove's way of handling the matter. I respect Spinlove, but that does not prevent my observing him to be a devoted ass. He has no lightness of touch. He goes boring down into the dregs of every misery. We may see Brash squirming in his chair as he writes his reply, which is in autograph.

BRASH TO SPINLOVE

Dear Mr. Spinlove,   30.4.24.

I consider that I have been involved in a sufficiently excessive expenditure over these wretched trial holes (the mare was shot yesterday) without being defrauded by overcharges. It is unfortunate that you did not ascertain the character of the firm *before* you employed them instead of *after*. I certainly have no intention of submitting to the extortion of these people, and if, as you intimate, their charge is preposterous—and it certainly seems outrageous to me—and, for some reason I do not understand, you are unable to negotiate with them, I apprehend my solicitors must take up the matter and I will instruct them to communicate with you. It is regrettable that at the very first outset, and in such a small matter, I should be involved in so many annoyances and vexations.

Yours truly,

SPINLOVE TO BRASH

Dear Sir Leslie Brash,   2.5.24.

I am more sorry than I can say to hear of the loss of your mare and for my unlucky part in the matter. I made inquiries of the standing of Reaker and Smith for the purpose of finding out whether they were suitable people to invite to tender, as you suggested they should do. It did not occur to me, after your recommendation, that they were not to be trusted to dig the trial holes. Messrs. Russ, Topper, Mainprice, Cornish and MacFee rang up to-day—I mean the firm did—and I have made an appointment to see them with correspondence, etc., on Wednesday at 2.30.

Yours sincerely,

There is a hiatus of six weeks. Drawing-boards and T-squares have been well employed, we gather, during that time.

PREPARATION FOR TENDERS

SPINLOVE TO BEDDY & TINGE, QUANTITY SURVEYORS

Dear Sirs,   14.6.24.

As arranged with Mr. Tinge I send you contract drawings Nos. 1 to 6 inclusive, and six sheets of rough $\frac{1}{2}$ in. and other details. I also send draft specification. The drawings have not been traced and will be completed, as usual, after the quantities are taken off. Will you please, as usual, complete specification to agree exactly with the bills. I shall be glad to see you and settle any matters not made clear.

Will you also be so good as to make a preliminary estimate of cost and let me know the figure?

I understood from Mr. Tinge that you could have the bills ready in four or five weeks' time. Will you please confirm this?

Yours truly,

Spinlove's arrangements are good. He has evidently "been there before". He secures that the bills shall include for no more and no less than he intends, and that the drawings and specifications shall show or describe the position of work measured. If particular care is not taken in these matters, work may be shown in the bills the position of which is not determined in the specifications—e.g. dowels—with the result that it is not included in the building, although paid for, or, on the other hand, the architect may intend a certain class of work and the bills not cover for it. He is wise to get an estimate before the bills are prepared and to let Beddy and Tinge know that time is an object. Quantity surveyors commonly work against time, and the architect who does not make a point of date of delivery will be likely to have to wait on those who do.

The next letter has been duplicated to seven firms of builders by Spinlove.

SPINLOVE TO VARIOUS BUILDERS

Dear Sirs, 14.6.24.

I shall be glad to know whether you will be willing to tender for a brick mansion, fourteen bedrooms, on a site at Thaddington, near Marlford.

In the event of your being willing to do so you may expect to receive bills of quantities and form of tender in about five weeks' time.

Yours faithfully,

Spinlove's object in writing thus is to secure that the firms he wishes to tender will be prepared to take up the work of pricing the bills when the time comes. If bills are sent out without such warning there is a chance that some builders may be so busy as to be unable to prepare a competitive tender within the time allotted. A builder will always send in a tender, because he feels that not to do so will prejudice his chance of being invited on a future occasion; but unless he has an opportunity of giving close attention to the business, his tender will be no serious bid and of no use to Spinlove nor to anyone else.

To save himself the trouble of arriving at a figure which will be too high for acceptance and yet presentable as a tender, he will, if opportunity serves, obtain such a figure from another builder who is making a bona fide offer.

RUSS & CO., SOLICITORS, TO SPINLOVE

Brash v. Reaker and Smith

Dear Sir, 16.6.24.

Messrs. Reaker and Smith have now offered to accept the sum of twenty-seven pounds (£27. 0. 0.) in full settlement of their account. We think the matter should be so agreed and propose to advise Sir Leslie Brash to that effect unless you have any objections to raise.

Yours faithfully,

SPINLOVE TO RUSS & CO., SOLICITORS

Brash v. Reaker & Smith

Dear Sirs,   17.6.24.

In reply to your letter I cannot agree that £27 0. 0. is a reasonable charge for digging the trial holes. I have referred the measurements to my quantity surveyor, who estimates £23 10s. 0d. as an outside figure.

Yours faithfully,

Spinlove's tenacity is worthy of a better cause. He is evidently soured against Smith and cannot endure that he should get more than strict measure.

BRASH TO SPINLOVE

Dear Mr. Spinlove,   20.6.24.

I have a communication from Mr. Russ intimating that Reaker and Smith are prepared to settle for £27, and as I am given to understand your own estimate is £23 10s., I have instructed him to signify acceptance of that offer. Will you oblige me with the sketch plans? You may remember that I intimated this request some time ago and you promised to transmit them. They have not, however, so far eventuated.

Yours sincerely,

Spinlove's reluctance to return the sketch plans is perhaps the wisdom of the once bitten. The contract drawings can only be made after the sketch plans have been approved, and the reopening of questions already settled, which ruminations over the sketch plans by the client is apt to provoke, is a disaster.

BEDDY & TINGE, QUANTITY SURVEYORS, TO SPINLOVE

Dear Sir,   20.6.24.

Drawings and specifications received and instructions noted. We cube front house at 2s. 8d., and offices and servants' quarters at 2s. 0d. The terrace will cost about £1,500. Total £20,140. We will endeavour to have bills ready in five weeks' time.

Yours faithfully,

B. and T. it will be noted, waste no words. Their speciality is facts. There here follow letters from all seven builders signifying readiness to tender. Then we find:

SPINLOVE TO BRASH

Dear Sir Leslie Brash,   21.6.24.

I enclose the sketch plans with apologies for not having sent them before. The drawings and specification are with the quantity surveyors and the tender forms will go out in five weeks' time. All builders have agreed to tender.

I note that you are proposing to settle Reaker and Smith's account for £27, but I should mention that my estimate of £23 10s. is an *outside* figure. My idea of the proper charge is £19 15s.

Yours sincerely,

What object Spinlove had in writing the last paragraph Spinlove himself could scarcely say. His grudge against Smith is probably accountable. Our James has the rattle-brained pertinacity of a blue-bottle, and his victim will feel the same wild, helpless irritation. The matter of the trial holes is well over and Spinlove should be thankful it is so. The whole history is a first-rate example, in miniature, of the way in which unlucky chances, favoured by faulty organization and lack of conscientious foresight, may lead from insignificant causes to disastrous catastrophes. If the owner's liability in this matter had been a thousand or ten thousand pounds instead of a hundred, we may be sure the architect would not have been left scatheless.

SPINLOVE TO BEDDY & TINGE

Dear Sirs,   23.6.24.

I am sorry your estimate is so high. The owner expects £18,500, and I am anxious not to disappoint him. I must try and knock off £1,500. On enclosed sheet I have made a list of suggestions to this end, and I shall be glad to go into the matter further with you.

Yours truly,

Spinlove's wisdom in getting down to estimates before the quantities are taken off is now proved. It is a sad business to have to cut down costs after tenders are in, with attendant supplementary bills and specifica-

tions, and notes in red ink on the drawings and other elements of confu-sion and future misunderstanding.

BEDDY & TINGE TO SPINLOVE

Dear Sir,   19.7.24.

Receive herewith copy of bills and form of tender sent to-day to seven builders as instructed. Also drawings and specifications com-pleted with notes of modifications agreed.

Yours truly,

LADY BRASH TO SPINLOVE

Dear Mr. Spinlove,   29.7.24.

I met an acquaintance to-day who told me that the kitchen win-dow ought to be on the left side of the range for the light and architects always put it on the other side but I want mine to be on the right side. What lovely weather we are having!! Sir Leslie is fishing in Cornwall till next week.

Yours sincerely,

SPINLOVE TO LADY BRASH

Dear Lady Brash,   30.7.24.

Thank you for your letter. You will be glad to know that the kitchen window *does* come on the right side. Yes, the weather, as you say, has been beautiful, but I am sorry to notice that it is cloud-ing over this morning. I hope Sir Leslie will enjoy his visit to Cornwall. I know of no part of the country where I would rather spend a holiday.

Yours sincerely,

Spinlove knows how to purr loudly, but there was an ambiguity in Lady Brash's letter which he appears to have overlooked. However, here are the tenders at last.

THE TENDERS GO WRONG

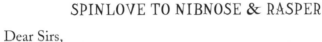

SPINLOVE TO NIBNOSE & RASPER

Dear Sirs,   1.8.24.

I have to thank you for your tender for £18,221, and to say that I am prepared to recommend it for acceptance. You may expect to hear from me in a day or two.

Complete list of Tenders received is as follows:

	£	s.	d.	
Carloop Building Co	25,000	0	0	18 months
Bintoch Bros.	24,000	10	9	18 months
Paul & Kirsh, Ltd.	21,050	0	0	18 months
Toller, Bunsen & Topp	19,500	0	0	18 months
George Robble	19,237	15	0	2 years
John Grigblay	18,970	0	0	16 months
Nibnose & Rasper	18,221	7	8	20 months

Yours faithfully,

Omitting the first two, which are not bona fide *tenders, but mere formal compliances, these tenders are a fairly close group except for the big difference of £750 between the lowest and that next it, where small differences only are to be expected. It seems that Spinlove has not realized the significance of this disparity.*

The following letter is marked as having been sent to all unsuccessful firms.

SPINLOVE TO UNSUCCESSFUL BUILDERS

Dear Sir,   1.8.24.

I have to thank you for your tender, but regret I am unable to recommend it for acceptance. The complete list of tenders received is as follows: [*List as above.*]

Yours faithfully,

Spinlove is right in notifying results to all firms as it is important to builders, for many reasons, to know at once what their obligations are. It would have been better, however, had he omitted the names of firms from the list, for as he will be likely to invite them to tender on a future occasion, he is opening the door to collusion.

SPINLOVE TO BRASH

Dear Sir Leslie Brash,   1.8.24.

I opened tenders to-day, and enclose list. I am glad to feel that the result will be satisfactory to you. You will see that Nibnose & Rasper's price is well within the figure I named. I recommend the acceptance of this tender. Twenty months is a reasonable time for carrying out the work.

I am sorry John Grigblay is not the lowest for he has a reputation for this kind of work, but I have good accounts of Nibnose & Rasper from architects for whom they have done work, and I was favourably impressed when I called at their premises one day when I was in Marlford. Have I your authority to accept their tender?

Yours sincerely,

BRASH TO SPINLOVE

Dear Mr. Spinlove,   2.8.24.

I am deeply gratified at the contents of your letter intimating the result of the tenders. It is, I can assure you, a great satisfaction to Lady Brash and myself after waiting so long a period to know that the estimate is not to be exceeded. Most certainly act upon your recommendation and accept Messrs. Nibnose & Rasper's tender, but only on the express stipulation that they complete the work within the period of sixteen months, for, as another firm undertakes to perform the erection within that limit of time, there is no excuse for Messrs Nibnose & Rasper not entering upon a similar engagement. I anticipate that there will be certain legal Contract documents for signature.

Since I am in credit on the tender in the sum of £300, I contemplate augmenting the dimensions of the reception rooms which I still consider somewhat restricted in area. I will determine these and communicate particulars in the course of a few days. The erection of the mansion will, I assume, now commence immediately.

Yours sincerely,

As it is impossible to know whether Spinlove first read this letter or the telegram that is filed next it, it is impossible to imagine his feelings on that second day of August 1924. We shall be safe, however, in giving him our sympathy.

(TELEGRAM) NIBNOSE & RASPER TO SPINLOVE

2.8.24.

Regret must withdraw tender writing Nibrasp.

NIBNOSE & RASPER TO SPINLOVE

Dear Sir,   2.8.24.

We much regret we were obliged to wire to you to-day withdrawing our tender, as per enclosed confirmation. On receipt of your letter, for which we thank you, we noticed the large difference between the amount of our tender and the next lowest price, and on checking over our prices we found an error of several hundred pounds. We may say that such a thing has not happened in our experience, and was due to an irregularity in the bills. The tiler's bill is paged 1, 2, 3, 2, 3, 4, and the clerk in collecting the castings of each page to arrive at the total did not observe the repetition of pages 2 and 3, and omitted two pages, which was not noticed in the check as they were stuck together by a blot of ink.

The correct total of our pricings is £18,953 4s. 7d., and we shall be obliged if you will substitute this figure for that entered on our tender, as the mistake arose through error in the particulars supplied to us, and although we would have corrected it had we noticed, we feel that we were led into the error which would not have occurred had the bills been correctly paged.

We shall be glad to send the bills to you or to your quantity surveyor for examination so that our statement may be checked.

Yours obediently,

Spinlove has again been unlucky, but his ill-luck is again attributable to his lack of perspicacity. He should have noted the incongruity of Nibnose & Rasper's tender, told them that before recommending their tender the priced bills were to be sent to the quantity surveyor for examination; and said nothing of the other tenders received.

The state of affairs now is that as Nibnose & Rasper know the amount of the tender they have to beat, they can increase their bid to one very little less than the next one above. This, it appears, is what they may actually have done. Bills are usually priced out in pencil and the rates could be readily reviewed and amended to give a more judicious total. Opinions would differ on the point whether, in the matter of business, this would be a dishonest act. The old-established building firms, in which the pride and tradition of craftsmanship still linger, are, with scarcely an exception, honourable and fair-dealing; but the field of business is very much a field of battle and has its own code, and when one side surprises a weakness in the defences of the other, it can only be assumed, in the course of business, that use will be made of that advantage. This revised tender is, however, a new tender; and as it has not been delivered before the hour fixed for the receipt of tenders it is, strictly speaking, inadmissible. On the other hand, the error in the original tender arose from irregularity in the particulars supplied and "Nibrasp" is entitled to some consideration.

Spinlove, also, has notified Grigblay and others that their tenders are not accepted, and any or all of them may have other irons hot in the fire or have given the go-by to options and quotations upon which their tenders were based, and thus will be unwilling to renew their tenders except at an increased price; and as each now knows who his rivals are, all can get together and arrange a lowest tender in collusion, so that the devices to secure bona fide *competitive tenders are now, in a great measure, stultified. It should be understood that this kind of collusion is not illegal.*

Another aspect of the case is whether Spinlove's notification to "Nibrasp" that he had recommended their tender for acceptance, constitutes actual acceptance, and therefore debars "Nibrasp" from withdrawing; but as the tender relieves the proprietor from obligation to "accept

*the lowest or any tender" we may assume the tender has not been ac-
cepted and that the "Nibrasp" withdrawal is good. In any case it would
be a foolish policy to compel him to build at a price which was known to
be disastrous for him: a house is not a sewer or a gasometer, and the
ready collaboration of the builder is necessary for its success. Spinlove's
predicament is, therefore, an awkward one; and he has also the painful
duty of swallowing his own complacency and deflating the exuberances
he has roused in the bosom of his client.*

SPINLOVE TO BRASH

Dear Sir Leslie Brash,   4.8.24.

I am extremely sorry to have to tell you that with your letter of
Saturday I found a telegram from Nibnose & Rasper withdrawing
their tender; and this morning I have received a letter from them
stating that they made a mistake in casting up their total, and substituting a tender of £18.953 4s. 7d. Such a thing is quite new in
my experience. This revised tender is only £27 less than Grigblay's
and I am very sorry to say, more than my estimate has prepared you
for. I should mention, however, that the tenders include the sum of
£300 for contingencies— that is a sum to cover unforeseen work
which may, only, be wanted—so that the actual tender for the work
can be considered to be £18,653 4s. 7d., which is only £153 4s. 4d.
more than my own estimate. I am extremely sorry this has happened and am much disappointed. Perhaps it would be well if I
saw you to-morrow. I can come over at any hour that suits you if
you would be so good as to ring up and let me know.

Yours sincerely,

*As Spinlove was before far too self-congratulatory, so he is here alto-
gether too apologetic. Although the uninitiated may suppose that an architect, by looking at the plan of a house, can name the lowest sum for
which unknown builders on an unknown day and under unknown conditions will bargain to build it, Spinlove's estimate of £18,500 was, in
fact, not so wide of the mark as such estimates go. He was probably too
ready to hope for the best in arranging modifications with the quantity
surveyor, but he is less than 2½ per cent below the tendered price. Brash
has nothing to complain of, and Spinlove should not, as he does, invite
him to think that he has. Spinlove ought to have found an early oppor-*

tunity of letting Brash understand that an architect can, at best, make only a shrewd guess at the cost of a building; and that even builders, with exact particulars before them of the measured amount of labour and materials involved in the work, arrive at results varying by 20 and even 30 per cent and, when all is done, often find themselves on the wrong side of the account. Spinlove, although his earnestness is exemplary, is worrying and wearying himself to no useful purpose by identifying himself so closely with his client's monetary anxieties. He should regard himself strictly as an agent conducting another's business; his own particular business being to get the house well, economically, and beautifully built. He should have written in some such terms as these: "Dear Sir Leslie Brash—Nibnose & Rasper have withdrawn their tender on the grounds of an error in their calculations, and have substituted an amended tender for £18,953 4s. 7d. Will you let me know what you wish me to do. Perhaps it would be better if I saw you. . . ."

If he had so written he would have exonerated instead of blamed himself, and put the plain question before Brash instead of confounding him with a confusion of issues. Such a letter, it is true, would appear to Brash curt and offhand in contrast with those he is used to receiving from his architect, and is to be regarded as the sort of letter Spinlove ought to be able to write without appearing curt and offhand. The meeting, we gather, duly took place, for we next read:

SPINLOVE TO WILLIAM WYCHETE, ESQ., P.P.R.I.B.A.

Dear Mr. Wychete,   5.8.24.

You have been so kind in letting me ask your advice that I hope you will not mind my writing to you, as I am in a fix. On the enclosed sheet I have set out the position of affairs. The question is what ought I to do? Sir Leslie Brash, my client, is fixed in his decision to accept the second lowest tender, that of John Grigblay, because Grigblay is the better builder. He says he has the right to accept any tender, and he can do what he likes. I can make no impression on him. If you could tell me what line I ought to take I should be very much obliged to you.

Yours sincerely,

WYCHETE TO SPINLOVE

My dear Spinlove,   7.8.24.

Your scrape interests me. Your client is morally bound to accept the lowest tender: that is clearly understood when particular builders are invited to tender, for if their tenders are not wanted there is no just reason for troubling them to prepare them. You can do no more than tell your friend this. He is, however, within his rights in not accepting the lowest or any, although this right is intended only as a safeguard.

I do not think Nibnose & Rasper's revised tender is admissible. It was sent in after the amounts of the other tenders were published, and for all we know their actual prices may originally have been *higher* than Grigblay's. If you accept it, Grigblay would have grounds for feeling aggrieved. You could write to N. & R. and say that as they withdrew their original tender their substituted tender is a new tender and was received too late for you to consider it; but I think the best course would be to tell them that the owner has instructed you to say that he cannot accept. Grigblay will certainly come to terms; you will have secured a good builder; will be free of responsibility for the choice, and relieved of the necessity for deciding a difficult point and finding reasons for your decision. You ought to be glad your client has taken the matter into his own hands.

Best Wishes from,
Yours sincerely,

SPINLOVE TO BRASH

Dear Sir Leslie Brash,   8.8.24.

I saw Mr. Grigblay to-day. He is willing to renew his tender, and I am meeting him to-morrow at the quantity surveyor's to see what reductions can be made in the matters I proposed to you. I will write to you to-morrow or call in the afternoon.

Yours sincerely,

SPINLOVE TO NIBNOSE & RASPER

Dear Sirs,   8.8.24.

I am instructed by the owner, Sir Leslie Brash, to thank you for your tender of August 2, but to say that he regrets he is unable to accept it.

Yours faithfully,

NIBNOSE & RASPER TO SPINLOVE

Dear Sir,   9.8.24.

We were naturally astonished to get your letter informing us that our tender is not accepted. We may say that we are unused to being treated in that style and we are quite as capable of making a good job as Grigblay or any other on your list. If we had known our tender was only going to be made use of as a check upon the prices of other firms we should not have accepted your invitation, and we may say that we are not anxious to tender again with any such purpose. We do not know what the meaning of all this business is nor why Grigblay is given a preference over us when we were invited to tender and our firm was well known long before Mr. Grigblay came on the scenes, but we may say that we consider that we have been treated in a very offhand and inconsiderate manner.

Yours obediently,

SPINLOVE TO NIBNOSE & RASPER

Dear Sirs,   11.8.24.

Permit me to assure you that in inviting you to tender I did so with the intention that you should be given the contract if you offered the lowest price. The decision not to accept your tender did not originate with me nor did I favour it. I can only say that I regret very much what has happened, and that I hope you will tender to me in the future and be successful in securing the contract, for I should have confidence in entrusting work to you. Believe me,

Yours truly,

Spinlove is distinguishing himself. Wychete's advice has been well observed by him. Without it he would characteristically have elaborated the matter of the substituted tender and involved himself in a wrangle.

As it is, he has written a letter which is obviously sincere and which will go far to soothe the "Nibrasp" chagrin— although not so fully, it appears, as to produce an acknowledgment—and he has not, for once, said too much.

SPINLOVE TO BRASH

Dear Sir Leslie Brash,   11.8.24.

I send you herewith memorandum of agreement in duplicate signed by Grigblay. If you will sign both with witness where marked and return to me I will let Grigblay have his copy and get yours stamped. I enclose copy of the schedule of variations you saw, showing the reductions by which the total of £18,440 is arrived at.

Grigblay signed drawings and specification to-day. He will begin getting his plant on the site on Wednesday and on Friday I am going on to the site. Can you come down on that day and approve the marks fixing the position of the house?

Yours sincerely,

GRIGBLAY, AND BRASH, GET TO WORK

SPINLOVE TO EWART HOOCHKOFT & CO., LTD.

Dear Sirs,   15.8.24.

I shall be glad if you will send me two or three samples, with prices, of your medium, red, broken-coloured, $2\frac{1}{2}$ in. sand-faced slop facing bricks such as I saw at last year's Building Trades' Exhibition. The samples should show extremes of variety in colour, texture, etc.

Yours faithfully,

GRIGBLAY TO SPINLOVE

Dear Sir,   22.8.24.

Our foreman, Bloggs, who is setting out house, has informed us that dimensions on plan do not work out correct. Shall be glad if you will give immediate instructions so that we can get on with the digging.

Yours faithfully,

We are to gather that Brash duly approved the position of the house on the ground, and that the builder has since been engaged in setting out the position of walls preparatory to laying their foundations.

Grigblay may be a good builder and a competent organizer, but he appears from this letter to be a man who means to get the job carried through and no nonsense about it. Spinlove would be justified in feeling a little uneasy. A really first-rate builder would be likely to show solicitude and say what the difficulty in question was. Grigblay may have had unfortunate experience at the hands of architects in the past and, having met Spinlove, may have sized him up. He does not intend to put up with flabbiness. As a successful builder he knows his job and he ex-pects the architect to know his.

BRASH TO SPINLOVE

Dear Mr. Spinlove,   23.8.24.

Lady Brash and myself have been considering the plans and have decided, after mature reflection, that we desire the drawing-room inverted the other way round—that is, turned at an angle of 90 deg. to its present orientation. There is still time to make the emendation, and as the dimensions will remain the same there will be no inflation in the expenditure. The alteration would permit the loggia to extend the whole extent of the length of the apartment instead of across its width, and it would then be possible for my daughter to play ping-pong there on wet afternoons.

Will you please instruct the builder accordingly.

Yours sincerely,

The foregoing letter evidently crossed the following one from Spinlove, as the dates are the same.

SPINLOVE TO BRASH

Dear Sir Leslie Brash,   23.8.24.

I think I ought to warn you of extras. Everything necessary for the completion of the building, with fittings and decorations, is included in the contract, and I can promise that there shall be no extras so far as I am concerned; but if you make changes in the work it will be impossible for me to avoid them creeping in.

Another matter I ought to mention is the importance of your making any request through me and never on any occasion saying anything to the builder's people that can be interpreted as an order; otherwise it will be impossible for me to keep control and extras are sure to arise.

I mention these matters because I am most anxious to avoid extras, and I can only do so with your co-operation.

Yours faithfully,

All Spinlove says is perfectly true, and he might have drawn a har-rowing picture of the confusion, disasters, cross-purposes, and ill-temper that interferences by the owner produce. At the same time it is most unusual for the architect to give the matter the weight of a formal warning that has almost the character of a threat. Spinlove might with better diplomacy have explained the point in conversation and perhaps confirmed in a brief sentence when writing. The hint is usually welcomed by the client, and observed. The letter which follows is one such as Spinlove ought to have written, but apparently did not.

SPINLOVE TO GRIGBLAY

(Supposititious)

Dear Sir,   23.8.24.

I write to remind you that the contract lays down that no claim for any extras shall rank unless that claim is made at the time the work is ordered and acknowledged by me as an extra.

I, on my part, agree to notify you of any omissions as the work proceeds.

Yours faithfully,

The object of this letter would be to make the builder understand that the stipulation in the contract as to extras must be observed. There are always some variations, and it is understood that omissions are set against extras unless the contrary is recorded at the time; and if the builder is to notify the architect of extras for which he claims payment it is only fair that the architect should similarly notify the builder of omissions in respect of which he claims credits.

Builders are shy of claiming extras while the work is in progress; to do so has an appearance of refractoriness. If, however, work is done which the architect knows *to have been an extra, he is bound in honour to allow it to rank in the final statement of account, and the fact that that extra was not claimed and acknowledged at the time it was ordered, and that it has, nevertheless, been allowed, makes the architect a party to the irregularity and opens the door for the builder to claim other unrecorded extras.*

As the architect has acquiesced in the one case it is very difficult for him to refuse to consider other claims on their merits. The result is that the stipulations of the contract are stultified, and the statement of account becomes not a plain question of fact, but of argument and wrangling of which the builder always has the best, for he has kept records of extras whilst the omissions, which might be set against them, have been forgotten.

For this reason it is well for the architect to notify the builder of extra work involved in his details, as well as of omissions. The builder has then no grounds for making claims at settlement which have not been agreed, and if he does so the architect can, with perfect fairness, refuse to consider them.

Our friend Spinlove, however, seems to have other ways of safeguarding extras. We shall perhaps see later on what his methods are and how far they succeed.

SPINLOVE TO GRIGBLAY

Dear Sir,   23.8.24.

I am at a loss to understand your foreman's difficulty. The dimensions on the plan were all checked up, and as you do not say what the discrepancy is I am unable to arrange matters. It is impossible for me to go on to the site until next Tuesday. Will you please wire to your foreman and ask him what it is he wants to know?

Yours faithfully,

BRASH TO SPINLOVE

Dear Mr. Spinlove,   25.8.24.

I can assure you that I am the last person to order extras of any description, and you may place reliance in my refraining from doing so.

I note that you desire all communications with the builder should be transmitted through yourself. This may, I apprehend, prove somewhat an inconvenient arrangement, but I commend your purpose and will keep it in mind.

Yours sincerely,

SPINLOVE TO BRASH

Dear Sir Leslie Brash,   25.8.24.

Your letter was a shock to me because the alterations you propose involve a radical change in the design, a new set of contract drawings and, I am afraid, a supplementary bill of quantities to determine the amount of the variation in cost, if any.

There are many objections and difficulties in the way of your proposal, and you will notice that it would not be possible to get from the hall to the drawing-room without turning the stairs round and making them begin on the other side of the hall. This would involve making other modifications in the plans and spoil the effect aimed at and which I have, I think, been fortunate in achieving.

I may also point out to you that the pump-house chimney would, as a result of the alteration, be visible from the end of the drawing-room and from the bedroom over, as the trees will not screen it from that point of view.

The alterations would also hold up the work for many weeks and, all being well, the digging for foundations may be expected to begin in a few days. I hope, therefore, you will reconsider your suggestion.

I am sure, when you are aware of all that is involved in the change, you will prefer to leave things as they are. I will take no further action till I hear from you.

Yours sincerely,

Spinlove's adroitness in himself making profit out of the pump house chimney is a master stroke. There is some advantage after all in having no sense of humour, for no one who had any would have dared such impudence.

SPINLOVE TO HOOCHKOFT

Dear Sirs, 26.8.24.

I like the samples of the bricks and the price is satisfactory. The very light-coloured brick seems soft and under-burnt, the red and purple brindled bricks will give all the variation in colour necessary. I have directed the builder, Mr. John Grigblay, to place the order with you.

Yours faithfully,

SPINLOVE TO GRIGBLAY

Dear Sir,   26.8.24.

Please order from Messrs. Hoochkoft & Co., facings of their multi-broken coloured red 2½ in. sand-faced slops to sample already approved by me, price 147s. per 1,000 on rail.

Yours faithfully,

Spinlove is looking well after his bricks, but it would have been wise, as he does not know them and has not ordered from a merchant known to him, to have seen the bricks in bulk at the brickyard.

GRIGBLAY TO SPINLOVE

Dear Sir,   27.8.24.

I enclose letter received from foreman Bloggs to-day. Shall be glad of instructions.

Yours faithfully,

(ENCLOSURE) BLOGGS TO GRIGBLAY

Sir,   26.8.24.

In reply to your wire *re* dimensions along main back front is figured 138 ft. 10 in., total of dimensions 138 ft. 6¼ in., error + 3¾ in. Where am I going to make it? Drawing-room right for window and fireplace cannot find where + is.

Yours humbly,

SPINLOVE TO GRIGBLAY

Dear Sir,   28.8.24.

In reply to your letter enclosing your foreman's note, the discrepancy will work itself out. I really do not understand why this trivial matter has been given such importance and progress delayed.

Yours faithfully,

Spinlove's experience must, indeed, be limited for him to write such a letter as this. He ought to be the first to know that the dimensions on a plan, like a bank ledger, must balance. Any error may be the difference

*between greater errors, but in any case errors of $3\frac{3}{4}$ in. do not readily
"work themselves out". $3\frac{3}{4}$ in. off the width of a narrow backstair makes
all the difference between one that is narrow and one that is too narrow.
$3\frac{3}{4}$ in. cannot be spared off a doorway, and the want of $3\frac{3}{4}$ in. may entail
omission of a window, and single inches in the width of a moulding
may mar the design of an important feature.*

*In the next place Spinlove is discouraging the builder from precision
in observing instructions, whereas he ought to take every opportunity to
make the builder understand that exact precision and minute conscien-
tiousness are expected of him. It would suit the builder to go ahead and
settle things for himself, and this letter will encourage him to shrug his
shoulders and do so. It is, further, the special duty of the builder, under
the terms of the contract, to call attention to all discrepancies, and it is
folly on Spinlove's part to deter him.*

BRASH TO SPINLOVE

Dear Mr. Spinlove,   29.8.24.

I am at a loss to comprehend what the difficulties are in altering
the plan, but as it appears to involve bringing the pump-house
chimney into visuality, Lady Brash has decided against the proposition. As you know, we greatly admire the plans; we observe, however, that the kitchen window is on the right-hand of the range.
Lady Brash informs me that you intimated you would have it located on the other side. I must ask you not to overlook this important matter—it is merely necessary, you will perceive, to put the
fireplace at the reverse end of the kitchen.

Yours sincerely,

SPINLOVE TO BRASH

Dear Sir Leslie Brash,   30.8.24.

I have looked at Lady Brash's letter to which you refer and find
that it asks that the kitchen window should be arranged on the
right side of the range, and this is what is shown on the plans.

I am very glad you have decided not to go on with the alteration
to the drawing-room. I may point out—

*Spinlove, with his fatal instinct for saying a great deal too much,
here goes on to elaborate a number of reasons why it would be impossible*

or objectionable to put the drawing-room "the other way round". He even goes so far as to say "perhaps your daughter may not care so much for ping-pong by the time the house is finished". This is not only entirely unnecessary, but will be extremely irritating for Brash to be troubled to read, and as Spinlove is already engaged in another tussle with Brash on the subject of plan alterations, it is unfortunate he should write a letter that will only stiffen the obstinacy of the man he wishes to placate.

BRASH TO SPINLOVE

Dear Mr. Spinlove,   1.9.24.

I deeply regret that I must venture to differ from you in considering that the right-hand side of the range is the right side for the window. The left is the correct side for perfectly obvious reasons, although architects, as I am informed, always put the window on the right-hand side. Lady Brash wishes the window on the left, which is the right side, and I must request you to make the necessary emendation, which, as I have intimated to you, can be done by merely shifting the range to the other end of the apartment.

Yours sincerely,

SPINLOVE TO BRASH

Dear Sir Leslie Brash,   3.9.24.

I have again read Lady Brash's letter and find that in one place the term "right side" is used in the sense of correct side, but I read it to mean the right-*hand* side.

It is quite true that it is best for the window to be on the left hand of the range, but this cannot always be managed without sacrificing more important considerations. If the range is put at the opposite end of the kitchen, as you suggest, the door from servery will have to be moved farther down the passage and the scullery and larder will be remote from the range instead of close at hand.

The range in the new position will require a chimney stack all to itself, and this will go very awkwardly in the external view of the house; and although the back bedroom can have its fireplace moved to the stack at its other end, the small bedroom will have no fireplace at all unless the stack for the present range is carried up for this purpose only. If so, you will have two chimneys each carrying only one flue, and unless they are extravagantly built they will be weedy and unsightly.

As now arranged, the kitchen has two large windows in the long side, and, as the walls and ceiling are to be painted with white enamel, the place will be flooded with light and there will be no shadows at the range. This I can promise you.

The plan provides for a very short course from kitchen to servery, and everything is compact and falls together well. It would, I assure you, be a great mistake to make the changes you propose and you would certainly regret it. Any such alterations will involve delay, and I hope to get the work on the trenches well forward by the end of the week. Unless, therefore, I hear from you to the contrary, I shall assume that the range is to be as shown on the plan.

Yours faithfully,

The last sentence assumes too much and is wanting in tact. It would be likely to provoke opposition. It would have been wiser if Spinlove had expressed himself as hoping he would be allowed to build according to the plan.

SPINLOVE TO GRIGBLAY

Dear Sir,   3.9.24.

When I was on the site yesterday I instructed your foreman to amend his adjustment of the error in the dimensions. In looking further into the matter, however, I find that I must alter the instructions I then gave him. The enclosed plan shows the dimensions to be followed. Please change the figures on your plan accordingly.

There seems to be a certain amount of surface water about the site and I shall be glad if you will arrange to pump out the trenches.

Yours faithfully,

Spinlove, it will be seen, is muddling along. He has discovered that the small error of $3\frac{3}{4}$ in. is not such an unimportant matter as he supposed. However, although he has had to give three contradictory orders in order to get matters put right, we may assume that he has definitely settled the matter at last and will not have to devise some ugly botch later on.

He has no right to call upon the builder to instal pumps. All he can do is to require the builder to keep the trenches free from water. It may suit the builder better to drain, as it is a sloping site; or perhaps to bail out from sumps may meet the case.

BRASH TO SPINLOVE

Dear Mr. Spinlove,   4.9.24.

I must request you to emendate the arrangements so that windows come on the left-hand side of the range. I do not object to the small bedroom having no fireplace.

Yours sincerely,

This is thoroughly bad judgment on Brash's part. Spinlove ought to have been able to persuade him to a right decision and it is probably entirely due to his irritating methods that he has not succeeded in doing so. Perhaps, too, Lady Brash is fretful. The unhappy Spinlove, however, with characteristic tenacity, does not admit defeat.

SPINLOVE TO BRASH

Dear Sir Leslie Brash,   5.9.24.

I was very sorry to read the contents of your letter. I think I ought to see you before altering the plans. I will ring up to-morrow if you will be so good as to leave word what time will suit you.

Yours faithfully,

GRIGBLAY TO SPINLOVE

Dear Sir,   5.9.24.

Revision of set-out figures received. We have told Bloggs to get on with digging. We will see trenches are kept clear of water; the site seems dry enough.

Yours faithfully,

The following letter indicates that Spinlove's last resort to persuade Brash to accept his kitchen arrangements was useless. It also supplies an instance of how an architect may be too ready to find alterations in his plans impracticable.

No doubt Spinlove had thoroughly explored alternatives, and it was only the torment of being compelled to revise his cherished schemes which led him to find that he had overlooked one possibility. This sometimes happens, and it also sometimes happens that the revised scheme is an improvement on the original arrangement. One gathers that it may be so in this case.

SPINLOVE TO BRASH

Dear Sir Leslie Brash,   8.9.24.

Since I saw you I have spent some time on the revision of the plan and I am glad to say that I have hit on an arrangement which meets the case excellently, as I think you will agree. I enclose sketch. You will see that by rearranging scullery, servery and den, etc., the kitchen can be lighted from the east instead of from the north, which I think an improvement; and that the length of the corridor to the back door, now a little nearer to the north front, is shortened. The bedroom arrangements, you will see, are improved, as both bedrooms have an east window, and you will note that one chimney stack serves all.

This chimney stack comes to place well on the ridge of the roof of the small gable formed by the projection of the den on the south, and this small gable makes an attractive feature on the south elevation.

Yours faithfully,

Spinlove, as usual, is fulsome in pointing out the beauty of his own devices and scarcely leaves Brash any opportunity for discovering any merits in them. He is, in fact, challenging Brash to make objections; but his very frank surrender, which is perfectly sincere and born of his wish to give Brash what it is best for him to have, will be likely to establish him more firmly in favour. Brash, we have noted, has been of late more than usually portentous and stiff, and not without reason.

BRASH TO SPINLOVE

Dear Mr. Spinlove,   10.9.24.

Both Lady Brash and myself entirely approve of the amended plan as the window is shown on the left of the range. Will you please instruct the builder to make the emendations?

May we have the pleasure of expecting you at lunch at 1.30 on Saturday? There are several matters which Lady Brash and myself would like to discuss with you.

Yours sincerely,

THE DISTRICT SURVEYOR INTERVENES

GRIGBLAY TO SPINLOVE

Dear Sir,   16.9.24.

Bloggs reports that Mr. Potch, the rural district council surveyor, called on site and took great exception to work being begun before plans approved. Shall be glad if you will communicate or he may make things awkward.

Yours obediently,

SPINLOVE TO SURVEYOR, MARLFORD DISTRICT COUNCIL

Dear Sir,   17.9.24.

It has been reported to me that you visited the site of the new house at Honeywood and commented on the trenches having been cut out before approval of plans. Please accept my apologies for the oversight.

May I point out that it is more than six weeks since I submitted plans and application form, but that I have heard nothing from you, although I have twice written calling your attention to the matter.

Yours faithfully,

BRASH TO SPINLOVE

Dear Mr. Spinlove,   17.9.24.

We were motoring in the vicinity of Marlford to-day and diverged on to the site. Both Lady Brash and myself were dumbfounded at the limited extent of the dimensions of the rooms as indicated by the trenches. We comprehended that the dimensions were restricted, but what we observed to-day alarmed us. Are you quite sure that the trenches are correct? The foreman assured us that they were exact, but have they been checked and certified? I cannot comprehend how these inconsiderable squares and oblongs can represent the apartments in which we have to reside. Please communicate by telephone between 2.30 and 3 at the office.

Yours sincerely,

The Brashes have suffered the usual shock with which the owner of a house views its plan entrenched on the ground.. The adequate dining-room of 22 ft. x 16 ft. appears before him as but a plot of grass four paces by six—for the width of the trenches eats up a foot or two along each wall—and nothing but a tape measure will establish his peace of mind. Spinlove no doubt poured assurances into the telephone next day.

SURVEYOR, R.D.C., TO SPINLOVE

Sir,   19.9.24.

In reply to your letter my council takes strong objection to the high-handed action of beginning operations in contravention of by-laws before plans have been approved.

I would recommend you to attend the next meeting of the Plans Committee which is at 8 o'clock at Marlford School House on Tuesday next, to make your explanation of your irregular behaviour.

Any work you may have done will be at your own risk.

The members of my council need holidays, the same as others do, and there have been no meetings of the Plans Committee since July 28, as you could have learned if you had troubled to inquire.

Yours faithfully,

V. POTCH.

The explanation of this extraordinary letter is that Marlford is a small provincial town with its own local architects, surveyors, auctioneers, agents and traders; and these men hob-nob together and play into each others' hands and are jealous of any who do not belong to the place taking money out of it. We have also seen that Nibnose & Rasper, who belong to the place, have a grievance against Spinlove which, in such a community, would become general knowledge; and if neither member of the firm is on the council their friends are sure to be.

It is also possible that Mr. Potch practises privately as an architect independently of his official duties, and that it is in his interest to make things difficult for all architects who trespass upon his local preserves, so that it may be generally perceived that any who employ Potch as their architect will have no trouble with interference by the district council, but that if they employ anyone else they probably will have. Potch's proposal that Spinlove should attend at Marlford at 8 p.m. is part of his system of inflicting annoyances upon his rivals. If Spinlove was so foolish as to act on the suggestion the surveyor would perhaps forget to mention that he was in waiting, or persuade his committee to decline to see him.

Mr. Potch has impudently ignored a fact of which Spinlove appears to be ignorant, namely that the Public Health Act ordains that approval or disapproval of intended work shall be signified by a local authority within one month of the deposit of plans.

SPINLOVE TO CLERK, MARLFORD R.D.C.

Sir,   20.9.24.

I enclose copy of my letter to your council's surveyor and of his reply, and shall be obliged if you will ask your council for an explanation of that reply.

I do not propose to attend the meeting of your Plans Committee on Tuesday.

I have to point out that I complied with your by-laws in submitting application form and plans nearly eight weeks ago, and that if I am called upon to stop the work your council will have to accept responsibility for breaking the contract.

Yours faithfully,

Spinlove has, apparently, "been there before". He wisely addresses himself to the clerk: he could scarcely reply to Potch's letter, and if he did so the council would probably never see the correspondence, but would have only the surveyor's hostile report.

THE CLERK, MARLFORD R.D.C., TO SPINLOVE

Dear Sir,   24.9.24.

Your letter and enclosures were laid before the Plans Committee on Tuesday and the surveyor was instructed to write you.

My committee instructs me to say that the dates of their meetings are fixed to suit general convenience and can be obtained on application, and that they have instructed the surveyor to stop work being commenced before approval of plans as much trouble is caused.

Yours faithfully,

POTCH TO SPINLOVE

Sir,   24.9.24.

I have to inform you that the Plans Committee of my council are prepared to recommend plans of Honeywood subject to alterations, see below. Plans and form returned under separate cover.

Attic to have vertical height at wall 5 ft. 6 in., and average height of ceiling over floor area of 9 ft. 6 in.

Window area to be not less than one-tenth floor area.

Independent vent, as per by-laws.

Walls of house to be increased in thickness down to ground to comply with by-laws for house of three floors.

Yours faithfully,

SPINLOVE TO POTCH

Sir,   25.9.24.

There is no attic. The third floor is roof space and is clearly marked *boxroom*.

I return plans and application form and shall be glad to receive notice of approval.

Yours faithfully,

POTCH TO SPINLOVE

Sir,   27.9.24.

I am obliged to you for pointing out that an attic occupies roof space. Unfortunately, my committee are not in the habit of regarding habitable attic rooms as roof space because the architect calls them boxrooms on the plans.

The plans and application form herewith.

Yours faithfully,

SPINLOVE TO POTCH

Sir, 29.9.24.

I have amended plans by writing *"roof space"* instead of "boxroom", as you ask. The concrete will be laid in trenches immediately. Plans and form are returned herewith.

The parcel containing your letter and the plans was not stamped. I enclose the label with excess stamp and shall be glad to receive refund of 1s. 6d.

Yours faithfully,

Potch's quibbling attempt to force Spinlove to alter his drawing, and his neglect to stamp the parcel, are all part of his method of obstructing and bullying those who, in his private practice, he regards as rivals. If he could infuriate Spinlove into some indiscreet act of protest or retaliation which could be adversely commented on at the council meeting and reported in the local paper, which loyally supports local interest, Potch would consider his trouble well rewarded.

One cannot but commend the characteristic tenacity of Spinlove as exhibited in his letter that follows.

SPINLOVE TO CLERK, MARLFORD R.D.C.

Dear Sir, 6.10.24.

A week ago I had to ask your surveyor to refund 1s. 6d. excess postage paid by me on parcel of plans sent unstamped. I enclosed label showing the excess stamp. I have had no reply except a form of approval of plans. I shall be glad to receive the money.

Yours faithfully,

CLERK, MARLFORD R.D.C., TO SPINLOVE

Dear Sir, 8.10.24.

In reply to your letter, Mr. Potch states that you did not enclose excess stamp, and also states that postage on parcel is recorded in his stamp book. It appears, therefore, that there must be some mistake or else the stamps came off in the post.

Yours faithfully,

SPINLOVE TO BULLJOHN

Dear Mr. Bulljohn,   9.10.24.

I know you to be a local magnate and I am writing to ask your help in what seems to me to be a public scandal, for if I submit to the obstructions of the Marlford Council I may get into serious difficulties in the building of this house at Honeywood.

I enclose copies of correspondence with the clerk and surveyor. I pinned the excess stamp on to the letter myself. I have no doubt the parcel was intentionally posted without stamps just as the reply to my request for refund was purposely ignored.

You will notice also the tone of the other letters. If this sort of thing goes on I shall have to make a strong protest to the council, but probably a word to the right person will act as a warning.

I am informed by the builder that Mr. Potch is notorious, and that he has a private practice so that it is to his interest to make difficulties for everyone who does not employ him as architect.

I should be much obliged if you could drop a hint in the right direction.

Yours sincerely,

BULLJOHN TO SPINLOVE

Dear Spinlove,   10.10.24.

Yes, it is all very bad. There have been lots of complaints, but the fellow has many friends on the council and among the local trades-people. However, I see the chairman sometimes—a very decent man—and I will give him a hint. I am keeping the papers you enclosed.

Ever yours sincerely,

POTCH TO SPINLOVE

Sir,   15.10.24.

I am glad to inform you that I am directed by my council to present you the enclosed postal order for the value of one shilling and sixpence. I regret that the requirements of the auditors of His Majesty's Local Government Board make it necessary for me to trouble you for a receipt, but no stamp is required as sum is less than £2.

>I have the honour to be, Sir,
>Your obedient servant,

Spinlove's action has not soothed the savage beast, but that was scarcely, in any case, to be hoped, for such men are swayed only by cupidity and funk, and Mr. Potch may be depended upon to make things as awkward for Spinlove as opportunity safely allows.

BRASH TO SPINLOVE

Dear Mr. Spinlove,   10.10.24.

I made a détour to-day and diverged to Honeywood for a brief period after the workmen had vacated the site. It will be necessary for you to immediately return to the makers the bricks, of which a vast quantity are already on the site.

It was clearly demonstrated, I must remind you, that the mansion was to be constructed of *red* bricks. Have you, may I inquire, seen what the builder is purposing to use? They are yellow, green, and all colours, and seem to be partly composed of cinders. I observed many to be broken and am at a loss to comprehend how Mr. Grigblay could suppose that I would tolerate such abominable rubbish. Has it not been explained to him that this is to be a gentleman's residence? I must request you to give this matter your immediate attention.

>Yours sincerely,

SPINLOVE TO BRASH

Dear Sir Leslie Brash,   11.10.24.

The bricks you saw are not the outside or "facing bricks", but the rough bricks of which the inner thickness of the walls, and where covered with plaster, will be formed. None of the facing bricks has yet been delivered, but I have chosen them. They are, of course, red bricks and are of the best make. No wonder you objected to the bricks you saw if you supposed they were for the outside face.

>Yours sincerely,

THE AFFAIR OF THE SPRING

BRASH TO SPINLOVE

Dear Mr. Spinlove,   13.10.24.

I enclose copy of a communication I have received from the solicitors of the proprietor of the estate on the other side of the road at the bottom of my property, and from whom I acquired Honeywood.

I have conferred with my own solicitors, who approved the conveyance of the land, and these gentlemen confirm that the spring must not be interfered with.

I trust that there will be no trouble *anent* this. I understood from you that the well was to be sunk previously to the other work being commenced, so that the builder could supply himself with water.

Yours sincerely,

(ENCLOSURE)
SPOONBILL & WELLSTAFT,
SOLICITORS, TO SIR LESLIE BRASH

Dear Sir,   10.10.24.

Mr. Gregory Witspanner, who is the tenant of Honeywood Farm, adjoining the property lately conveyed to you by our client, Mr. Rallingbourne, has written to our client complaining that the water supply to Honeywood Farm, which flows from a spring in Honeywood Spinney and along the watercourse on the land conveyed to you, has been recently, and now is, badly discoloured with clay, marl, vegetable soil or other foul matter, causing pollution of the water flowing from the said spring on to the said land in Mr. Witspanner's tenancy.

Our client understands that building operations are being carried out on your property and supposes that the pollution is due to the action of the men employed by you in those operations.

We have to remind you that it was expressly laid down in the conveyance to you of Honeywood Spinney that our client's user in the water flowing from the said spring should be maintained unimpaired and that there should be no interference with the flow of pure spring water on to his Honeywood Farm property as heretofore.

We have to call upon you to take immediate steps effectively to abate the pollution and shall be glad to hear that the matter has your attention.

Yours faithfully,

In other words, "The spring at Honeywood is being fouled contrary to the terms of the conveyance. Stop it!"

SPINLOVE TO BRASH

Dear Sir Leslie Brash,   14.10.24.

I have written to Grigblay and told him the spring must not be fouled. I will let you know what can be done. I shall be on the site on Friday. I had intended getting the well sunk, but when I noticed the spring I deemed it not necessary to take that step.

Yours sincerely,

SPINLOVE TO GRIGBLAY

Dear Sir,   14.10.24.

The owner of the property lying below Honeywood has written complaining that the water delivered on to his land from the spring in Honeywood Spinney is being fouled and requires that pollution and interference with the flow shall cease. He has a right to the flow of the spring water on to his land. I must ask you, therefore, immediately to arrange for another source of water supply.

Yours faithfully,

Spinlove is here altogether too aloof and disinterested. He ought to identify himself with this misfortune to the builder and at least make a gesture of readiness to help him, if possible. How is the builder to find water? The position is serious.

GRIGBLAY TO SPINLOVE

Dear Sir,   16.10.24.

It will be a serious matter for us if we are not to draw water from the spring. Where else are we to find water? When we went to the site before completing our tender we naturally assumed that we could make use of the spring as there was no stipulation in the contract that we should not make use of it. We can only suggest that the well should be sunk immediately and that we should be allowed to draw from it. This will involve a considerable delay, and we shall have to ask for an extension of the contract date corresponding to the time it takes to find water. In the meantime we have told Bloggs to use all possible care not to foul spring.

Yours faithfully,

SPINLOVE TO GRIGBLAY

Dear Sir,   17.10.24.

The contract stipulates that the builder is to make his own arrangements for the supply of water. You would be at liberty to use the spring if it were available, but, unfortunately, it is not. I will give orders for the well-sinking to be put in hand as soon as possible; in the meantime it will be necessary for you to make temporary arrangements of some kind, as Sir Leslie Brash would never consent to let the work stand while the well is being sunk.

Yours faithfully,

If Spinlove thinks that he can settle the matter in this fashion he is very much mistaken. Does he suppose that the builder is to carry water up hill on to the site? The question is, how is water to be found? The circumstances are awkward.

GRIGBLAY TO SPINLOVE

Dear Sir,   17.10.24.

Since we last wrote, Mr. Grigblay has been on site and arranged for Bloggs to dig out ditch and form a weir, and lay a 1 in. pipe from above weir to 1,000-gallon tank to be sunk into ground further down slope. This amount of water will not affect the flow from the spring and we shall not go near ditch or foul spring in the future. We shall be glad to have your approval of this proposal.

We have now got cellar excavated and shall be glad if you will approve same. The ground is dry and compact marly clay, and, as we should like to get concrete in and walls up before chance of rain, we shall be glad of your approval at once.

Yours faithfully,

SPINLOVE TO GRIGBLAY

Dear Sir, 18.10.24.

I am sorry I cannot accept your proposal to form weir and draw water from spring as Sir Leslie Brash has no right to interfere with the flow. I will, however, communicate with Sir Leslie Brash and ask him to refer the point to his solicitors.

Yours faithfully,

GRIGBLAY TO SPINLOVE

Dear Sir, 20.10.24.

I rang up to-day and asked you to put off writing to Sir Leslie Brash *re* spring. If permission is asked of solicitors it may very well be refused, as there is no inducement why it should be granted. The amount of water I shall take from the spring is nothing at all and no one will be any the wiser or know what is being done, as all pollution will cease. There will be no objection to the work proposed, as all will be removed at completion and no harm done.

Yours faithfully,

Grigblay is perfectly sound in his judgment in this matter, nor is there anything sly or deceitful in his proposal. All that the adjoining owner requires is that the spring shall not be polluted and that his right to the flow shall not be interfered with.

SPINLOVE TO GRIGBLAY

Dear Sir, 21.10.24.

If you care to carry out the arrangement you propose at the spring at your own risk and to indemnify Sir Leslie Brash from all liability, I will not object, although I cannot approve of or consent to the spring being made use of.

Yours faithfully,

Spinlove is taking a great deal too much upon himself here. He is, as accredited agent to Brash, engaging him in words which, to say the least, are ambiguous. Supposing that in some way Grigblay's interference with the spring violates a covenant of the conveyance and involves Brash in some penalty or forfeiture, is it to be imagined that Spinlove's letter will fix liability on Grigblay? This is not likely. It is difficult to know what Spinlove's letter stands for if it is not a formal consent to Grigblay's proposal by the owner's accredited agent. It appears, too, that Grigblay never acknowledged that letter so that he would be entitled to say, "Yes, the architect said he would hold me responsible, but I never agreed to accept responsibility for more than having to dismantle the arrangements."

It would have been better for Spinlove to have written to Grigblay saying he had no power to authorize him to interfere with the spring and leave him to interpret that letter by such a hint as is sometimes conveyed by a wink.

SPINLOVE TO GRIGBLAY

Dear Sir,   22.10.24.

I confirm authority for you to get on with concreting of cellar. You will note that the cellar damp course is to be carried up outside walls to the level of the normal damp course; this cellar damp course will come below the bottom of the concrete floor and above the bottom of the hard core.

I was glad to see such good progress had been made and to note that the concrete seems quite satisfactory. I have, however, to take exception to the facing-bricks, one load of which has been delivered. In ordering these from the makers I expressly excluded the bright red bricks, which are soft and probably under-burnt. I yesterday selected and marked three samples covering the whole range of variations in colour, etc., which your foreman has set aside in his office. The soft bright red bricks must be thrown out and no more must be delivered.

Will you please let me know in good time what detailed drawings you want?

Yours faithfully,

BRASH TO SPINLOVE

Dear Mr. Spinlove,   21.10.24.

I am in receipt of a strongly-worded communication from Mr. Rallingbourne's solicitors stating that the pollution of the spring continues and is worse than formerly, and requiring me immediately to have the state of affairs ameliorated and even hinting at proceedings. The occupier of the farm asseverates he cannot water his livestock and has to draw from a well.

This is all extremely regrettable and alarming, as I desire to maintain amicable relations with Mr. Rallingbourne, who will be my adjoining neighbour and is a most influential gentleman. It is now eight days since I desired you to give attention to this subject and yet nothing has eventuated.

Yours faithfully,

SPINLOVE TO BRASH

Dear Sir Leslie Brash,   22.10.24.

The matter of the spring has been attended to and there will be no pollution in future. The necessary work, unfortunately, involved muddying the water for a few hours.

Yours faithfully,

TROUBLE WITH BRICKS

GRIGBLAY TO SPINLOVE

Dear Sir,   23.10.24.

We note your instructions *re* facing-bricks. We may say we ordered bricks as selected by you according to your instructions, but have now taken up the matter with the brickyard.

Yours faithfully,

Spinlove, it will be remembered, dealt directly with the brick manufacturer in selecting bricks and merely told Grigblay to order bricks as selected, without defining, with samples or otherwise, what bricks exactly he was to receive. Grigblay accordingly did not know what bricks to expect and was not in a position to approve or disapprove of what was sent. Spinlove ought to have carried out his negotiations with the brickmaker through Grigblay and made Grigblay responsible for the bricks being up to sample

GRIGBLAY TO SPINLOVE

Dear Sir,   25.10.24.

With regard to the common bricks specified and seen and approved by you, Bloggs reports that some built into the foundation walls have blown already. We have had no experience of these bricks, not having used them before, and understand they come from Belgium; but Bloggs says that quite a few have lime in them and will blow, and for our own satisfaction we would prefer not to use them on the face of plastered walls. The price is very low, but we should be willing to substitute Strettons for this purpose.

We shall be glad to have your approval.

Yours faithfully,

Grigblay means by this that the clay of which the bricks are made has not been thoroughly ground so that there are lumps of lime in it. These become quicklime when the bricks are kilned, and when such bits of quicklime occur near the surface of the brick the lime swells when the brick is wetted and a flake is lifted from the surface. For a very few such bricks to blow and push the plaster away from the walls, perhaps after papering and painting is completed, is a terrible disaster, and the defect may go on appearing months after the house is finished.

SPINLOVE TO GRIGBLAY

Dear Sir,   27.10.24.

I am much obliged for your letter. I had a good report of these bricks which pleased me when I saw them. I do not like Strettons for facing plaster walls. What other proposal can you make?

Yours faithfully,

Spinlove is right. Stretton bricks have a smooth, greasy face and square edges and show a narrow joint, so that even when the joints are carefully raked the key for the plaster is not good. A rough-surfaced, irregular brick is what a builder likes for plastering upon, and there is nothing better for this purpose than the London stock.

GRIGBLAY TO SPINLOVE

Dear Sir,   28.10.24.

Our proposal was for grooved Strettons, although the cost to us would be a little higher than the bricks specified. We understand you have no objection to these and have ordered as we shall require them at once for cellar.

Yours faithfully,

The bricks referred to have grooves formed by pressing rubber ridges into the brick; the rubber expands with the pressure and contracts on its withdrawal, so that the groove is slightly dovetailed in consequence and forms an excellent key for plaster.

Grigblay is a little inclined to take charge of matters and tell Spinlove what he ought to do, but his quickness to notice the defect in the specified bricks is one of the advantages which an architect gains by employing a good builder

SPINLOVE TO GRIGBLAY

Dear Sir,   29.10.24.

I was on the site yesterday and found that your foreman had not carried out my instructions to throw out the soft facing bricks. I have to ask you to see that this is done.

Another trolly load of these bricks arrived while I was on the site, and it seemed to me that it contained as large a quantity of the objectionable bricks as the earlier consignment. These must be picked out.

Yours faithfully,

GRIGBLAY TO SPINLOVE

Dear Sir,   30.10.24.

We have noted your instructions *re* facings and will see that no unsuitable bricks are used, as the bricklayer will have instructions to throw them out. It is not necessary to handle the whole lot over first. We have written again to the brickyard calling attention to the matter.

We enclose list of detailed drawings as per your request. Bloggs points out that the 14 in. return where Den breaks for ward (see revised plan No. 8) will not give room for gable knee to match other gables (see $\frac{1}{2}$ in. detail No. 6) as indicated on $\frac{1}{8}$ in. scale elevation. It is too late to alter now, but call your attention to same.

Yours faithfully,

It will be recalled that this projecting gable marking the Den was one particular of the kitchen range modification. Here is an instance of the mishaps that are too apt to follow revision of the design. Spinlove, in making his design as a whole, would have kept this point in mind, but pecking at it against time he has overlooked the condition imposed by his $\frac{1}{2}$ in. detail of the gable knees. Some sort of contrivance or botch will have to be made to meet the case. It may perhaps lead to an interesting variation; on the other hand it perhaps will not, and in any case the matter is an annoyance to the architect, as his letter in reply makes clear.

SPINLOVE TO GRIGBLAY

Dear Sir,   31.10.24.

I am sorry to learn of the mistake with the Den gable. You say it is "too late to alter now", but I have to point out to you that you are responsible for the building according to the true intent and meaning of the drawings and for referring all discrepancies to me. I am not in this case going to require you to take down the wall and build 1 ft. 10½ in. break, but I must reserve to myself the right to require strict observance of this condition of the contract. The list of details you enclose does not help me much as they are general and cover the whole building. What I ask is that I may be kept informed beforehand of details that may be immediately wanted.

Yours faithfully,

This will not do! Spinlove is unfair and he is even foolish. The condition he quotes is a saving clause. It determines that the builder is responsible for the correct building of the house, but it does not make him responsible for the architect's definite instructions any more than it does for the design. Spinlove directed a break of 14 in. it seems, and he ought to be grateful to the builder for warning him of what lies ahead, and not discourage him, as he has done, from looking beyond what is strictly his business. The dimension was a definite instruction; the detail of the particular gable knee is suppositious. The tone of Spinlove's letter is wrong; he ought to make the best of the matter to the builder, and not the worst. Disparagement is always an error; expostulation or even reprimand may be necessary, and a builder will not be put out of countenance even if he feels grieved; but disparagement serves no good end whatever and destroys that atmosphere of common purpose on which good results depend.

GRIGBLAY TO SPINLOVE

Dear Sir,   1.11.24.

We note your remarks and have to say that we quite understand what we have to do and are giving this work our best attention; but when an architect sends us a figured dimension to work to we work to it unless it disagrees with other figured dimensions, which please note and see conditions of contract, page 2.

With reference to our foreman's question *re* finish of Den gable knee, of which we have not yet received details, we are instructing him not to take any such action again. The details which we immediately require are those which vary from contract drawing and specifications now in our hands, as you may deem it necessary for us to have and as per our list.

Yours faithfully,

This is a very stiff letter for a builder to write to an architect.

Grigblay is naturally annoyed. His letter states the case fairly and entirely demolishes Spinlove. No contract can be carried out at all if the letter of the conditions only is to be observed. A common spirit of good intention and fair play and good sense is necessary.

SPINLOVE TO BRASH

Dear Sir Leslie Brash, 6.11.24.

Before I arrange for the well to be sunk, would it not be worthwhile to consider whether the spring cannot be made use of? I understand that you are under covenant not to pollute or interfere with the flow, but you could lay on to a storage tank without infringing either condition. Two thousand gallons a day, which would be more than you would use for all purposes, would in no measurable way interfere with the flow. I took the opportunity when last on site to observe the flow where it discharges into the stream below Honeywood Farm, and it seemed as strong as at the source, so that the owner seems to have little use for the water. If the spring were tapped as I propose, the cost of well-sinking would be saved and also most of the cost of installing and running a pump, for the fall of the ground makes it an easy matter to put in an efficient ram. The waste water from this would be returned to the spring. I assume the spring water to be fit for drinking purposes, etc., but it ought to be reported upon by an analyst. I will take no steps until I hear from you.

Yours sincerely,

Spinlove, it will be noticed, has put himself to some trouble to master the facts and devise a scheme that shall give Brash a better service and save his pocket. Such action is not merely the prerogative of the architect, but a privilege which brings dignity to his office and adds joy to his activities to do a thing well for the sake of so doing it, and not for the money it brings, is what distinguishes the professional from the commercial code. It is because the commercial man is conscious of this that he bleats continuously: "I wish to serve you", and protests that his performances are "genuine", and "real", and "bona fide", and "super". I make this comment because there are signs that the spirit of disinterested initiative here displayed by Spinlove is in some degree discredited by the architects of a new generation. It will learn better when its own children revolt against the sophistication which numbs the sense of true life values for their parents, and puts the architect in a hopeless rivalry with the shopkeeper.

BRASH TO SPINLOVE

Dear Mr. Spinlove,   8.11.24.

I am extremely gratified at your communication *anent* water supply. I have transmitted a copy of your letter to my legal advisers who approved the conveyance in my behalf and who will no doubt be able to inform me what the correct interpretation of "pollution" and "interference" is to be understood to signify. I will communicate with you when I have received this information. In the interim please desist from all operations in regard to water supply.

Yours sincerely,

MORE DIFFICULTIES

GRIGBLAY TO SPINLOVE

Dear Sir,   8.11.24.

We are sorry to say that Bloggs reports difficulty with damp course. He has carried up cellar to near level of ground, but in fixing level of damp course at bottom of cellar wall he did not allow for main damp course also running round, so that joint is 1½ in. too high at ground-floor level. What we propose to do is to take down a couple of courses and level over wall below ground to give the correct joint level. Shall be glad of your approval.

Yours faithfully,

The fact that Grigblay has confessed to this blunder and referred his proposal for making good to Spinlove is a sign that he has a particular sense of his obligations The foreman of some builders would have levelled over with cut bricks in cement, and when the architect objected to the botch would have made excuses and belittled the matter, confident that as the wall was sound and the work finished and out of sight, the architect would not call upon him to demolish it.

SPINLOVE TO GRIGBLAY

Dear Sir,   10.11.24.

Your foreman had no grounds for assuming that the main damp course would not run round the top of cellar walls, and if he did suppose so he should have realized that the width of the two courses of slates in cement had to be made up somehow to allow the joints of facings to run through. I am not prepared to accept your proposal to level up. It will be necessary to pull down, say, fifteen courses and save the 1½ in. out of the joints in rebuilding.

Yours faithfully,

Spinlove is right in pointing out that the foreman made a stupid mistake, but his letter is unsympathetic; so long as a builder does his best the architect ought to try to help him out of difficulties. There is no weight on the walls, and the half course would be out of sight in the thickness of the floor or perceived only by an expert eye below the ceiling of the unplastered cellar. On the other hand, it is a good thing at the beginning of a job for an architect to be exacting in his demands on the builder; for if he passes over small irregularities at the outset, the builder may assume that the architect is easy-going and some later deviation from exactness may lead to dreadful difficulties and makeshifts. It will take perhaps two hours to pull down the wall and a day to rebuild, and the cost to the builder will be perhaps £7. The foreman will "know all about it", and he and the builder will be warned to be wary. On the whole, Spinlove's decision is probably the best one, but he can write polite, and even ingratiating letters to his client, and he should know better than to write crusty and domineering ones to the builder.

GRIGBLAY TO SPINLOVE

Dear Sir,   12.11.24.

We enclose letter we have received from Messrs. Hoochkoft *re* facings. Please return with your instructions.

Yours faithfully,

(ENCLOSURE) HOOCHKOFT TO GRIGBLAY

Sir,   8.11.24.

We do not understand the complaint of the architect. The bricks we are sending are same as approved by him. If we are required to pick over we shall have to charge 35s. per thousand extra. There is nothing wrong with the bricks.

Yours faithfully,

SPINLOVE TO GRIGBLAY

Dear Sir,   14.11.24.

I return Hoochkoft's letter, of which I have kept copy, and enclose copy of my letter to the firm.

Yours faithfully,

(ENCLOSURE) SPINLOVE TO HOOCHKOFT

Dear Sirs,   14.11.24.

Mr. Grigblay has shown me your letter to him of 8.11.24. My objection to the bricks you have delivered on the site is that they include a quantity of the soft bright red bricks which I expressly said I could not use at the time I ordered the bricks.

Yours faithfully,

BRASH TO SPINLOVE

Dear Mr. Spinlove,   14.11.24.

I have been in correspondence with my solicitors, Messrs. Russ, Topper, Mainprice, Cornish and McFee, and have further discussed with them the proposition of obtaining water from the effluent of spring, but they are unable to advise me what interpretation should be given to the covenant limiting my use of the water. They approved the conveyance in my behalf so that I should have expected them to be able to tell me what the words mean, but this they seem unable to do. I am given to understand that only a judge can say what the words mean and that probably different judges would have different views as to their meaning. I am now, at my solicitors' suggestion, obtaining the opinion of an eminent K.C. as to what opinion a judge would be likely to give on the matter. When I have this information I shall know better how I stand. I inform you of these minutiae in order that you may comprehend that a considerable period must elapse before anything can be definitely determined.

Yours sincerely,

The way Brash sets forth this matter makes it appear ludicrous. The predicament of his solicitors is in fact grotesque—the more so as there are five of them—though Brash does not perceive it. We do not know what the terms of the clause in question are, and should be little the wiser if we did, but it may be that Brash is under covenant not to "interfere" with the flow of the spring, and that the question is what exactly constitutes "interference", having regard to the terms of the conveyance as a whole and the physical circumstances of the case? We lately saw Spinlove light-heartedly committing Brash in ambiguous words, and now we find skilled lawyers all at sea as to the meaning of their own carefully weighed phrases. A great part of the business of lawyers is to determine the meaning of words used by other lawyers. The law is what is known as "a lucrative profession".

HOOCHKOFT TO SPINLOVE

Dear Sir,   15.11.24.

We have respectfully to point out that you accepted our quotation for bricks *ex kiln*. It is true you said you did not care for the bright-red bricks and we are accordingly extra firing the bricks for your order, but we cannot guarantee that there will not be a small number of bright reds unless we send you picked, for which our price is 182s. per thousand instead of 147s.

Yours faithfully,

Spinlove's letter accepting quotation for facing bricks was as follows: "I like the samples of the bricks and the price is satisfactory. The very bright-coloured bricks seem soft and under-burnt; the red and purple brindled bricks will give me all the variation in colour necessary. I have directed the builder, Mr. John Grigblay, to place the order with you." This is a sloppy letter. Spinlove means to say that he accepts the tender on the understanding that the bright, under-burnt bricks are excluded, but he does not say it. He first approves of the samples and the price, and then expresses a preference, only, for the better-burnt and darker bricks— that, at any rate, is an interpretation which the "shrewd, hard-headed business man" that Samuel Smiles taught us to admire (before we taught ourselves to recognize the commercial sharper) would put upon the letter if it helped him to a half-sovereign. In some firms the taking advantage of verbal ambiguities and the dealing in them themselves is part of a daily routine. It is best for an architect to buy only from merchants and manufacturers of established reputation; but whether he does so or not it is his duty to be exact and precise in his directions, or he may mislead an honest man to his disadvantage by the same loose phrases by which he places himself at the mercy of a dishonest one. Hoochkoft's talk of extra firing is nonsense; if all the bricks were thoroughly burnt some would be over-burnt and there would be waste. Hoochkoft seems to have got our friend Spinlove on toast.

SPINLOVE TO HOOCHKOFT

Dear Sirs,   17.11.24.

My order was for facing bricks to sample, but omitting the soft bright-reds. It was for you to amend your price if necessary, but you did not do so, but took the order on the tendered price. I cannot use the soft bricks and no more must be sent on to site.

Yours faithfully,

HOOCHKOFT TO SPINLOVE

Dear Sir,   19.11.24.

We respectfully regret that we cannot agree that the price we quoted and which you accepted was for picked. We are doing our best to reduce the number of bright-reds and do not know what you have to complain of, but we cannot supply picked at same price as *ex kiln* as quoted, but to meet you will offer you special rate of 175s. per thousand picked.

Yours faithfully,

SPINLOVE TO GRIGBLAY

Dear Sir,   20.11.24.

I enclose copy of my correspondence with Hoochkoft. Can you arrange to take over the bricks thrown out and credit them? The extra cost of the picked bricks will be about £70, as nearly as I can judge.

Yours faithfully,

GRIGBLAY TO SPINLOVE

Dear Sir,   22.11.24.

Another lorry of facings has been delivered with about the same number of soft reds as before. We were willing to throw out from the first load, but you will realize this is going to be a serious matter for us if we are to pick over the whole facings. We estimate 15 per cent will have to be thrown out. The only offer we can make is to credit the throwouts against the cost of picking and use them in the back walling. We await your instructions.

Yours faithfully,

Grigblay's proposal is fair, but the bargain would, no doubt, favour him. The result would be that Brash would pay 175s. a thousand for perhaps 7,000 extra useless bricks. It seems, therefore, that when Spinlove said he would engage not to run into extras he flattered himself, for his difficulty with the brickyard is entirely his own fault. It will be remembered, however, that Spinlove has included the sum of £300 as a provision for contingencies upon which he can draw without involving Brash in an extra; but I do not recall that he explained to Brash that this £300 provision was to cover the contingency of the architect making mistakes, although it is available for this purpose, as all architects are thankful to know. This is not unfair. A small margin for error is the due of the most exact human machinery.

SPINLOVE TO HOOCHKOFT

Dear Sirs,   24.11.24.

A third load of your facing bricks similar to those to which I have objected has been delivered. I have told Mr. Grigblay not to allow any more to be brought on to the site, and I must ask you to send only bricks equal to approved sample as ordered.

Yours faithfully,

SPINLOVE TO GRIGBLAY

Dear Sir,   24.11.24.

I am obliged for your letter but the bricks were ordered to approved sample. If I accept your proposal it appears there will be an extra of about £120. I enclose copy of my letter to Hoochkoft of to-day. Please refuse to allow any further consignments including defective facings to come on to site.

Yours faithfully,

Spinlove has not realized the consequences of this prohibition.

GRIGBLAY TO SPINLOVE

Dear Sir,   25.11.24.

May we remind you that we have some face work now built on part of the south front and that we shall have to close down the work if we send back facings. We have been urging delivery. It will also be impossible to match the bricks from another yard, and it seems necessary to come to some arrangement with Hoochkoft at once.

Yours faithfully,

HOOCHKOFT TO SPINLOVE

Dear Sir,   26.11.24.

We can only repeat that we did not quote for picked and that the bricks we have sent you are as per your order.

We gather from your letter informing us that no more unpicked will be accepted that you wish us to send picked facings in future.

Yours faithfully,

SPINLOVE TO HOOCHKOFT

Dear Sirs,   28.11.24.

It is no concern of mine what steps you take to supply facings similar to samples approved by me, but further consignments containing the soft bright-reds will not be received on the site. If, therefore, you cannot supply to sample without picking, the bricks must be picked.

Yours faithfully,

Spinlove has now dropped into the trap in which Hoochkoft, with skill acquired by long practice, has maneuvered to catch him. Spinlove's contention is that it was part of the bargain that the soft reds should not be included. Hoochkoft has identified this with "picking", for which he has quoted a higher price; Spinlove, by here adopting the term "picking", gives Hoochkoft an opportunity for charging for "picked facings".

It should be added that the tone of Spinlove's letter is too aggressive—a common fault with him. Such a letter will not, in fact, disturb the equanimity of Hoochkoft, who, in common with his kind, has the hide of a rhinoceros; but it is undignified, and not the sort of letter a professional man should write. It may also be remarked that power largely subsists in self-control; any exhibition of feeling is a mark of weakness.

GRIGBLAY TO SPINLOVE

Dear Sir,   2.12.24.

Bloggs informs us that yesterday another lorry load of facings arrived. They are much as previous lots, but as Messrs. Hoochkoft would not have received your letter before loading up, we did not send them back. We shall have to stop work if the facings don't come regular.

We notice that your brick detail of front entrance, drawing No. 10, omits mat-sinking and shows the front step $1\frac{1}{4}$ in. above finished level of ground floor as fixed by bench mark to your approval. As the $\frac{1}{8}$ in. scale plan shows a mat-sinking we set out the brick joint on the floor level, so that the top steps should line up with brick joint. If we raise step $1\frac{1}{4}$ in. it will mean cutting the bricks to build in step, which we think you will not care for. Have we your authority to drop the bench mark and the ground floor level $1\frac{1}{4}$ in.?

Yours faithfully,

We may gather from the above that the horizontal brick joints have been set out to a bench mark approved on the site by Spinlove as the level of the ground floor. The $\frac{1}{8}$ in. scale drawings show a sinking for the mat at the front entrance, but Spinlove in his $\frac{1}{2}$ in. detail of the entrance has eliminated the mat-sinking, which harbours dirt, and has, as an alternative, raised the top front step $1\frac{1}{4}$ in. above the level of the floor. Grigblay points out that to build in the step in this position will involve unsightly cutting of the bricks and proposes to make the top of the step agree with the bench mark and brick joint, and to lower the floor $1\frac{1}{4}$ in. below bench mark. That Grigblay should write on such a matter shows him to be a good and careful builder.

HOOCHKOFT TO SPINLOVE

Dear Sir,   1.12.24.

We note your instructions *re* facings, which shall have our best attention.

We are, dear Sir,
Yours faithfully,

This letter is so worded as to support a claim for picked bricks at the increased price, while it gives Spinlove to understand that the objectionable bricks are to be eliminated at the rate originally quoted. Sly deceit of this kind is practised by many business firms, but an experienced architect readily protects himself by exact methods and precision in the use of words, and he soon learns to distrust ambiguous phrases and to spy out the treacherous purpose hidden in them. Spinlove seems to have no suspicion, although the affable subscription to this letter might well have warned him.

SPINLOVE TO GRIGBLAY

Dear Sir,   4.12.24.

Thank you for your letter. Please drop the floor 1¼ in. as you propose. The finished ground floor will now be 1¼ in. below bench mark from which all vertical heights are figured.

Hoochkoft has now agreed to pick out the soft bright-red bricks to which I have objected, and further consignments containing them are not to be unloaded, but must be sent back.

Yours faithfully,

SPINLOVE TO GRIGBLAY

Dear Sir,   14.12.24.

I was on the site yesterday and saw the last delivery of facings, which are quite satisfactory, but they will show up a little darker in tone than the facings you have already built. Luckily there is not much of this and I have arranged with your foreman that he shall mix what remains of the old with the new, and see that the redder and brighter faces of the new bricks are shown in the next few courses so that there will be a gradation of tone from new work to old.

I was glad to notice that the bricklayers have now got into the way of pressing the mortar out of the joints and cutting off with the edge of the trowel as specified; but they are apt, from force of habit, to press the mortar home with the flat, which they *must not do*. I spoke to your foreman on this matter. He seems to have trouble with one or two of the men, and I told him he would have to get rid of them if they did not do what they were told.

Yours faithfully,

The matter of finish to the brick jointing is of great importance, as Spinlove has evidently learnt. He seems, however, to think that the only occasion for a letter is to find fault. Bloggs appears to be doing his best under troublesome conditions, and the architect ought at least to hint appreciation.

BRASH ON BRICKS

BRASH TO SPINLOVE

Dear Sir,   19.12.24.

I visited my Honeywood property to-day and was aghast to view the house. I was given to understand that it was to be a *red* brick mansion, but the bricks are of all colours and they are not smooth, but rough, with wide rough spaces; in fact, thoroughly cheap bricks. I rubbed one of them and it *came off* on my finger. I never saw worse house building in my life; not like a gentleman's house, but appertaining to the similitude of a barn. The bricks I desired and which I assumed would be embodied in the fabric are the pretty pinky-red smooth bricks with straight white lines and all matching and not diversified in tint.

There is nothing more elegant and charming than these smooth, neat pink bricks, but the bricks I see are brown instead of red, and exhibit a dirty appearance and are not of one tint, but discoloured and *spotty* and *uneven* instead of being smooth. Is it really too late to put the matter right? Cannot the walls be coloured in some way and the spaces made straight and white and not so rough and broad? I have seen such work being performed in London, I think.

I am afraid to contemplate what Lady Brash will say when she views the edifice on her return from Buxton next week.

I have just arranged to rent a furnished house, "Roselawn", Thaddington, where we shall reside during the spring and summer so that Lady Brash and myself may be on the spot.

I must request your attention to the question of the bricks which is most urgent.

Yours sincerely,

One may feel sorry for Brash. No doubt he will learn to like his "uneven, dirty coloured, spotty" house, but the disappointment is probably a heavy one. The "operation" he refers to seems to be raddling and tuck-pointing. The penultimate paragraph will not be the tidings of great joy to his architect that he seems to imagine.

SPINLOVE TO BRASH

Dear Sir Leslie Brash, 22.12.24.

I am sorry you are disappointed with the facing bricks, but it is difficult to judge the effect of the finished house from a near view of the small piece of walling now built. The bricks are, I assure you, good quality, hand-made red bricks, and the variations in colour will not give a spotty effect as you fear, but a deep, soft colour, instead of the rather thin, hard, insipid tone of uniformly-tinted smooth bricks.

The pinky-red uniform smooth brickwork with fine white joints you speak of would be quite unsuited to the architecture of your house: it belongs to a quite different style of building. You will realize this if you have seen, for instance, Spronton Whytgates, and the Orangery at Kensington Palace. The former represents something of the brickwork effect aimed at in your house; the latter shows the kind you have in mind. I can assure you it would not only be a disastrous anomaly and confusion of ideas to build your house in the style of the Orangery, but almost impossible to do so. I have given close attention to the appearance of the brickwork and I feel sure you will like the effect when the walls begin to display themselves.

Wishing you the compliments of the season,

Yours sincerely,

Spinlove has not chosen the best of all happy moments for wishing Brash a merry Christmas by tagging the message to a letter telling him he does not know what he is talking about. It was certainly an awkward one to have to write, for there is no ground of common intelligence upon which to approach Brash; it would have been better, instead of saying: "You are an ignorant donkey. Wishing you a happy Christmas". . . . if Spinlove had written: "The bricks are all right. I will explain when I see you".

BRASH TO SPINLOVE

Dear Mr. Spinlove,   23.12.24.

You may be quite correct in what you say from your own personal attitude of view, but you must permit me to inform you that I *admire* the pinky-red smooth bricks with straight white space lines, which you appear to hold in such contempt. Our diversity of tastes differ in this matter, which I much regret. I desire to add that I visited Kensington Gardens and viewed the Orangery yesterday and I entirely fail to visualize the least resemblance between that building and your design for my mansion. No two) e iifices could be more dissimilar in their diversity, and I am astounded that you should express the contrary view.

Reciprocating your seasonable good wishes,

Yours sincerely,

The explanation of this letter probably is that Brash was so irritated by Spinlove's that he did not read it with any care.

SPINLOVE TO BRASH

Dear Sir Leslie Brash,   24.12.24.

You have misread my letter. I did not instance the Orangery as having anything in common with my design for your house, but as *not* having any; and I do not dislike the bricks you say you admire, but delight to use them in a design to which they are appropriate. If I had known that you particularly wanted your house faced with them I would gladly have made a design to suit, but nothing was said to suggest this. I feel confident that when you see the house taking shape you will be pleased, and not find the walling too rough or lacking in warm red colour.

Thank you for good wishes.

Yours sincerely,

BRASH TO SPINLOVE

Dear Mr. Spinlove,   28.12.24.

Lady Brash has returned home and has perused your letters on the subject of the bricks and is sure that if they are similar to those at Sponton Witgate (*sic*) they will be extremely pretty. I should mention that Lady Brash has the pleasure of acquaintance with the Rt. Hon. Lady Issit (*sic*) whose husband the Vicount (*sic*), as you are probably aware, is the owner of the house, which Lady Brash has heard much of. I apprehend that your judgment in selecting the bricks was quite correct, although they happen to be an innovation to me.

Yours sincerely,

Spinlove has struck it lucky: but poor old Brash! As Lady Brash does not know her acquaintance's name (Issy) nor the name of her house, and Brash cannot spell her husband's title, we may imagine that the great lady once opened a bazaar at which Lady Brash was a stallholder; and that the reason Lady Brash never wears a ring in her nose is that on that memorable day the Viscountess did not do so. How deep, therefore, will be the dear woman's gratification in possessing a house whose bricks are similar to those used in her friend's famous mansion. I make these comments to elucidate what I gather to be the inner meaning of Brash's letter. Whether Spinlove caught its significance depends upon how far he is sensitive to the manifestations of social snobbery.

GRIGBLAY TO SPINLOVE

Dear Sir,   27.12.24.

We are now several courses above datum all round and have a good deal of material prepared and shall be glad of a certificate for £2,000.

Yours faithfully,

A BOX OF CIGARS

SPINLOVE TO HOOCHKOFT

Dear Sir, 29.12.24.

On my return to the office to-day I found a parcel containing a box of fifty cigars. I am led to think that these have been sent by you, as your trade card with the season's greetings was found on the floor.

I appreciate your friendly intentions, but you will understand that it is impossible for me to accept presents from those with whom I do business in my professional capacity.

If you will confirm that you sent the parcel I will return it to you.

Yours faithfully,

Spinlove is right in returning the parcel and in the reason he gives for doing so: and, as he lays claim to no superior virtues, he will wound no susceptibilities—if Hoochkoft should harbour any, which is unlikely. It occasionally happens that a builder or specialist or merchant, yielding to a feeling of good fellowship or personal regard or gratitude for some friendly act, will, as an individual, send an architect the kind of gift that passes between convivial friends at Christmas, but all such ingenuousness has been rendered suspect by commercial enterprise, which is ready to falsify the purest motives of humanity at sixpence a time, and which fouls everything it touches. To accept gifts from firms is impossible; and an architect who accepts from individuals must expect to lose the respect of the giver as he deserves to do, for he has in like degree lost his own self-respect.

There are practising architects who are contemptuous of those who refuse gifts, and laugh scornfully at the idea of a couple of boxes of cigars or a case of champagne weighing with them when, as arbiters, they have

101

to determine the measure due from and to the giver, and to interpret the contract against his interests. The scornful tone of that laugh is the reaction from the laugher's contempt for himself in accepting; and if his impartiality in meting out justice is not, in fact, swayed, it is because his nature is insensitive to obligations that do not involve self-interest. The gifts are offered as an investment by those whose business it is to get full return for their investments, and they are accepted by those who desire possession and whose greed outweighs their self respect.

HOOCHKOFT TO SPINLOVE

Dear Sir,   31.12.24.

We thank you for your kind appreciation and trust that you will not put yourself to the inconvenience of returning the small customary token we venture to send at this time of the year to our more valued customers, with whom we trust we may be permitted to include your good self.

With our respectful compliments for your good health and prosperity in the coming year,

We are, dear Sir,
Yours faithfully,

Hoochkoft sent this greasy letter in view of the fact that they have deceived Spinlove and intend to press the claim for picked bricks which they know he will resist. The reference to the architect as a customer is a deceptive gloss. Spinlove is the agent of Brash, who is the customer—a very different matter—though Spinlove's habit of ordering goods without stating that he does so on behalf of his client would lead us to believe that he is not fully aware of the distinction. There is no reason why Brash, as a customer, should not accept Hoochkoft's cigars, but this he will never have a chance of doing. It is never the principal to whom the gift is ordered, but his agent; it is not the lady of the house to whom the grocer sends the drum of candied fruits, but her cook.

SPINLOVE TO HOOCHKOFT

Box of cigars posted to-day under separate cover.

for J. SPINLOVE,
R. S. PINTLE.

A distinguished architect tells me that when any gift is sent to him he accepts it with a grateful letter of appreciation and thanks, and an expression of his very deep regret that his doing so will make it impossible for him to place any orders with the giver in future. If his example were widely copied the practice would soon end.

SPINLOVE TO GRIGBLAY

Dear Sir,   1.1.25.

In reply to your letter asking for certificate, will you let me know how you arrive at your estimate of £2,000?

Yours faithfully,

GRIGBLAY TO SPINLOVE

Dear Sir,   5.1.25.

We enclose estimate for certificate, as requested. If not convenient please draw certificate for such less amount as you may think proper.

Yours faithfully,

SPINLOVE TO TINGE, QUANTITY SURVEYOR

Dear Mr. Tinge,   7.1.25.

The builder has applied for certificate for £2,000. I enclose his estimate. The walls are up an average of two courses above ground floor all round—there are about 10,000 common and 3,000 facing bricks on site and ground-floor window frames are practically made. His claim for materials prepared and on site seems excessive, and the inclusion of £400 out of preliminary and general provisions does not appear justified. Will you please examine the figures?

Yours truly,

TINGE TO SPINLOVE

Dear Sir,   10.1.25.

Value of work done and materials prepared or on site £2,250, less 20 per cent retention, £1,800.

Estimate returned herewith.

Yours faithfully,

SPINLOVE TO GRIGBLAY

Dear Sir,   12.1.25.

I have examined your estimate, but am unable to agree that you are entitled to a certificate of £2,000; and as the contract stipulates that certificates shall be for not less than £2,000, you are not entitled to any certificate.

Yours faithfully,

Spinlove has no business to write these graceless letters to the builder, which will wound his self-respect and make bad blood. The tone is that of Scotland Yard addressing a ticket-of-leave man. No doubt Grigblay is "trying it on", but there is no harm in asking, for some architects are easy-going and, knowing their man, are willing to stretch a point to oblige him, for the architect usually has the right to draw a certificate for less than the minimum named if he thinks fit. A builder has to pay his merchant or lose the 2½ per cent discount usually allowed for settlement within three months, and if he is to make full use of his capital, as most of them do, he must get his money in promptly or borrow at interest, in which case his profits will vanish.

Spinlove ought to identify himself with the builder's interests as well as with his client's, and the sort of letter he ought to have written is somewhat as follows: "As I was not able to follow the details of your estimate I referred it to Mr. Tinge, who arrives at a figure, less retention, of £1,800. I should be glad to certify for this amount, but you will see that the contract stipulates a minimum of £2,000. I am afraid, therefore, that the matter must stand over for a few weeks".

No builder could object to such a letter as this. The quantity surveyor is an impartial authority; the terms of the contract are inviolable. Spinlove is right in keeping to the letter of the contract, however, and Grigblay will not be likely again to lay himself open to a similar repulse.

LADY BRASH TO SPINLOVE

Dear Mr. Spinlove,   15.1.25.

I am writing as Sir Leslie is shooting with a friend at Westerham. I went down to-day and was horrified to find them *soaking it with water!!!* I spoke to one of them, but I am afraid he did not pay much attention, so will you please be so good as to have it *stopped* as I particularly want it *dry?* All my family are subject to rheumatism, so you may imagine my feelings to-day when I saw *water being poured over them!!!*

How very cold the wind has been lately!!

Yours sincerely,

It is a pity Lady Brash's regard for her family does not extend to another kind of relatives—grammatical!

SPINLOVE TO LADY BRASH

Dear Lady Brash,   17.1.25.

Your house will, I can promise, be a thoroughly warm and a perfectly dry one. Bricks are always wetted so that the mortar will set hard. The walls will become quite dry in due time.

Yes, as you say, the wind has been very chilly. I hope Sir Leslie has had good sport.

Yours sincerely,

In point of fact it is difficult to get bricklayers to use enough water with absorbent bricks which, if not kept very wet, suck up moisture out of the mortar and give it no opportunity of setting properly. The bricklayer's hand gets softened by being constantly wet, and the sand on the handle of the trowel cuts his skin.

CARRYING ON

SPINLOVE TO GRIGBLAY

Dear Sir,   22.1.25.

When I was at your yard yesterday I had to condemn five cills, seven jambs, and two mullions on account of sap or shakes; I notice also a certain amount of sap in the timber coming from the sawmill. Will you please see that none is included in the worked-up stuff?

Yours faithfully,

GRIGBLAY TO SPINLOVE

Dear Sir,   22.1.25.

Our shop foreman tells us that you objected to some of the oak prepared for window frames. We may say that this is one of the best lots of oak we have seen for a great many years; it is ten years old, Sussex white, grown on the chalk, and not weald oak, and we defy anyone to show you finer timber as it is not to be had and there is very little as good as this anywhere. These slow-growing trees do not come very straight, so we are bound to get a little sound sap wood running in and out in places, and if we threw out all that showed a trace we should have to throw out more than half. Some of your jambs are near 9 ft. long. We will carefully select and keep any sappy angles on the back face; we will also creosote or tar the backs and underside of cills if you wish.

Yours faithfully,

It was easy for Spinlove to specify "the timber to be well seasoned, free from sap, large loose or dead knots, waney edges"—and all the rest of it. The point is, how is he to interpret words which describe the general characteristics of timber and which mean a different thing to different persons and have a different value according to the purpose for which the wood is to be used? In what degree is the timber to be free from those particular defects? To apply the rule literally and rigidly would drive any builder into flat revolt, and no arbitrator would support the interpretation. A bit of sap running in and out on the back angle of cill or jamb is of no account, and large live knots are characteristic of English oak, as also are shakes, which cannot be objected to when they are superficial and the wood is well seasoned. If Spinlove has no stomach for the robust, rugged integrity of English oak he ought to have used Austrian or Danzig or Japanese.

Grigblay's letter strongly suggests that the stuff he is cutting is first class, and that Spinlove's objections are due to ignorance. The fact is that the established form of specification with its impracticable stipulations is not the best for securing first-rate work; a more discerning and indulgent description, which shows that the person specifying knows what he can get and means to have it, is the right thing, and enables a builder to understand what he is actually expected to provide. For instance, what exactly does "well seasoned" mean? How long seasoned and in what form? Seven years felled and three years in plank can be had, and the builder will provide it, or its equivalent, if he has allowed for it in his tender.

SPINLOVE TO GRIGBLAY

Dear Sir,   27.1.25.

I raise no objection to the general quality of the oak, but the specification is definite in ruling out sap, shakes, etc., and I must require you to conform to it.

Yours faithfully,

James is riding for a fall.

GRIGBLAY TO SPINLOVE

Dear Sir,   3.2.25.

Our shop foreman has now selected and got out the whole of the planks we propose to use for window and door frames for your inspection, and we shall be glad to have your approval of same before they go to the mill.

We may say that the planks we are selecting from have been in store for more than four years.

In the event of your not approving same perhaps you will let us know where we are to get it.

Yours faithfully,

This is a distinctly stiff letter for a builder to write to the architect. It is clear that Grigblay has no great respect for Spinlove's practical knowledge or experience and has no great regard for him personally. Spinlove, one imagines, is helpless: how is he to tell Grigblay what he wants or where it is to be got when he does not know? He ought, however, since he has approved of the general quality of the oak, to refuse to approve it in detail in plank, for the suitability of the components of the window frames to be cut from the planks will depend entirely upon the skill and judgment of the joiner in laying out the work and scheming to avoid defects. If Spinlove accepts definite planks he will prejudice his position if, in avoiding waste, defective timber is worked up into jambs and cills.

GRIGBLAY TO SPINLOVE

Dear Sir,   12.2.25.

We shall be obliged if you will now favour us with certificate for £2,000.

We are sorry to say the frost has got into the upper course of brickwork and some of the pointing has been caught. We have the green work well covered, but the papers say frost is to continue, so we have stopped bricklayers. Bloggs has set out the main drain to sewage outfall and we should like to get on with this if you will approve same. We notice there is a provision of £350 for septic tank and filter beds and shall be glad to have your instructions.

We are awaiting details of brick window-cills; there is a lot of bed and back cutting to these and we should like to put bricklayers to work on it.

Yours faithfully,

SPINLOVE TO GRIGBLAY

Dear Sir,   16.2.25.

I enclose certificate No. I for £2,000. I was on the site yesterday and agreed set out of main drain. The branch drains I will deal with later on. The exact level of the outfall will be fixed by the anaerobic tank; I will send you particulars of the work covered by the provision for this as soon as possible. I enclose detail No. 21 of brick window-cills and weatherings; the lengths of these cills, you will note, vary, so that in order to keep joint widths constant, i.e. $1\frac{1}{2}$ in., and the bricks equal in width, it will be necessary in some cases to reduce the bricks by cutting or rubbing so that exact regularity is maintained.

You will note that the cills and all weathered members are to be bedded, jointed, and pointed in cement waterproofed with Puddlyt. This must be carefully attended to as the bricks are absorbent and not to be relied on to keep out water.

Yours faithfully,

GRIGBLAY TO SPINLOVE

Dear Sir,   17.2.25.

We are obliged for detail No. 21 showing brick cills, etc., and note your other instructions. With regard to gauging the brick cills we shall be glad to have your authority for the extra as same is not included in the contract. Are we to understand that the same rule applies to brick heads and to the brick gable copings, etc.?

Yours faithfully,

SPINLOVE TO GRIGBLAY

Dear Sir,   18.2.25.

You are right in understanding that the whole of the brick cills, heads, and weatherings are to be cut to show equal widths and uniform $\frac{1}{2}$ in. joints. I do not agree that you are entitled to an extra for this work, which is required under the general condition that all work shall be of the best quality.

Yours faithfully,

BRASH TO SPINLOVE

Dear Mr. Spinlove,   18.2.25.

At long last, after this interminable period, I have received counsel's opinion on the proposal you suggested for making use of the spring; I append a copy as its perusal may interest you. I have conferred with my legal adviser on the appropriate action to be taken and I desire you will be so good as to wait upon Messrs. Russ, when you have made your arrangements, and inform those gentlemen of the work contemplated, as they anticipate they may wish to take counsel's opinion again, for I consider it advisable to make things secure and not to incur any liability of a lawsuit or to be compelled to dismantle the arrangements after they are instituted.

I should mention that it is not desired that attention should be attracted to the operations, and I apprehend that when the work is completed there will be nothing visible to see. Perhaps it would be desirable to direct the work to be performed during the night.

I am considerably indebted to you for propounding the suggestion for utilizing the spring. Will you please arrange for the necessary sample of water to be procured for analysis, if this precaution has not yet been safeguarded. I am informed that the receptacle should be thoroughly cleansed before the water is enclosed, to avoid contamination.

Yours sincerely,

(ENCLOSURE) OPINION

Re Rallingbourne v. Sir Leslie Brash

1. The Defendant is not entitled to use the spring in Honeywood Spinney of which he is the owner for any purpose that will interfere with the natural pure flow of the stream on to the Plaintiff's land injuriously to the Plaintiff and in addition is bound to maintain such pure natural flow.

2. Any building or works extending into the stream is *prima facie* an encroachment upon Plaintiff's rights and is a cause of action in respect to the possible consequences to the pure natural flow without the necessity for Plaintiff proving actual injurious interference or proving the probability of any particular specified damage by such interference the onus being upon the Defendant to show that no act or omission to perform any act by or in his behalf or with or without his knowledge by any person in his employ or otherwise does in fact amount to interference with the pure

natural flow and also that the said acts or omissions have not and cannot in the nature of things have any perceptible injurious effect upon the natural flow of the stream. *cf.* Bickett v. Morris L.R. 1 Ap.47 L. Blackburn. Orr-Ewing *v.* Colquhoun L.R. 2 Ap. ca. 853.

3. Having regard to the facts in this case I am clearly of opinion that the Defendant will be able to show that his installation of a ram as proposed can in no perceptible degree obstruct pollute or diminish the pure natural flow of the stream on to the Plaintiff's land and that therefore an action for breach of covenants cannot be successfully maintained. *cf.* Per Cur Rhodes *v.* Airedale Commiss: L.R. 1 C.P.D. 392 45. L.I.C. P. 341.

(Sg) GEOFFREY CHAWLEGGER,

2 Midden Court,
Inner Temple.

So help you!

GRIGBLAY TO SPINLOVE

Dear Sir,   19.2.25.

We regret that we cannot agree to gauge brick cills and weatherings. No gauged work is described in the specification or measured in the quantities, and our price does not cover for it.

We may say that in all our experience we have never been called upon to gauge in work of this character. We are accustomed to turn out brickwork which will equal the best done anywhere and to the satisfaction of leading architects, and we will pick the bricks and keep the joints as near to $\frac{1}{2}$ in. as no matter, and we believe that this will meet with your satisfaction. If anything more is required, payment for extra time and waste must be allowed us.

Yours faithfully,

This is a perfectly right and reasonable view of the matter.

SPINLOVE TO GRIGBLAY

Dear Sir,   21.2.25.

It is you who have introduced the description "gauged brick work". I have not asked for it. I am not concerned with what is included in the quantities; the bills are not part of the contract and any question arising out of them must be settled between Mr. Tinge and yourselves.

Yours faithfully,

Spinlove is right in what he says of the quantities, which have no place in the contract except as a schedule of prices fixing rates at which any variation shall be valued, but he is perfectly wrong in every other particular. His letter is lamentable in its arrogant disregard of the builder's point of view, and his requirements are childish. What he asks for is, in point of fact, not gauged work—for gauged work is a particular process employed with particular bricks—but his demand is akin to it, and a special clause in the specification could alone entitle him to make the demand.

GRIGBLAY TO SPINLOVE

Dear Sir,   23.2.25.

We beg to say that we are perfectly aware the bills are not part of the contract, but if your requirements for gauging the cills, etc., were included in your specification Mr. Tinge would have measured the item, and the fact that he has not done so supports our contention that the work is not included in the contract. We have given special instructions to Bloggs *re* this work and have no doubt that it will give you satisfaction, but we cannot handle the cills as gauged work without being allowed the extra price, which we are willing to agree with Mr. Tinge.

Yours faithfully,

SPINLOVE TO TINGE

Dear Mr. Tinge,   24.2.25.

I enclose copies of correspondence with Grigblay on the subject of brick cills and weatherings. Surely the general requirement of "work to be of the best description" and "to the architect's satisfaction", includes this necessary cutting and jointing?

Yours faithfully,

TINGE TO SPINLOVE

Dear Sir,   26.2.25.

We did not measure any gauged work nor describe any special labours in cills of the kind you describe, as such work was not asked for in your specification nor shown in the drawings.

Yours faithfully,

We probably admire Tinge's pithy style more than Spinlove, who wants to have his view of Grigblay's obligations. That, however, has nothing to do with Tinge; it is a point for the decision of that tremendous person widely known as "the Harshtec". Spinlove evidently did not know how to reply to Grigblay, for there is no letter on the file. He has obviously allowed his mind to be obscured by his drawing-board, which has presented to him a problem that, in practice, does not exist. Spinlove (who cannot lay bricks) has been trying to show a bricklayer (who can) how to lay them by representing bricks and their joints as equal rectangular blocks with straight edges ranged out with dividers. The resources of the craftsman are out of mind for the draughtsman; the problems presented by set-square and dividers do not exist for the craftsman.

A SANITARY
EXPERT APPEARS

SPINLOVE TO WREEK & CO.,
SANITARY SPECIALISTS

Dear Sirs,   28.2.25.

I enclose layout of drains for house near Marlford, with con-
tours, and shall be glad if you will let me have a scheme for sewage
disposal. Before you do so, however, I should like you to see the
subsoil and discuss things with you, preferably on the site. Will
Tuesday next suit you? I shall be travelling by the 2.5 from Charing
Cross on that day.

Yours faithfully,

WREEK & CO. TO SPINLOVE

Dear Sir,   2.3.25.

We duly received your esteemed communication, with plan, and
we will have pleasure in arranging for our Mr. Peter Schwarb to
place himself at your entire personal disposal and visit the site in
your good company on Tuesday next, as per your letter.

As one of our fleet of motors is available on that day we shall be
favoured if we may be allowed to place it at your personal disposal,
and would arrange for Mr. Schwarb to call for you at one o'clock at
your office, or any other place or hour convenient to your good self,
for the purpose of personally escorting you to and from the site.

We are, dear Sir,

Your obedient servants,

*Wreek & Co. evidently believe in "personal charm as a commercial
asset", and by "personal charm" they appear to understand a fawning
sycophancy directed to establish in the charmed one a sense of obligation*

114

which shall make it difficult for him to reject their proposal, question their price, or condemn their performance. To experience three hours boxed up in a motor with Mr. Schwarb's unflinching personal charm—sublimed, perhaps, with a touch of scent—will probably settle Spinlove's hash, or, on the other hand, perhaps it will not. The needs of personal charm have, we may guess, led Mr. Schwarb to scheme to join Spinlove at lunch and pay for both; and, at a hint, it would probably find him ready to carry the architect upstairs on his back and put him to bed.

SPINLOVE TO WREEK & CO.

Dear Sirs, 3.3.25.

As I understand you are motoring down to Marlford on Tuesday I shall be glad to accept a seat in your car. I will expect it after lunch at 1.30.

Yours faithfully,

One cannot here altogether regret the graceless style Spinlove adopts to those under his direction, but although the insincerity of Wreek's obsequious letter smells strongly, there is no reason why Spinlove should not thank them on the frank assumption that the intention is to save their own, and his, time.

SPINLOVE TO THUMPER & CO.

Dear Sirs, 7.3.25.

I write to confirm arrangements made with your manager by telephone to-day for your representative to call here at 1.25 on Tuesday to go with me by road to site near Marlford for the purpose of taking particulars for ram. There is a level and staff on the site.

Yours faithfully,

Spinlove's action in inviting the representative of another firm of kindred activities to take a seat in the car put at his disposal with such unctuous blandishments by Wreek & Co. is the last thing that Wreek & Co. would expect or desire. Thumper's man will greatly dilute the personal charm of Wreek's Mr. Schwarb, and we have to picture James Spinlove beset as by rival beauties, each trying to ingratiate herself and displace the other in his favour.

SPINLOVE TO THUMPER & CO.

Dear Sirs,   11.3.25.

I am obliged for your report with specification and tender for water supply. You say nothing of the guarantee of rate or discharge from the ram, which was promised.

I will write to you further when I have inquired into the rights of the adjoining owner.

Will you please send down and take sample of water and send it to Sir Geoffrey Whittle for analysis. I am writing to him.

Yours faithfully,

SPINLOVE TO SIR GEOFFREY WHITTLE, F.R.S., M.I.C.E.

Dear Sir,   11.3.25.

I have instructed Messrs. Uriah Thumper & Co. to send you sample of water from spring rising in Honeywood Spinney on high ground at the top of Honeywood Hill, four miles north of Marlford, Kent. The water is wanted for domestic use and is to be pumped by ram to storage tank under roof of house.

I shall be glad if you will make your report cover the question of ram-lining, pipes, and tank.

Yours faithfully,

Spinlove seems to have had experience of water supply, judging from the exactness of his arrangements. He directs the sample to be taken by those who will take it at the source and in a clean flask of ample size, which they will seal and mark. A sample taken from a limey bucket thrust into a ditch below a dead crow and put into an imperfectly washed embrocation bottle, the cork of which has been moistened in the mouth of a labourer who is chewing tobacco, often gives unsatisfactory and per-plexing analysis.

Spinlove is evidently aware that pure spring water is not pure, but is a highly diluted chemical; and that pure soft water, i.e. rainwater, will dissolve lead by oxidation. Spring water contains carbonic acid in quan-tities that sometimes rusts iron so fiercely that galvanized pipes are no protection against stained, iron-smelling water; and there are acids dis-solved from heather roots and peat beds which act disastrously in a simi-lar way in hot water service pipes; and various other dangers. These awkward conditions can be met, but they must be first known. Freedom from organic pollution and fitness for drinking has obviously also to be proved. Water analysis is a special subject and the expedients demanded by the analysis are also a matter of special knowledge and practical experience.

GRIGBLAY TO SPINLOVE

Dear Sir,   12.3.25.

We are sorry to have to mention the matter, but Sir Leslie Brash has not yet honoured your certificate of 16.2.25 for £2,000. We wrote him on March 1 calling his attention to same, but have received no reply. If you will mention the matter to him we shall be grateful.

Yours faithfully,

When an architect has drawn a certificate, the owner is bound to honour it within a certain time defined in the contract, and usually thirty days. The architect has a duty to the builder of drawing certificates when due, and to the client of seeing that the amounts certified are, in fact, due. Spinlove ought, however, to have notified Brash that he had drawn a certificate and in a letter somewhat as follows: "The contractor has applied for payment on account. I find that he is entitled to the sum of £2,000, and I have to-day sent him a certificate for that amount." Such a letter warns the owner and gives him the assurance, otherwise only implied, that the certificate duly conforms to the requirements of the contract.

SPINLOVE TO BRASH

Dear Sir Leslie Brash,   14.3.25.

Mr. Grigblay happened to mention to me that he thought you might not perhaps understand that the payment of instalments is due on presentation of each certificate. I think you will like me to let you know this.

The work, as you will see, is going ahead now. A few days were lost by frost, but progress is good and I think Grigblay is well up to time.

With kind regards,
Yours sincerely,

This letter of Spinlove's is so extremely circumspect and tactful as to suggest he thinks Brash is trying to avoid payment. It would have been better had he written: "Grigblay seems to want a cheque rather badly. Perhaps I ought to have explained to you that it is customary to honour certificates on presentation."

We may remember that Brash is by profession an expert economist, and he has perhaps calculated that if he holds back each certificate (and there will be ten of them) for three weeks he will gain the interest on £2,000 for six months. Brash, apparently, is what is known as a "bad payer". Spinlove, however, is a much younger man than Brash and his sensitiveness is natural. He has probably never had to write such a letter before and will perhaps never have to do so again.

BRASH TO SPINLOVE

Dear Mr. Spinlove,   16.3.25.

I certainly did not comprehend that the builder was to be paid cash immediately. The contract, I may remind you, stipulates that certificates are to be honoured within thirty days, of which twenty-eight have only so far elapsed. I have not, I may inform you, over-looked the matter, and it is unnecessary for Mr. Grigblay to suppose that I shall not complete my obligations, but at the time you drew the certificate there was very little to be perceived of the building.

I shall be visiting the site again shortly and am gratified to know that the progress made meets with your satisfaction.

Yours sincerely,

SPINLOVE TO BRASH

Dear Sir Leslie Brash,   17.3.25.

The stipulation in the contract for payment within thirty days of date fixes the *outside limit*. I enclose copy of the clause from the conditions, from which you will see that the builder is entitled to be paid at once, and this is the established custom.

You will understand, of course, that at the date each certificate is drawn you have security in the work done to the value of 20 per cent more than the amount certified. This first certificate included for all the digging and foundations.

Yours faithfully,

SPINLOVE TO TINGE, QUANTITY SURVEYOR

Dear Mr. Tinge,   18.3.25.

I enclose letter, plan, specification, and drawing of sewage disposal together with Wreek & Co.'s tender. You will see they have connected two of the baths and six of the lavatory wastes to a separate tank, as they say that the considerable flow from baths, which are all used at one time when the house is fully occupied, will flood out the anaerobic tank and put the filter out of operation. If they make the anaerobic tank big enough to deal with this flow it will not operate satisfactorily with the normal flow. This second tank will involve an extra, I am afraid, but their estimate of £525 greatly exceeds the provision you fixed. Will you please examine their estimate and report.

Yours faithfully,

TINGE TO SPINLOVE

Dear Sir,   23.3.25.

Wreek & Co.'s price is at least 30 per cent too high; they could also do much less extravagant work. I see no object in bronze bushes to tip, or of grid over the filter; the white glazed outfall channel and fireclay detritus chamber could quite well be replaced by concrete and brick; stone cover to septic tank is all that is wanted.

Why not let Grigblay do the building work under their direction at scheduled rates? The cost ought to be about half of that proposed.

Yours faithfully,

Personal charm seems to extend to the flattery of suggesting that an architect of Spinlove's distinction and social eminence will require a kingly sewage outfall.

SPINLOVE TO WREEK & CO.

Dear Sirs,   24.3.25.

I have carefully considered your estimate, but your proposal is too extravagant and your prices too high, and I will ask you to send me an amended competitive estimate omitting bronze bushes to tipper, and the grid over filter and substituting brick and concrete for outfall channel and detritus chamber, and excluding building work, which I will arrange for the general contractor to carry out under your direction.

I am not able to invite you to tender for ram and water supply, as you ask. That matter is already arranged for.

Yours faithfully,

Mr. Schwarb has evidently seized the opportunity suggested by meeting Thumper's man in the motor, to follow the first precept of commercial enterprise and "do the other fellow in the eye".

WREEK & CO. TO SPINLOVE

Dear Sir,   27.3.25.

We are gratified to know that our proposal for sewage disposal installation meets with your esteemed satisfaction and only regret that you are not in a position to spend the sum necessary to secure that your client's drains shall be of the finish now in favour with the leading architects and included in the modern equipment of the great houses recently built.

We may mention that refined and dainty sanitary works are becoming the rule rather than the exception among the nobility and gentry, and we should like to feel that you and your good client will not in the future have to regret that his septic tank and filter will not compare favourably with those possessed by his more distinguished friends and neighbours. We may say that many gentlemen who are our clients take pride in their sewage plant, which they frequently view, as they would their conservatory, and introduce to the notice of their friends.

In order to give your client this satisfaction, and out of consideration for your good self and with a wish to make our super high grade Antystynk plant better known, we will make you the special offer of $12\frac{1}{2}$ per cent reduction on our previous estimate. In case, however, your client cannot afford our super high grade Antystynk, we enclose specification and estimate for our lower grade plant, such as we instal at police stations, factories, etc. We regret that we always keep the building work in our own hands. We may mention that we absolutely guarantee our effluent, the purity of which is well known. Our Mr. Sinclair Vennom, the celebrated septic tank expert, who lately retired from our board of directors owing to ill-health, frequently demonstrated the fact by drinking a wineglass of it.

Yours faithfully,

The flunkeyism displayed in this letter is the same as that with which certain shops shame the parvenu into buying the most expensive goods by suggesting that if he does not he is ignorant of the correct thing and a stranger to the best circles. Their Mr. Sinclair Vennom seems to have demonstrated the purity of the famous effluent once too often; but as Brash's enthusiasm for his sewage plant is not likely to lead him to similar exuberances, the effluent may be considered satisfactory.

SPINLOVE TO WREEK & CO.

Dear Sirs,   1.4.25.

I have to acknowledge your amended tender. Your proposal is satisfactory, but your price is not, and I shall be glad if you will see what you can do to reduce it before I invite proposals from other firms.

Yours faithfully,

As different firms of specialists use different methods and different materials, plant, and workmanship, competitive tenders, in the strict sense, are not possible. All the architect can do is to compare the proposals and prices of reputable firms, and choose what best suits the case. Apparently Wreek & Co. do good work, or Spinlove would not take so much trouble to get an acceptable tender from them.

BRASH TO SPINLOVE

Dear Mr. Spinlove,   1.4.25.

I have to-day transmitted cheque to Mr. Grigblay. I was certainly much gratified by the advance progress has made, which I observed when I viewed the operations yesterday.

Yours sincerely,

This letter gives the impression that Brash would not have honoured the certificate had not the appearance of walls above ground satisfied his ideas of "progress". To the uninitiated there is always dismay at the early stages, delight when the walls rise rapidly, as they do, and final despair at the interminable operations of interior work and finishings.

WREEK & CO. TO SPINLOVE

Dear Sir,   4.4.25.

In reference to your esteemed request, we have carefully reconsidered our proposal and enclosed revised estimate.

By using less expensive bricks and making other immaterial alterations we are able to reduce our price to a figure which we trust will be acceptable to your good self. The price we are quoting is made specially low in order that we may have the satisfaction of not disappointing you.

We are, dear Sir,
Yours faithfully,

The indications are that Wreeks have stood out for a price much higher than the value of the work justifies, as specialists of high reputation are able to do. Their substitution of a "less expensive brick", etc., is to "save the face", as the Chinese say; the real consideration is that if they do not cut down their figure they will lose the job. Spinlove appears to have understood the game they were playing.

SPINLOVE TO WREEK

Dear Sirs,   7.4.25.

I write to accept your amended estimate of £375 for sewage disposal plant. The outfall drain is now in hand, and I shall be glad if you will make arrangements with Mr. Grigblay and get the work started at an early date.

Yours faithfully,

THE THICK OF THE FIGHT

❋ ❋

SPINLOVE TO RUSS & CO.

Dear Sirs,   9.4.25.

By Sir Leslie Brash's instructions I enclose complete particulars of water supply from spring. I am to await your approval of these proposals before putting the work in hand.

Yours faithfully,

RUSS & CO. TO SPINLOVE

Dear Sir,   14.4.25.

We return particulars for drawing water from spring at Honeywood. We see no objection to these proposals so long as the pure natural flow of the spring is not interfered with injuriously to the owner's interest by any act or omission in the carrying out of the works or in subsequently withdrawing and pumping the water.

Yours faithfully,

The charge for this letter will be, we may suppose, 13s. 4d.

SPINLOVE TO RUSS & CO.

Dear Sirs,   15.4.25.

I have duly received your letter and enclosures, but you have not answered the question I had to refer to you. I am aware of the stipulation you describe, and what I want to know is whether my proposals infringe those stipulations.

Yours faithfully,

Spinlove's unappeasable tenacity is here very much to the point. Brash's solicitors have burked the question partly because of their habit, as lawyers, of using extreme caution, and partly because they cannot say whether the installation and operation of the ram may, or may not, impress the House of Lords as an infringement of the covenants, the House of Lords being the only decisive tribunal for the interpretation of these covenants.

RUSS & CO. TO SPINLOVE

Dear Sir,   17.4.25.

In reply to your letter on the subject of Honeywood spring, we see no objection to the proposal providing that the restrictions of the covenant of conveyance are not infringed.

Yours faithfully,

"Say 6s. 8d."

SPINLOVE TO BRASH

Dear Sir Leslie Brash,   18.4.25.

In accordance with your instructions I referred proposal for installing ram to Messrs. Russ & Co. and enclose copy of correspondence. Will you please let me know what action I should now take?

Yours faithfully,

Spinlove is handling this matter creditably. For this occasion at least we may say that no flies are settling on him.

BRASH TO SPINLOVE

Dear Mr. Spinlove,   22.4.25.

I conferred with Mr. Russ to-day and he signified to me that he perceives no objection to the contemplated ram proposal if carefully executed; and he advises me that the chance of the probability of Mr. Rallingbourne taking action is extremely remote, and that if he were so ill-advised as to do so he would certainly not succeed. Will you, therefore, be so obliging as to ensure that the work shall be carried out *at night* with as little ostentation as possible.

Yours faithfully,

It will be noted that Mr. Russ can give an opinion in conversation that he will not embody in a letter. This is perfectly understandable: the risk of being proceeded against is one for Brash's shoulders alone; Russ can only accept official responsibility for advising what those risks are.

The temper of the adjoining owner; his health and sanity; his attitude towards his rights in general; whether he is easy-going and generously minded, or jealous of his rights and grasping; and also the actual nature of his interest in the property, which may be entailed or held in trust; all are vital considerations of which Russ knows nothing. His judgment, however, as a man of the world, which he puts at the disposal of his client in conversation, is entirely a different matter.

SPINLOVE TO GRIGBLAY

Dear Sir,   25.4.25.

I enclose Thumper's estimate, specification, etc., of work in connection with ram and piping to house. The cover of chamber enclosing the spring should be kept a few inches below surface of ground and well banked in and covered over and turfed so as to be inconspicuous.

Will you please carry out your work at the spring head *at night*. To be done day-work and set against provision for pump.

Yours faithfully,

GRIGBLAY TO SPINLOVE

(Personal)

Sir,   27.4.25.

I have seen your letter on the subject of spring head and venture to write to you privately as I gather that your instructions to do the work at night is to keep it secret.

You will pardon me pointing out, with all respect for your superior judgment, that to have men up in Honeywood all night with lights visible from road and for miles round to the south and west, is not the best way to keep it secret. Down there they wouldn't have any excitements if they did not all look sharp after other people's business, and the whole country will be in a buzz. Some of my men are sure to mix it up with a drop of beer at the public, and we shall have the New River Company and the London Water Board and Thames Conservancy round to have a look at us, and "Mystery of Honeywood Spinney" on the evening papers.

Bloggs does not allow any on the site, and there is no one about would be the wiser if you let us do the work all in the ordinary

course and get it finished out of hand. You will pardon me addressing you, but I thought best after I got home to-night as it will save
a bit of trouble.

Yours faithfully,

*This friendly letter reveals Grigblay to us as he is under his skin. He
writes privately as he could not well question the order to work at night
officially, since the reason is no business of his. He has already prevented
Spinlove from hanging up the whole work while the solicitors negoti-
ated permission for the builder to use the spring, and he has again come
to the rescue. The letter displays the honest good-nature and practical
wisdom of the writer; and we recognize in his kindly, dry, ironical
humour the salt of sterling British national character. Spinlove ought
long ago to have established friendly personal relations with such a man.*

SPINLOVE TO GRIGBLAY

(Private)

Dear Mr. Grigblay,   28.4.25.

 I am very much obliged for your letter. Of course you are perfectly right. Please act as you suggest. I was on the site yesterday
and I wish to tell you that I am entirely satisfied with the brick
window cills that I saw. Please work the flat arch heads and
weatherings in the same way. I appreciate the attention your foreman has given to this matter and also the way he has managed the
gradation from the first lots of facings to those now being sent.
This has been done extremely well; no one would notice the change
unless his attention was called to it.

Yours truly,

*This is a private unofficial letter, and it would not be amiss if Spinlove
used it as a model for his official letters to the builder in place of those he
is so ill-advised—and ill-mannered—as frequently to write. It is clear
he understands that Grigblay takes a pride in his work and wishes to
please the architect, and he ought always to keep it in mind.*

BRASH TO SPINLOVE

Roselawn,
Dear Mr. Spinlove,   Thaddington.
2.5.25.

You will perceive from the above address that we have now gone into residence here until the autumn. I visited the site last evening and am gratified to observe that progress is advancing, but there are several matters which I do not quite comprehend. Could you meet us on Saturday? I shall be travelling by the 12.27 from Cannon Street and we might go down together in concert and visit the site after luncheon.

Yours sincerely,

P.S.—Lady Brash requests me to say that our daughter is expecting some young friends to tennis in the afternoon, and it is desired that you will bring your bat, etc., if you like disporting yourself in that pastime.

We may conclude that Brash has never played lawn tennis.

SPINLOVE TO BRASH

Dear Sir Leslie Brash,   4.5.25.

As the builder's people will have left in the afternoon and I want to see the foreman, I will go down early on Saturday and come to the house at 1 o'clock.

Yours sincerely,

P.S.—Will you be so obliging as to inform Lady Brash that I shall be charmed to comply with her invitation to tennis.

I detect a touch of east wind here. Spinlove's postscript—as recorded on the carbon file copy of his letter—is in autograph, as was that to which it replies, and as we know Spinlove well enough to judge that he would not so answer an invitation from a lady without being aware of a gaucherie, we may gather that he has deliberately retaliated on Brash by accepting in the same form and through the same channel as the invitation. His adoption of Brash's stilted diction and condescending tone cannot possibly be accidental; in fact, we appear to have surprised a bit of the Old Adam in our friend James. It seems clear that he has come to resent the condescending self-sufficiency of Brash (discernible to us only in his letters) and has reasons for being wide awake to social slights. Lady Brash would have written her own invitation had she not felt it incompatible with her social eminence to so condescend to her architect—that, at any rate, is my sense of the matter—and, if I am correct, Spinlove has shown a very proper spirit, although, without knowing what lies in the background, it is impossible either to commend or condemn his manner of showing it.

SPINLOVE TO GRIGBLAY

Dear Sir, 8.5.25.

I was on the site on Saturday and was greatly concerned to notice that two of the brighter of the red bricks in the facings are *already beginning to decay.* The surface is coming away in a powdery dust near the edges of the brick. I expressly prohibited the inclusion of these red, under-burnt bricks in facings; you promised that you would throw them out, and I selected and handed to your foreman samples of the bricks which only were to be used. It is really inexcusable that, after my particular and exact directions to the contrary, these soft bricks have been built into faces. Your foreman is going over the work and marking the doubtful bricks, and when I have checked over I must ask you to cut out and replace them with the bricks sent under the new arrangement with Hoochkoft.

It is a great disappointment to me that the frost spoilt so much of the jointing. It is a pity this work was not protected, as the top of the wall was, with sacking. It will be impossible to match the cut-off joint by pointing, so that the whole of the facings will now have to be raked and pointed. I have asked your foreman to have different samples of pointing done so that I can decide which to adopt.

I also had to call your foreman's attention to the clearing of the battens in the hollow walls.

Yours faithfully,

The battens referred to are those which are hung in the 2 in. space of hollow walls and carried up with the brickwork to prevent mortar falling into the space and collecting at the bottom, where it might conduct damp from the outer to the inner wall and block the ventilation inlets which, by allowing air to circulate, keep the space dry. These battens have to be pulled out and cleared of accumulations of mortar at frequent intervals if they are to serve their purpose thoroughly.

GRIGBLAY TO SPINLOVE

Dear Sir,   9.5.25.

Referring to your remarks *re* decay of facings, we cannot accept responsibility for same. If this matter had been left to us we should never have accepted such bricks as Hoochkoft first sent, but it was not in our hands as we acted on your orders and were told you had approved the bricks. We picked over the bricks to oblige you without charge, and Bloggs worked to your instructions and you saw what he was doing. It does not seem likely there can be many of the defective bricks and we will arrange to cut out and replace, but shall have to charge men's time for same and shall be glad of order for extra.

The frost getting at joints is no fault of ours, as faces cannot be protected. We were obliged to take off top course and rebuild, as you know, although that work was protected.

Yours faithfully,

Grigblay is not to blame for frost attacking the green mortar joints; and he is not only entitled to disclaim responsibility for the decaying bricks, but is obliged to do so, for if he agreed, as part of his obligations under the contract, to remedy the defect in only one or two bricks, he would be accepting liability for the soundness of the whole of the facings.

SPINLOVE TO GRIGBLAY

Dear Sir,   12.5.25.

As you are well aware I have all along objected to the red soft bricks and expressly forbidden their use. I actually selected samples of what I did approve, and your foreman had these to guide him. I asked you to pick over the bricks, but you said the bricklayers would throw out the soft bricks as they came to hand. This has not been done and I must call upon you to make good.

Yours faithfully,

Spinlove, we know, is responsible for the bricks supplied. But for his vigilance 15 per cent or more of the whole of the facings would be defective; he would not be able to avoid direct responsibility to Brash, and it is very doubtful if he could by any means fix liability on Hoochkoft. Again we see how a small lapse from formal exactness in organization may lead to disastrous consequences.

Under-burnt facings have been known to decay before the roof of a new house was on, so that the whole had to be pulled down and rebuilt with the architect unable to fix responsibility on any one because the samples he had approved had not been marked and could not be identified.

GRIGBLAY TO SPINLOVE

Dear Sir,   16.5.25.

We have to say that we accept no responsibility for defective bricks for reasons given. We note that the bricks delivered under the new arrangement with Hoochkoft meet your approval.

Bloggs tells us that bricklayers threw out all bricks that did not agree with samples. He did not keep samples after work completed as no reason to. He writes that about forty bricks had ought to come out.

Yours faithfully,

It will be noticed that in his first paragraph Grigblay repeats that he accepts no responsibility for the facing bricks, and then records that Spinlove has approved present deliveries. He does this in order to consolidate his position—so to speak—and put on record that he has always disclaimed responsibility.

GRIGBLAY TO SPINLOVE

Dear Sir,   19.5.25.

We shall be glad if you will pass us a further certificate for £2,500.

Yours faithfully,

SPINLOVE TO BRASH

Dear Sir Leslie Brash,   25.5.25.

The builder has asked for a further payment on account, and I have to-day sent him certificate No. 2 for £2,500.

Would it be convenient to you, I wonder, to let me have, say, £400 on account of my own fees?

Yours faithfully,

It would have been just as well if Spinlove had not asked for any fees at this time.

In dealing with business firms, public companies, corporations, Government offices, and so forth, it is well for an architect to send in claims for fees on account according to the letter of the custom (see R.I.B.A. scale of charges), for it is no one's business to ask the architect whether he wants any fees, and later on he may be called on to explain why the claim was not made earlier. The case is different, however, when the architect's employer is a private person. There is an etiquette which directs that, when employed by the nobility and gentry, the architect waits until invited to send in an account. This etiquette, which is linked with the past, flatters the architect by dissociating him from commercial activities, and it is a pity for the architect to discourage the sentiment.

In a certain high social plane it would be a gaucherie for the architect to ask for his fees; it would not so particularly mark a man in sore straits for money, as one who did not know what was what.

GRIGBLAY TO SPINLOVE

Dear Sir,   28.5.25.

Bloggs reports that he finds that the heads of window-frames come $1\frac{1}{2}$ in. too high to allow top of brick-on-edge head to line with horizontal joint of facings. The frames are made as figured on your detail No. 11, but we think you overlooked that ground floor is now $1\frac{1}{4}$ in. below bench mark datum from which the height of brick cills was figured. We might have saved it out of the joints, but we are up twenty courses now. Shall be glad of your early instructions.

Yours faithfully,

SPINLOVE TO GRIGBLAY

Dear Sir,   30.5.25.

I am annoyed to hear of the mistake with the frames. If the detail had been checked with the actual work this would not have happened. I shall be going on to the site next Tuesday and will see what can be done.

Yours faithfully,

It is difficult to see what exactly has happened, but the mistake has arisen from Spinlove having confused the ground-floor line with the bench datum with which it was originally identified. The builder is here at fault. All joiner's details are—or should be— sent on to the site so that they may be checked and figured up to agree with the actual work. It is likely that Spinlove's blunder trapped Bloggs; and it is also likely that the detail of the brick cills was prepared after the detail of the win-dow-frames which had to be made early for building in. There are plenty of openings for slips and mistakes, but the builder who allows any join-ery to be prepared which will not fit the building is to blame.

SPINLOVE TO BRASH

Dear Sir Leslie Brash,   30.5.25.

I have received report of the analyst, Sir Geoffrey Whittle, and enclose his account. The report is quite satisfactory, but it will be necessary to use specially lined pipes and lead tanks; and a water softener, at least for drinking and special purposes, is recommended. I should like to discuss this with you at an early opportunity. I shall be on the site on Tuesday.

Yours sincerely,

P.S.—Since dictating the above I rang you up and have now received your message and will arrange to meet you on site at 5.30 on Tuesday and stay to dinner. I will bring analyst's report with me.

SPINLOVE TO GRIGBLAY

Dear Sir,   3.6.25.

I was on site yesterday and arranged with your foreman to ad-just error in height of window-frames by building a 6½ in. brick-on-end flat arch in place of 4½ in. brick-on-edge, so that the top of flat arch will now come one course higher than originally intended and shown on ½ in. detail.

I approved the bricks in facings marked by your foreman as to be cut out. I agree to an extra (day-work) for this work.

I also approved sample of pointing. A flat joint makes the joint appear too wide, and the irregularity of the bricks makes it untidy. The mortar is, therefore, to be slightly pressed back into the joint with a rounded piece of wood. This is to be done *as the work proceeds.* Facings already built to be raked and pointed to match.

The work looks very well and Sir Leslie Brash, you will be glad to hear, expressed himself as delighted with all that has been done and with the progress being made.

Yours faithfully,

There is a healthy change of tone in this letter. "The band has come." Probably the Brashes, now first able to see the house taking understandable shape, are appreciative, and Spinlove's heart is lightened. It will be noticed that he has admitted his responsibility for the faulty bricks by allowing Grigblay an extra for replacing, and has found a satisfactory way of getting over the undue height of window-frames without the loud lamentations and complaints we have learnt to expect from him.

SPINLOVE TO THUMPER & CO.

Dear Sirs,   5.6.25.

I enclose analyst's report and recommendations, and shall be glad to receive an amended specification and estimate for ram installation and piping to storage tank, all in accordance with the recommendations of the report. I should also be glad to receive proposal from you, later on, for water softener. This is to serve one bath and bib cocks in pantry and scullery and H.M. closet.

Yours faithfully,

THE LAST OF THE SPRING

GRIGBLAY TO SPINLOVE

(Private)

Sir,   11.6.25.

Rather an awkward thing happened to-day, but no harm done, I believe, and lucky for us. Just before I got on to site Mr. Witspanner, tenant of Honeywood farm, came on to our ground and wanted to know whether we had right to hay in meadow below, and then he noticed our water tank. "Hullo, you've a nice lot of water," he says. "Yes, and we wants a nice lot, too," Bloggs told him. "That's my water," he says, "and you've no right to take it." Well, I suppose Bloggs gave him a bit back, and off he goes saying he'd complain to Mr. Rallingbourne.

When I drove up he was just getting over the gate at the bottom, but Bloggs sent a whistle after, and he saw me and waited while I went down. Well, to make a short story I took him to the hotel, and it's like this. He will not interfere with us taking the water, but he wants that bit of grass which is not of much account, anyway, after horses have been on it, so the business can be put right if Sir Leslie Brash will agree. But I was asking him about his landlord, Mr. Rallingbourne, and he says he's the sort that has got to be cock of his own dunghill. If you're polite, and not unreasonable, and don't presume, he will agree to near anything, but if he thinks you're trying to better him or steal an advantage he gets all his hackles up and nothing will move him. He does not care for money; it's bossing up he values.

Now, Witspanner knows we are using the water and if the ram is put in your client will be at his mercy, and he's a sour-tempered fellow and no mistake. What I suggest is that Sir Leslie should get Rallingbourne's consent to the ram by offering to pipe the spring on to his land. More water is lost travelling the ditch than the ram will pump.

With apologies for troubling you.

Yours faithfully,

The remarkable lucidity and completeness of Grigblay's presentment of the position will be noticed. Not only do we get the facts, but Bloggs, Witspanner, and Rallingbourne stand before us as actual persons, and we have an intimate and minute understanding of the state of affairs. Brash could not do it; the whole forces of Russ & Co. could not attempt it, nor could Spinlove. Grigblay has no educated knowledge of the use of words; but he has humour, practical insight, and the habit of single-minded frankness.

SPINLOVE TO BRASH

Dear Sir Leslie Brash,   12.6.25.

The letter of which the enclosed is a copy is marked private, but I have Mr. Grigblay's permission to show it to you. It seems important to open negotiations with Mr. Witspanner at once and get in touch with Mr. Rallingbourne. I estimate cost of piping ditch, which is 320 yds. long, at £20.

Yours faithfully,

Oh, do you, Mr. Spinlove!

This estimate is wildly at sea. One can only suppose that Spinlove has light-heartedly mixed up yards with feet and made no allowance for consolidating and levelling ditch and filling in with earth, wheeled or carted, and making good to ram waste and spring-head. Assuming that a 4 in. pipe will serve, a reasonable estimate is from £60 to £100.

Spinlove has here airily tossed a trifle from his richly-stored bins of knowledge to Brash as he might throw a scrap from his plate to a dog; but Brash will make the figure the basis of his negotiations with Rallingbourne. Facile, off-hand estimates ought not to be given. Spinlove would do well to notice the stolid ignorance of Bloggs, who, in common with every other foreman, never has any idea of the value of any kind of work and, when rallied, merely grins wisely. Spinlove's lapse is here quite inexcusable; he has not been confronted by a sudden demand for an estimate, but offers it gratuitously; he does not describe his figure as a

*rough approximation and he has not paused to visualize the work in-
volved or even to scrutinize his absurd figure.*

BRASH TO SPINLOVE

Dear Mr. Spinlove,   15.6.25.

I thank you for your communication transmitting copy of Mr.
Grigblay's letter. Will you please convey to him my sensible appre-
ciations of his action. I have indited a letter to Mr. Witspanner,
which I have entrusted to a gentleman who will call and negotiate
with him, and I will open the subject with Mr. Russ to-morrow on
the lines suggested in Mr. Grigblay's proposal.

Yours sincerely,

SPINLOVE TO BRASH

Dear Sir Leslie Brash,   17.6.25.

I have received the enclosed from Grigblay. Perhaps you, or your
solicitors, will write to Grigblay direct, as there appears to be no
time to lose.

Yours sincerely,

(ENCLOSURE) GRIGBLAY TO SPINLOVE

(Personal)

Sir,   16.6.25.

Bloggs writes that Witspanner was on site to-day and wants 5s.
a thousand gallons for all water used past and future. We do not
hold with this, but would rather pay than be stopped, though we
are using a thousand gallons a day or more while the hot weather
lasts. We do not want, however, to prejudice your client's position,
so write to ask instructions. Bloggs held him off for a day or two,
but he means to have the money so we shall have to agree to something.

Yours faithfully,

*This impudent claim by Witspanner is, frankly, blackmail. It is rather
a highly-coloured instance of the subtle undercurrents that constitute
business, with a big B, in which concessions are made in one matter on
the tacit understanding that mischievous interferences will be withheld
in another. Witspanner has no property in the spring; and even if*

Grigblay diverted the whole of it, his claim would be against his land-lord, Rallingbourne, and not against Grigblay or Brash. The price he is asking is such as he might charge if he were pumping as well as supplying the water.

It is to be noticed that if Grigblay had not adopted a false position by drawing the water secretly, he could not thus be victimized by Witspanner.

BRASH TO SPINLOVE

Dear Spinlove (*sic*),   20.6.25.

I am happy to intimate that all future anxiety *anent* the spring is finally eliminated.

My secretary interviewed Mr. Witspanner, and offered thc hay for nothing if he would desist from objecting to our use of spring, but he said the crop would not be worth taking and desires me to pay him for mowing and carrying. He has also a claim against Grigblay for the water he has used.

This evening I met Mr. Rallingbourne, quite unexpectedly, at the house of friends by whom Lady Brash and myself were being entertained at a dinner-party. I found an opportunity of informing him that the builder was using water from the spring. I found him a most affable gentleman. He intimated he had no objection so long as Witspanner had sufficient flowing to him. I then asked if he would complete an arrangement for me to utilise the water, and acquainted him what our proposal was. He said he anticipated there would be no objection, but desired to appoint a surveyor to report, and, of course, some agreement will have to be executed. He made a memorandum of your address, and I will request you to represent me and meet this surveyor.

I desire to record my appreciation of the great assistance you have been in enabling me to secure the spring for my use, and which would never have eventuated but for your initiation of the proposal.

> Believe me,
> Yours sincerely,

This letter is in autograph, written at night and after a very pleas-ant dinner-party. The champagne is not out of Brash's veins and the glow of a social triumph newly fills them. These facts account for the unusual warmth and intimacy of the letter, and for the generosity of its concluding acknowledgment, but Spinlove is entitled to gratitude. He could not have been more concerned for Brash to benefit by the spring if the house had been his own

GRIGBLAY TO SPINLOVE

Dear Sir,   22.6.25.

On receipt of your telephone message yesterday telling us that rights to spring were agreed and not to deal with Witspanner, we wired to Bloggs to warn him. We enclose his letter received to-day, which you may like to see.

Yours faithfully,

(ENCLOSURE) BLOGGS TO GRIGBLAY

Sir,   21.6.25.

Your wire received and noted. Two o'clock Witspanner clomb over fence so I thought better use a bit of tack. What are you bargin in for I says dont you see the notice board. What do I care for you and your blinking notice boards he says, when are you going to pay me for my water he says. Blinking yourself I says you can go to blazes out of here you lousy tup I says or I'll chuck you out. After that he began to get a bit saucy and I admit we add a few words till Alf Cheese chipped in and offered him a thick ear and I thought it would come to a scrap, but the men wouldnt have it and he cleared off saying as how he was going to talk to Mr. Rallingbourne on the telephone.

Yours humbly,

SPINLOVE'S SPECIAL ROOF

SPINLOVE TO GRIGBLAY

Dear Sir,   7.7.25.

I yesterday saw first delivery of roofing tiles, which are quite satisfactory, but I noticed no tile-and-half tiles for verges. The tiles are cogged, as well as prepared for nailing and, as on further consideration I do not think it necessary to nail the whole as specified, will you please nail every fourth course on south and west slopes only, and verges and eaves throughout. I have noted this as an omission.

Will you also let me know how you intend to mix the three different colours so as to give the "broken colour" tiling specified? Patches of uniform colour must not show, nor must there be any appearance of arrangement.

I asked your foreman to build a yard run of eaves and verges with one of the kneeler oversails, all as shown on drawing No. 27, for my approval. I also directed that rafters should *not* be lined up on plate and at ridge, but allowed to range a little unequally so that the finished surface of tiling will show undulations; and directed that the tiling battens should not run truly parallel, but vary $\frac{1}{4}$ in. each way, and the battens themselves be bent or "sprung" as necessary, so that gauge of tiles will *not* show in rigid parallel courses. Please give these matters particular attention.

Yours faithfully,

We may sympathize with Spinlove's solicitude and applaud his vision—although Grigblay is unlikely to do either—without necessarily commending the principles of the game he would be at. All architects who have the right salt acquire affections—or affectations—which they afterwards discard in favour of others, and we have no right to decide that Spinlove is either precious or silly because the immediate colour of his architectural creed may not be also ours. Spinlove has, clearly, lifted the idea bodily from a book, for it would scarcely have jumped into his head in such complete detail, and he has never tried to get the thing done before or he would not suppose carpenters and tilers to be ready, at a word, to do haphazard and crookedly the particular work which it is the pride of their skill and experience to perform by a rule of perfect exactness. He would also have known, had he before experimented in this way, that his demands upon the builder in these matters are intolerable.

GRIGBLAY TO SPINLOVE

Dear Sir,   8.7.25.

We note your instructions *re* nailing tiles. The tile-and-half bonnet and ridge tiles are on order. With regard to mixing tiles, specification calls for "broken colour tiling", from which we understood they would be supplied ready for hanging as they came to hand. The tilers will want more money, but we will have the three different kinds sent up in equal quantities and the tilers can be trusted to use them haphazard, as you wish, but we must ask you to set off this against omission of nailing.

We have directed our foreman to build sample eaves, etc., as you ask, though we were not prepared for this; and with regard to the other matters you mention, will do our best to meet your wishes, but we must point out that this is special work not covered by the contract, and we may have to claim an extra for it.

Yours faithfully,

If Spinlove had not launched out with his prescription for a sham medieval roof, Grigblay would not have been likely to comment on his other exactions. That comment is made, on principle, to remind his young friend, the architect, that a builder pays for his compliances in hard cash, and that favours should be sought and not demanded. In the circumstances, Grigblay is not unreasonable, and he evidently foresees that the stolid inertia of the carpenters and tilers will put the extinguisher on Spinlove's crotchety roof. He knows that they will listen respectfully to his directions for battening and tiling, while perhaps sharing a few winks behind his back, and then carry on much as usual. On a later day it will appear that the architect has not been understood; and if he is tenacious in his purpose, he will be asked questions he cannot answer and will be left to surrender the position either before provoking a mutiny, or after doing so. All this Grigblay perfectly understands. It is possible to build such a roof as Spinlove has set his heart on, but only with foresight and after careful preparation and with selected workmen.

SPINLOVE TO GRIGBLAY

Dear Sir,   9.7.25.

I agree to the omission on nailing tiles being set against the extra work you say I have asked for, but the method of roofing I described must be included. I do not agree that it is "special work". The whole of the work, I may remind you, has to be done "to the architect's satisfaction".

Yours faithfully,

Spinlove has once already tried to bludgeon Grigblay with this God-given power conferred upon him by the contract, and his second attempt will probably be as futile as was the first, for Grigblay's claim is sound: the field of the architect's satisfaction is, of course, limited to the work described in the contract.

GRIGBLAY TO SPINLOVE

Dear Sir,   10.7.25.

We regret we cannot accept your view that the special work in roofing you have called upon us to do is included in the contract, and we must respectfully ask you to note that we can undertake it only on the clear understanding that it is an extra. We will ask you to give directions to the carpenters and tilers on the spot, so that your exact wishes may be understood as these are not clear, and to note that we cannot accept responsibility for the soundness of this method of work, which is new to us. When we know exactly what is required we will give you estimate of the extra value of carpenters' work, and subsequently of the tiling,

Yours faithfully,

This stiff letter is not remarkable if we consider the extremely provocative one to which it replies. We notice Grigblay's assumption of authority. We have before observed this, and found the explanation in

Grigblay's sense of Spinlove's practical inefficiency. If Spinlove had the gumption to treat Grigblay as a colleague, the interchange of such un-pleasant letters would be avoided. Another builder might well have taken Spinlove's orders; made a dreadful botch of the roof, and brought in a heavy claim for extra at settlement; and Spinlove ought to be grateful to Grigblay for his plain speaking.

BRASH TO SPINLOVE

Dear Mr. Spinlove,   7.7.25.

I enclose specification *anent* inserting pipes in ditch from Mr. Rallingbourne's surveyor. I understand you have signified your approval of the proposition and shall be obliged if you will direct Mr. Grigblay to proceed with the operations.

Lady Brash and myself are much gratified with the advance in progress and anticipate eventually moving into the house considerably in advance of the expiration of the contract period, as the chimneys are now completed and the roof commenced and little remains but the interior work. I inquired of Mr. Bloggs as to the signification of the flag I observed to be affixed to a staff on one of the chimneys, and as I ascertained that many of the workmen were addicted to total abstinence from alcoholic liquor, we arranged for a picnic tea to be served to them on Friday. Our hospitality, I gather, was greatly appreciated, and the event will, I trust, serve still further to expedite progress.

All our friends join with us in admiring the fine appearance the edifice is assuming. The effect promises a very pretty and charming residence when complete.

I beg the pleasure to enclose cheque for £250 on account of your fees.

Believe me,
Yours sincerely,

P.S.—I am requested to remind you that your anticipated presence for lawn-tennis is expected on next Saturday prox. Jump in to eats and toe the line at 2 before the patters scrum starts, Woggles and Biff will be here. Snooty tried the tea-tray toboggan stunt backwards and is nursing her bumps, poor dear.

The last lines are in a hurried, bulgy hand so different from the body of the letter, that we may decide Sir Leslie Brash did not write them.

The pleasure Brash begs will find Spinlove begging. On May 25 Spinlove applied for £400 on account of fees, and now, after an interval of six weeks, Brash sends his architect £250 as a mark of approval and by way of encouragement. It will probably be a very long time, indeed, before Spinlove again has such an experience; but if he continues long in practice he will learn that the reaction of the private client to claims for architect's fees—knit up, as it is, with personal relations and respective social standings and financial circumstances—is as varied as any other of the characteristics of which every individual is compacted. Broadly speaking, an architect who is reasonably competent and conscientious may, saving disasters, expect not only to have his bill paid in full, but to be thanked for his services; yet he may not always be paid as and when he expects. There are also sensitively honourable men and women who confuse the architect with the commercial agent, and who are taken aback at being charged for services which they have not made use of—such as advice, sketch plans, or even contract particulars; and there are others who feel that they should not be called upon to pay for advice which has misled them, e.g. where contract particulars have been authorized under the architect's estimate and no tender near to his figure is obtainable. There are also men and women who are not sensitively honourable and who resist on principle all obligations, and will make unjust quibbling objections to the amount of both builders' and architects' accounts in confidence that the matter will be settled to their own advantage without recourse to lawyers. It is impossible to instance all the different kinds of treatment an architect may receive from private clients in the article of fees; they cover every degree of meanness and of generosity which human nature knows. It is a fact that will appear odd only to those whose experience of men and affairs is slight, that trouble over payment of fees is most to be expected when the scale or amount of them has been particularly and exactly agreed beforehand. The sort of man who bargains with his architect on the point of fees is precisely the sort who boggles at paying anything, and who will seek to interpret the understanding unfairly against the architect. This is the "shrewd, hard-headed" principle which is better admired at a distance than near at hand, although most architects obtain a close view of it sooner or later.

SPINLOVE TO BRASH

Dear Sir Leslie Brash,   8.7.25.

Thank you for cheque, I enclose form of receipt.

There is a misunderstanding for which I may possibly be responsible. I gather from the amount of your cheque (£250) that you suppose I asked for payment on account of £400 fees, whereas I asked for £400 on account.

Please do not trouble to rectify. It will prevent all chance of confusion in future if I follow the established business custom and invoice architect's charges as they fall due for payment. I will take an early opportunity to get things straightened out on this footing.

Yours sincerely,

Spinlove is always at his best when his resentment is awakened and he forgets himself. He was evidently hurt, and composed his letter with the care which the task of being decorously venomous deserves. He pays Brash the compliment of assuming that the thing Brash has done is so unthinkable that a clear impossibility can alone be the explanation. Unless Brash has forgotten how to blush—and in view of his self-conscious aspirations to the genteel this is not unlikely—we may imagine him as growing pink when he reads his architect's letter. He will probably be thankful to avail himself of the fantastic excuse offered him, and it is difficult to see how, in the future, he is to avoid completing with reluctant cheque book the "formal business arrangement" which the solicitous Spinlove, entirely for his client's convenience, has promised to adopt. We need not, however, be hard on Brash: he means well. He sent his cheque, in fact, on an impulse of generous appreciation; but his activities have left him aware of little but his own importance and his own gain, and he knows no better than to behave in this way. Spinlove has taken a strong line, but, from what we know of Brash, it is justified and will be unlikely to do any harm. He was not merely entitled to make protest, but it was so necessary for him to do so as to be almost a duty.

SPINLOVE TO BRASH

Dear Sir Leslie Brash,   9.7.25.

It gave me great pleasure to know that you are so well satisfied with the work that has been done, but I think I ought to tell you that you must not expect to get into the house *before* the contract date. There has been delay from frost and bad weather and also that arising from alterations in the plans, and this lost time will unavoidably delay completion. The interior represents the greater part of the work, but I am satisfied with the progress Grigblay is making.

I enclose list of grates and sanitary fittings. Will you let me know, when I see you, whether you would like to choose any of these? The prices are those included for in the contract.

Yours sincerely,

BRASH TO SPINLOVE

Dear Mr. Spinlove,   13.7.25.

I was extremely disappointed to conclude from your last communication that our residence will not be completed till subsequently to the expiration of the contract date. I clearly comprehended that the contractor was under penalty to complete the house *previously* to the day designated. Surely the vagaries of our climate are an eventuality which the contractor must risk, and an alteration does not necessarily involve elaboration! I desire to be informed when the house will be completed for occupation so that we may make necessary arrangements.

I am obliged for the list of grates and conveniences. I will purchase them myself through the intermediary of an acquaintance who is in a position to secure them at wholesale trade discount prices.

Yours sincerely,

SPINLOVE TO BRASH

Dear Sir Leslie Brash,   15.7.25.

The whole question of delay in building contracts is intricate and not readily to be explained in a letter, I fear, but the root of the whole matter is that, as the contract allows consideration for bad weather, extra work, strikes, etc., time is not of the essence of the contract. As a practical fact, the only security for prompt completion you have is the builder's care for his reputation, and you could not be in safer hands than Grigblay's.

Please do *not* buy grates or sanitary goods. The former have to suit the fireplaces which I am designing; and the latter have each to fit special conditions, so that it is absolutely necessary that all should be ordered by the builder after you have settled the pattern and price.

It will be of no advantage to you to buy at trade prices. The builder can buy at least as cheaply as you can, and he has already credited trade discounts in making up his tender. If you buy, the builder will be entitled to add a fair trade discount to his contract price and you will certainly pay more in the end. This matter of trade discounts is carefully safeguarded in the contract. The sums set aside for the various goods are the actual sums paid to the merchant and not, as I think you suppose, the catalogue retail prices. The builder has already included in his contract for packing, carriage, etc., and it will be impossible for me to prevent extras creeping in if those arrangements are upset. I hope I have succeeded in making the matter clear.

Yours sincerely,

He has, at any rate, had a good try! It would have been better if Spinlove had kept his explanations for Brash's ear, for his letter is likely to raise more questions than it answers. Spinlove, however, appears to enjoy writing letters, although he cannot always enjoy reading those he receives: the next on file, for instance!

MR. POTCH AGAIN OBJECTS

GRIGBLAY TO SPINLOVE

Dear Sir,   18.7.25.

We are sorry to have to report that the District Surveyor refuses to pass the main drain to sewage tank on the ground that it leaks. As you are aware, there is a very sharp fall on this drain, and we used particular care in making the joints with waterproofed cement so that they should stand the pressure of water test which, between the second and third manholes, has a head of 32 ft. Only four joints showed a drop or two of water after standing several hours, and these have been remade to the Inspector's satisfaction; but water sweats out through the pipes themselves. It only shows in beads after standing for hours, and does not run, but Mr. Potch, the Surveyor, came down yesterday, and has condemned the whole drain. We shall be glad of your instructions.

The pipes are "tested" as specified and there is no flaw in one of them. Bloggs would have put on labourer to keep the pipes wiped dry against the Inspector's visit, he says, but he never thought objection would be made.

Yours faithfully,

We have already seen that, at a pinch, Bloggs can be depended on for "a bit of tack".

SPINLOVE TO GRIGBLAY

Dear Sir,   20.7.25.

I have written to the District Surveyor on the subject of the drain. Please take no further action of any kind, but keep the drain charged, and ask your foreman to mark standing level of water in manholes and keep the covers on. I will visit the site on Tuesday next.

I note the contents of your letter on subject of roofing. If Mr. Grigblay can meet me on Tuesday on this matter I shall be glad.

Yours faithfully,

Spinlove has come quietly to heel in this matter of the roof. It will be noted that the head of water gives a pressure, in the lower pipes, of some 15 lb. a square inch. The "tested" pipes are subjected by the makers to a hydraulic pressure of about 20 lb. a square inch, but this test is applied for a few seconds only, to detect flaws.

SPINLOVE TO POTCH, SURVEYOR, MARLFORD DISTRICT COUNCIL

Sir,   20.7.25.

It is reported to me that you have refused to pass the main soil drain at Honeywood. I shall be obliged if you will tell me: (a) the grounds for your objection; (b) the by-law infringed; and (c) the work you require to be done.

Yours faithfully,

Spinlove has evidently not forgotten previous interchanges with Mr. Potch. He does well to remind Potch that his powers are limited by the by-laws. Many small builders and others may forget this and Potch, in his ambition to flourish as a public terror, may not trouble to remember it.

POTCH TO SPINLOVE

Sir,   24.7.25.

Honeywood drain loses water and must be relaid. *See By-laws.*

Vent of settling tank to be replaced with 4 in. heavy cast-iron soil vent. *See By-laws.*

I am surprised to be informed by my assistant that copy of our by-laws was sent you last year. As it is unfortunately lost I shall be very glad to present you a second copy to go on with for a time, on receipt of 1s. 2d., post free, as my Council disapproves of putting A.R.I.B.A.'s and others to the trouble to ask unnecessary questions.

I am, Sir,

Yours faithfully,

The insolent intention of this letter, although veiled by its illiteracy, is undoubted, and is just what Spinlove must expect from Mr. Potch, who, as has already appeared, practises privately as an architect in the district in which he operates in his official capacity, and so finds it to his interest to pile up official difficulties in the way of his private rivals. To irritate them into precipitate action, to their public discredit with the Council, is all part of his system.

SPINLOVE TO POTCH

Sir,   27.7.25.

You must permit me to inform you that the Honeywood drain does not "lose water", as stated in your letter. After standing for three days fully charged, the drop in level of water in manholes is scarcely perceptible—$\frac{1}{4}$ in. or $\frac{12}{16}$ in., not more, in fact, than would be accounted for by absorption and evaporation. The joints are perfectly tight and a slight sweating of water through the substance of the pipes is due to the excessive head of water imposed by the sharp fall in the ground. This condition of head would not arise in practice and the sweating would be of no consequence if it did. The pipes are Dallop's deep-socketed "Tested" laid on concrete and are the best procurable. I have to ask you either to pass the drain or to say in what way the work can be improved, either as regards workmanship or materials.

There is no "Settling Tank". The thing you refer to is an anaerobic tank; its successful action depends upon absence of air, and the ventilation pipe you call for would tend to spoil its efficiency by admitting air. The 1 in. galvanized pipe you object to is to prevent gases accumulating at pressure in the tank and breaking the seal of the trap, and was put in by my orders.

Yours faithfully,

Spinlove does well to ignore the offensiveness of Potch.

POTCH TO SPINLOVE

Sir,   31.7.25.

I note you now admit water leaks through substance of pipes at Honeywood and which is the reason I stated drain leaks and must be relaid. Unfortunately my inspector cannot wait three days at manholes to check figures as he has other business as well. I have been told drains sometimes gets stopped. The water test is against that happening and not against it does not happen.

My Council does not expect of me to tell Institute architects where to get drain pipes, but most people know such trouble would be cured by treating with one or two coats of pitch, boiling hot.

I happen to be aware what a settling tank is and also all soil vents to be 4 in. heavy cast iron, *see By-laws*. If everyone who did not agree with by-laws could do what he liked my Council would not have adopted same.

I am, Sir,
Yours faithfully,

Potch seems to know that Spinlove is young and lacking practical experience, for his pitch proposal, not a joke, is a mischievous attempt to get Spinlove into worse difficulties or, at least, make a fool of him. The "boiling hot" pitch would crack all the pipes and it could not hold back water which is forcing itself, under a pressure of some 15 lb. to the square inch, through glazed earthenware. We may judge from the letter which follows that Spinlove fortified his opinion by discussing the matter with Bloggs.

SPINLOVE TO POTCH

Sir,   4.8.25.

Your letters on the subject of Honeywood are clearly intended to avoid the questions I have put to you. In the circumstances I must ask you to note that the drain you object to demonstrably conforms with your by-laws and is of the best possible workmanship and materials, and that I claim on behalf of Sir Leslie Brash a formal certificate of acceptance from your Council.

I also have to ask you to note that your by-laws do not require that septic tanks should be ventilated, and that, as it is insanitary and against established practice to do so, I have no intention of ventilating the tank at Honeywood.

Yours faithfully,

Spinlove is winning this tussle in fine style. Potch, of course, is only bluffing, and prevaricating, and obstructing; but Spinlove could scarcely arrive at the point of confidence in which, alone, he could write such a letter, without anxiety and stress. As I was led to remark on an earlier occasion, Spinlove seems to have "been there before", for in nothing does he show such firmness as in thwarting the machinations of Potch.

SPINLOVE TO POTCH

Sir,   14.8.25.

It is now ten days since I wrote to you stating the position I take on the subject of Honeywood drains and calling upon you for certificate of acceptance. As I have received no acknowledgment or reply, I have to ask you to note that unless I receive immediately a satisfactory answer, I must refer the whole correspondence to the Chairman of your Council, in which case I shall protest against the way I have been treated by their official and the offensive tone of the letters I have received.

I am, Sir,
Yours faithfully,

Spinlove seems, in a previous existence, to have been a prize fighter.

POTCH TO SPINLOVE

Sir,   16.8.25.

Re drains at Honeywood. I have been busy and the matter is a difficulty, but have now decided to give you the benefit and enclose certificate, which no doubt meets your satisfaction.

The vent to settling tank must be at your own risk.

I resent your remarks and regret you should feel cause to make same as no intention on my part.

I remain, Sir,
Yours faithfully,

What Potch means by "vent must be at your own risk" he probably could not himself exactly say. He no doubt considers his last paragraph to be an ample explanation and apology. Much of the offensiveness of his letters is, perhaps, due to native ungainliness of mind. He is like a fox which cannot help smelling and is unaware that he smells.

THE STAIRS GO WRONG

GRIGBLAY TO SPINLOVE

Dear Sir,   5.8.25.

As you know, we are at work on the staircases, and we venture to call your attention to the headroom at No. 3 step of back stairs. We think you overlooked that the binder carrying partition runs across door-opening to bathroom, so that unless the bathroom floor is raised one step the binder must be dropped 5 in., and owing to the revised arrangement of the stairs shown in detail No. 27, we do not think headroom will be satisfactory.

Awaiting your immediate instructions,

Yours faithfully,

P.S.—We shall be glad of a further certificate for £3,000.

Apparently Spinlove has done what it is perilously easy to do: he has improved on the contract in his detail drawings without investigating fully all the consequences of the change.

SPINLOVE TO GRIGBLAY

Dear Sir,   6.8.25.

I confirm telephone message directing all work on back stairs to be stopped. I note that the strings have already been got out and sunk, and treads of winders, etc., prepared, so that it is too late to go back to the arrangement shown in the contract drawings. I do not understand why my attention was not called to this matter when the work was set out.

I widened the landing at top to give more room for the swing of the door; this pushed the bottom step out and brought No. 3 step into the position of No. 2, so that it was obvious I had mistaken the position of binder. If you had called my attention to this at the time, the difficulty would not have arisen, as I might have managed with one step less.

I do not like the idea of raising the bathroom door one step. Will you please return drawing No. 27. I do not at present see what can be done. A 9-in. steel joist in place of binder will not settle the trouble. You will notice that I splayed off the angle of the binder to ease the headroom, which I knew was tight.

Yours faithfully,

A ridiculous letter! It is clear Spinlove does not know what the devil to do and wants the builder to tell him. He allows us to suppose that in the contract drawings there was an 11-in. binder which carried 5½ in. floor joists. This binder came below the ceiling and was probably cradled and installed as a beam. In making his detail he pushed the binder up flush with ceiling to give to the starved headroom the extra height required by the alteration in the steps; and overlooked the opening to the bathroom door across which the binder runs.

GRIGBLAY TO SPINLOVE

Dear Sir,   8.8.25.

We regret to say that we have to-day learnt that the binder, floor and partition, are now all in place as shown on the contract drawings. Your drawing No. 27 gives exact particulars of the stairs, but the position of the binder is only slightly indicated. The section of it is not coloured on our drawing, and we had no means of knowing what your intentions as regards other parts of the work were. The binder had been prepared and sent on to the work, and probably fixed, before we received your detail.

It will be necessary either to scrap the strings and winders or take down the binder, etc., which will be the simplest way. We suggest that the difficulty could be got over by putting in a 5½-in. sill in place of binder and trussing the partition, which might also be hung up by tie strapped to purlin. The easiest thing, however, would be to raise the binder and floor. If you do not care to go up one step to bathroom floor, the bathroom might be entered from the corridor instead of the landing of back stairs, in which case the floor need not be raised with the binder. Drawing No. 27 herewith. We shall be glad of immediate instructions.

Yours faithfully,

Spinlove is a conscientious fellow and we may sympathize with his predicament. It is more than humiliating for him to scrap the strings, etc., for to do so will probably cost about £30. We know, too, that he was not satisfied with the contract arrangement. On the other hand, Grigblay's other proposals are all hand-to-mouth expedients or botches.

SPINLOVE TO GRIGBLAY

Dear Sir,   9.8.25.

I return drawing No. 27 amended. You will see the binder and bathroom floor are to be raised. It is a particular point of the plan that the servants' bathroom should open off their own landing and not off the main corridor, and, as it is only for the servants, the step will not matter so much. [*Ahem!*]

I consider that the discrepancy should have been pointed out to me, as this is a duty specially placed upon you by the contract, and it must be clearly understood that no extra is involved by the making good which I consider to have become necessary owing to your oversight.

Yours faithfully,

Spinlove is pushing things too far. The mistake seems to be entirely on his shoulders.

SPINLOVE APPLIES FOR FEES

SPINLOVE TO BRASH

Dear Sir Leslie Brash,   9.8.25.

Grigblay has applied for a further certificate for £3,000, which I have sent him.

I take this opportunity of enclosing particulars of my own fees, as arranged. The first item—4 per cent on £18,440 became due on the signing of the contract. The second item, 2 per cent on £7,000 is the residue of the 6 per cent on value of work done.

I hope you like the dining-room fireplace which the bricklayers are finishing. The bricks are specially made for this purpose, and Grigblay has imported a particular bricklayer to carry it out.

Yours sincerely,

Two or three months ago Spinlove asked for a modest £400 on account of fees, and after waiting six weeks was fobbed off with £250. As we remember, he then promised to put the matter "on a formal business footing so as to prevent further misunderstandings". He now sends in an account for the fees which, by custom and under the Institute Scale, he is entitled to. The amount indicated is £876 less £250 already paid, or £626.

BRASH TO SPINLOVE

Dear Mr. Spinlove,   10.8.25.

You must permit me to convey to you that I did not at all anticipate that at this early period I should be requested to disburse so preponderant a proportion of your fees. I conceive I am correct in asseverating that professional gentlemen are, by habitual custom, paid their fees *after* the services they refer to have been performed and *not previously* thereto. The mansion is a considerable distance—

a very considerable distance I am led to apprehend—from being completed, and yet I am now requested to disburse a sum approximating to 80 per cent of the whole remuneration eventually accruing to you when the works have been satisfactorily completed and your engagement with myself terminated. I confess that I am amazed at a claim which is—if you will allow me permission to so express myself—most extravagantly preposterous.

Although it is not a matter to which I should, under happier circumstances, desire to make deviation, I, nevertheless, consider that you are under serious responsibilities and obligations towards myself which, as in all such monetary matters, have a financial signification. I observe that the contract document protects me with a not unsubstantial guarantee; that is to say, the sums I periodically disburse are amply secured to me by the value of the operations performed. It is on the face of it—if you will permit me to say so—an utterly anomalous conjunction of eventualities which gives me no such security against my architect, to whom I am requested to disburse—by clear demonstration—not 80 per cent of, but *more than double*, the proportion of fees represented by the work accomplished.

I observe that the certificate, which you inform me has been transmitted to Mr. Grigblay, is for the augmented amount of £3,000. May I be permitted to remind you that £2,000 is the payment I am accustomed to anticipate disbursing on these occasions.

Yours sincerely,

Brash's protest is not unnatural, and his reasoning would be sound if his premises were true. This is a very different letter from those he wrote to his young friend in the early days; in fact, it is such a letter as he might write to one of his own years and standing. Spinlove's firm resistance to being bilked seems to have jolted Brash into a higher esteem of him. His wordy expostulation is a little pathetic.

GRIGBLAY TO SPINLOVE

Dear Sir,   12.8.25.

We are unable to agree that the error in back staircase is a matter for which we are in any way accountable, as we had no means of knowing what your intentions *re* bathroom door were. We must ask you to note this, as we cannot accept any such responsibilities for oversights in joinery details, although we do our best to detect them. As the alteration now required is a small matter we will, however, in this instance make no charge, although we are entitled to do so.

Yours faithfully,

I judge this letter to have been dictated by Grigblay himself. He has no doubt had a sharp word to say to his shop foreman and to Bloggs, but as a matter of principle he finds it necessary to remind Spinlove that his bland assumption that the architect is not responsible for misdirections, and for discrepancies in his own thoughts, will not do at all.

SPINLOVE TO BRASH

Dear Sir Leslie Brash,   13.8.25.

Had I known you were not aware of the custom concerning payment of architects' fees I would have explained the matter. I now enclose particulars of architects' charges issued by the Royal Institute, from which you will see that two-thirds of the 6 per cent fees—that is, 4 per cent of the amount of the accepted tender—represents fees earned before the contract is signed. The remaining 2 per cent is for general supervision and direction of the work, and is payable in instalments as the works proceed, so that the architect is in the same position as the builder in giving what you term "financial security". At no time is the architect paid for what he has not done.

I shall be glad if you can make it convenient to send me a cheque. One has, of course, to get in one's money.

Grigblay is entitled to £3,000. He would have been entitled to £2,000 several weeks ago had he applied for it. The contract states that certificates shall be for not *less* than £2,000.

With kind regards,

Yours sincerely,

Spinlove seems now to have got Brash's measure in this matter of fees. He has knowledge, of course; but the letters also show him to be the stronger man. By comparison Brash appears to be—if I may be given permission to be allowed to so express myself—a flabby old jelly.

THE WATER COMES IN

SPINLOVE TO GRIGBLAY

Dear Sir,   15.8.25.

I was on the site yesterday and was disturbed to see water standing 15 in. deep in cellar. Some months ago I noticed water, but
supposed it was due to rain, only. There is no sign of its coming in
through the walls above the standing level of the water, so that
there must be a defect in the vertical damp course below that line.
Your foreman says he pumped the cellar dry a fortnight ago, when
there was nearly 2 ft. of water. I directed him to dig down outside
and open up vertical damp course for my inspection. Please let me
know directly the work is ready for me to see.

Yours faithfully,

GRIGBLAY TO SPINLOVE

Dear Sir,   16.8.25.

Our foreman has reported to us your instructions to open up
vertical damp course; but this is a big undertaking and, as we are
certain there is no defect in the damp course, we do not think any
purpose will be served by opening up. We have directed our foreman to pump the cellar dry, and we will keep it under observation.
In our opinion the water comes up through the floor.

Yours faithfully,

SPINLOVE TO WILLIAM WYCHETE, P.P.R.I.B.A.

Dear Mr. Wychete,   18.8.25.

I am in difficulties with a cellar which lets in water; but where it
comes from or how it gets in I cannot understand. The ground is
perfectly dry; there was not a sign of water when the excavation

was made, and the lower 7 ft. of excavation is in impervious clay. The vertical damp course of 1-in. thick waterproofed cement is continuous with the horizontal damp course which is below the level of the cellar floor. This is 4-in. concrete with $1\frac{1}{2}$ ins. of 3 and I cement rendering trowelled to a polish, with skirting carried up 6 ins. and turned into joint of brickwork.

I went on site yesterday after the cellar had been pumped out and wiped dry. We could find no flaw anywhere, but after a time the whole surface of the floor became wet, and after a couple of hours water had collected in one part. The foreman says the floor is "sweating", but does not explain what he means, and I don't think he knows. Can you give me any idea what is wrong, and how I can make the place tight?

Yours sincerely,

WYCHETE TO SPINLOVE

My Dear Spinlove,   20.8.25.

I think the explanation of your scrape is that the impervious excavation holds surface water, which collects against the outside of the walls, like a tank. This gets under the foundations and through the footings, and floods the space under the floor—which, I assume, has 4-in. or 6-in. of loose filling—and the water is forced up by its standing head through the concrete. The probability is that this process began while the concrete and rendering were green, so that minute channels were then formed in it; but under the conditions stated the cellar could scarcely be a dry one, as the floor was not dampproofed.

If there is such a fall in the ground that you can drain the water away by connecting a pipe through the wall into the hard core under the floor, the cure is easy. If not, your only course, in my opinion, is to cover the floor with asphalt and put a concrete floor on top, to prevent the water forcing the asphalt up. This concrete, however, may not be necessary. It is important to dig a sump and keep the water pumped out until the whole of the floor is finished and perfectly set. The builder should have done this originally.

With best wishes to you,
Ever yours sincerely,

SPINLOVE TO WYCHETE

Dear Mr. Wychete,   21.8.25.

Many thanks for your letter. I understand the matter perfectly now. There is a sharp fall in the ground, so that there will be no difficulty in draining. Can I make the builder pay for this work? Also, would the District Surveyor be likely to object to the drain going under the walls? If so, perhaps it would be best to put an iron pipe through the wall and under the house, but the rest of the drain, I imagine, could be earthenware? Or could the whole be earthenware if care were taken to carry walls, etc., clear of it?

Yours very sincerely,

Spinlove is here so elated to find himself master of the awkward situation that he loses his head and acknowledges Wychete's careful reply to his question by asking him a hatful of entirely idiotic and unanswerable ones. Needless to say, there is no reply from the great man.

LADY BRASH TO SPINLOVE

Dear Mr. Spinlove,   21.8.25.

Sir Leslie is so *dreadfully* sorry not to be able to have answered your last letter, but he has gone to The Moor quite suddenly! He did not in the least expect it, and asked me to write and tell you.

My daughter is expecting some young friends on Saturday, and we shall hope to see you in the afternoon.

How very close it has been to-day!

Yours sincerely,
MAUDE BRASH.

Will you be my D.P. to Bingham's and stay night? Biff has let me down. *Split-tail behaviours.* Phone early. P.

For "The Moor", I read the moors; Brash has been invited north to shoot grouse. I do not know how Lady Brash manages to convey that her husband is a most unsafe gun, but she certainly does so.

As it is eight days since Spinlove wrote, this stampede to "The Moor" is an imperfect explanation of his getting no answer. The intimation that he lies heavy on his client's conscience will, no doubt, hearten him.

It was "P", by evidence of the handwriting, who wrote a footnote to an earlier letter! "P" must be the daughter.

LADY BRASH TAKES CHARGE

GRIGBLAY TO SPINLOVE

Dear Sir,   27.8.25.

We enclose copy of letter from her Ladyship and await your instructions *re* same. We understand that the partition referred to is that between bedrooms Nos. 5 and 6, and is to be moved to increase size of dressing-room.

Yours faithfully,

(ENCLOSURE) LADY BRASH TO GRIGBLAY

Mr. Grigby (*sic*),

Lady Brash wants the wall in the other big room—not our room—moved nearer from the end as the big wardrobe must go in the dressing-room.

Sunday.

Grigblay knows better than to take instructions except through the architect, although inferior kinds of builders might not be so circumspect. Some might even welcome this opportunity of making hay of the contract and establishing an uncontrolled account for extras.

Lady Brash has here adopted the style of the great lady gratuitously, for this sort of thing has been far to seek since the war. One has only to consider that the person she addresses is superior to her in heart, in mind, in wisdom, in humour, and also—if the word is to have any right meaning—in education, to realize the absurdity of her assumption. We may imagine Grigblay, a middle-aged man, shouldering a pack in Flanders, while Lady Brash was hoarding provisions, decorating her car with flags of the Allies as if for a boat-race, and speaking of Grigblay and his kind as "Tommies".

SPINLOVE TO GRIGBLAY

Dear Sir,   30.8.25.

I have written to Lady Brash. Please tell your foreman to get on
with the work.

Yours faithfully,

*Decisive but ambiguous! The manner of it expresses "Lady Brash be
blowed!" but the sense is "Alter the partition as directed".*

SPINLOVE TO LADY BRASH

Dear Lady Brash,   30.8.25.

Mr. Grigblay has sent me a copy of your letter of Sunday. I understand you want the partition moved so as to make the dressing-
room wider. Are you really quite sure you would like this? No. 6
was designed as a dressing-room only, though big enough to take a
bed on occasion, and there is a door from it to the bedroom of No.
5. If you widen the dressing-room by, say, 3 ft., you will *reduce the
bedroom by 3 ft.* Have you realized this, I wonder? The result will be
that you will have a quite small single bedroom with a door opening into a double bedroom also so much on the small side that I am
afraid you will be disappointed with it. I mention this because I
have used particular care not to have any mean-looking rooms, and
because I was originally asked to arrange for a good double room
with dressing-room *en suite,* and the plan provides this.

If the partition is moved, the windows will be displaced and
both rooms will look lop-sided and ungainly—in fact, they will be
spoilt so far as appearance goes. Do you not think it would be sim-
pler to put your big wardrobe in another room and, generally, fit
the furniture to the rooms? It is really too late now to attempt to
alter rooms to suit furniture. It would be a great pity to shift the
partition, and I am sure you would be sorry if it were done.

I hope Sir Leslie is having good sport.

Yours sincerely,

*Spinlove's difficulty is no less because it is a common one. He is under
obligations to be courteous and patient and amenable to his employer's
ambitions; but he cannot ignore his own reputation nor that of his profession, and with this is associated the duty of rendering unfailing ser-*

*vices so that his client shall be guided to make wise decisions and pro-
tected from hasty and foolish ones. The indications are that Lady Brash
is so light-witted and so spoilt that appeals to her better judgment will
impress her merely as opposition. When such a woman wants anything
she has no attention to give to reasons against it; and in this case the
lady's mind is probably incapable of holding two ideas at the same time.
The best thing for Spinlove to do would be to make up his mind that
Lady Brash does not understand what she is asking, and take an early
opportunity of cajoling and flattering her to a sounder judgment.*

*One awkwardness of the position is that even if Spinlove found suf-
ficient justification to do what the wife demands, he could scarcely act
without the authority of the husband. If he writes to Brash for that
authority and does not get it; or if the lady knows he has written; or if he
acts without writing and is taken to task, he is in danger of becoming
involved in—well, let us say, an intermission of marital bliss, which
may thereafter encumber him with petty dilemmas, make his work a
misery instead of a pleasure and his best offices a personal failure instead
of a success.*

LADY BRASH TO SPINLOVE

Dear Mr. Spinlove,

I do not want any door and I want it in *that* room as it is the
room my sister will have when she comes and it was in our old
home and she is used to it so I cannot have it anywhere else as it
does not go with the other furniture. Of course I do not want the
windows changed only the wall. [*"It" is, evidently, the wardrobe.*]

A man came about sweeping the chimneys. He said his name
was Mr. Williams and in new houses the chimneys cannot be swept
unless you get on the roof and break the tiles so I really do not
know *what* to say. I wish Sir Leslie was at home to see about it.
How chilly the wind has been!

With kind regards,
Yours v. sincerely,

Friday.

*A touting chimney-sweep has apparently been telling the poor woman
that flues are sometimes so built that they cannot be swept.*

SPINLOVE TO LADY BRASH

Dear Lady Brash,   3.9.25.

I will see that the chimneys can be swept without anyone having to get on the roof. I will call at eleven on Saturday morning and
settle with you what is to be done. Yes, the wind has certainly been
rather chilly.

With kind regards,
Yours sincerely,

This looks more hopeful.
The letter which follows deals with so many points of detail that I
will interpolate my comments.

GRIGBLAY TO SPINLOVE

Dear Sir,   4.9.25.

Our foreman took down the partition between rooms Nos. 5
and 6, but her Ladyship now says that it is the one between Nos. 8
and 9 she wanted moved. Her Ladyship seemed very much upset
and directed Bloggs to take down the latter partition which he has
now about finished. This, as you know, is a double breeze partition.
Her Ladyship said you decided to increase dressing-room 3 ft., but
we do not think you can intend that on account of linen cupboard.
See plan.

[*Spinlove mentioned 3 ft. as an illustration only, and had in mind*
another partition.]

Four feet nine seems the least we can manage with, and that will
bring the wall very close up to window. You will remember there
was a post on this partition supporting purlin. Bloggs has got this
pinned up temporarily, but we shall want a steel joist to take this
post, which we think is the best way out of the difficulty. We take it
the binder carrying this partition, which is finished as a plastered
beam on ceiling below, will remain, and the new binder put in above
level of ceiling.

The heating engineer says he does not see how to run his return
which came down in the corner of this partition. We told him we
would chase wall, but that is an awkward job, as it is only $4\frac{1}{2}$ ins.

[*The inner lining of hollow external wall, presumably*], and we are afraid the casing cannot be made flush with wall, as it is a 2-in. pipe, even if we sink back of casing where the unions come. We shall be glad of your immediate instructions as the work is being delayed; also authority for extra.

Watkins started glazing their casements, but we had to stop their men as her Ladyship says they are wrong. We understand sheet or plate is wanted. We had to let Watkins's men go away, which is a pity, as we have had a lot of trouble to get them.

[*Watkins must be sub-contractor for the iron casements, and his fixing of leaded glazing is referred to.*]

There is a sweep been hanging about who said he was engaged by her Ladyship to sweep the chimneys. Bloggs told him he had no orders for him, but he afterwards found the man at work and two of the labourers had to see him off the premises. We mention the matter as we should like her Ladyship to understand that we had no instructions to admit the man, and as we are responsible for this work we prefer to entrust it to our own workmen. The parging is green as yet.

[*The builder is under contract to sweep flues to prove they are clear and have been properly built for sweeping.*]

The alteration to the partition will push the lavatory basin in the bedroom so far over that we shall not be able to get the waste into the same head taking those of dressing-room and room beyond, and a separate head and vertical waste will be necessary, and we do not see how this can be made to clear the garden entrance and window below.

[*The dressing-room is perhaps 7 ft. wide, and Spinlove has been able to scheme so that the waste from lavatory-fitting in this room, and those in the bedrooms adjoining on each side, shall all discharge into the rainwater head and be conducted to the ground by one inconspicuous vertical pipe.*]

A lead waste carried diagonally over the head of garden entrance and across to the gully receiving the vertical waste would, however, meet the case.

We shall be glad of your early instructions.

Yours faithfully,

A lead pipe trailing conspicuously across the wall in close proximity to one of Spinlove's architectural prettinesses, and reaching out frantically to the gully, would be a calamity. Such botches are unworthy of a competent speculative builder—they disgrace an architect.

This letter is an example of the disinterested solicitude of Grigblay for the success of the work. Few builders would lay the matter out so fully, but would either put the work in hand, or say they could not go on and ask for instructions. It also displays in a remarkable manner how the carefully contrived economies of means to ends and neat perfections of a skilful design may be cast into hopeless confusion by merely one act of capricious interference. However, here is some more of it!

SPINLOVE TO GRIGBLAY

Dear Sir,   5.9.25.

I was dumbfounded to learn that you have allowed your foreman to pull down and alter the work in face of my written instructions to the contrary. I tried to get into touch with Mr. Grigblay on telephone to-day. Will he please ring me up without fail to-morrow morning?

I confirm my telephone instructions that no further alterations are to be made except by my explicit directions. I am at a complete loss to understand why it should be necessary for me to remind you of so well-established a rule. It will certainly be necessary to put the work back as it was before, and I must look to you to do so, but kindly note that *nothing is to be done* until I am in a position to give complete instructions. I shall see Lady Brash on Saturday and will write to you next week.

Yours faithfully,

GRIGBLAY TO SPINLOVE

Dear Sir,   5.9.25.

Since we wrote yesterday we have heard from our foreman that her Ladyship has referred to hot and cold water to be laid on to the drawing-room. We know nothing of this, and ought to have instructions *at once* as the service pipes are being got out and this will mean a change in the layout, as it is a long run for the pipes and we do not quite see how we are going to get proper circulation. We understand her Ladyship intends an aquarium to stand in bay, so there will have to be a gully to take waste, and as the Surveyor may object to this being treated as rain water [*Sure to do so!*], we shall have to lower the top manhole. [*So that the extension may drain to it.*] We were about to build this manhole, but have stopped the work and also that on drains beyond, as levels and falls will have to be altered, and it is no good doing the work twice over. We think the Surveyor will insist on a vent pipe by gully. [*The extension is at the top end of drainage system and a vent pipe is required in that position.*] Would you wish this on the gable beside the bay window, which seems the best position? We shall be obliged by your immediate instructions.

Yours faithfully,

Spinlove, we may be sure, has exercised his best ingenuity to arrange that this unsightly 4-inch pipe running up walls and sticking up above eaves of roof, shall be hidden away; and the prospect of its becoming the salient feature of the most sappy part of a studied elevation will cause him anguish.

GRIGBLAY TO SPINLOVE

Dear Sir,   6.9.25.

We write to confirm and record statement made to you by Mr. Grigblay on telephone this morning that he acted in accordance with your instructions (see your letter of 30.8.25) to "go on with the work", which we naturally read to mean to do the work ordered by her Ladyship. Our understanding that the partition between Nos. 5 and 6 was intended, was, we hold, confirmed by your letter.

We note that no further work is to be done until we have your explicit directions, but must point out we are being stopped and that we shall not only have to claim extension of time as well as the extra, but shall have to compensate heating and other sub-contractors and ask you to consider our own position, as we have had to pay off labourers and drain-layers, and we may have to send away plasterers shortly, and these are difficult to get. We shall be glad of a certificate for £2,000 further on account.

Your last certificate, dated 6.8.25, has, so far, not been honoured. If you can help us in this matter we shall be obliged.

Yours faithfully,

Lady Brash, at a touch, has not only brought confusion to the work, but has given both the architect and builder sore heads. Grigblay has been indefatigable in good offices, but the dislocation of his organization is a serious matter for him and he evidently has no intention of being victimized. He is entitled to look to his architect to protect him.

LADY BRASH TO SPINLOVE

Dear Mr. Spinlove,   *Wednesday.*

The men took away the wrong wall!!! It really is all most trying and difficult and so very vexing when they will not do what they are told and putting it in all little squares one cannot see out of and the servants cannot clean properly because of the corners and complaining about it. The men have made a path through the wood all along where the bluebells come for a short cut through the hedge instead of going out at the gate, what Sir Leslie will say when he comes back I really do not know and I thought I should never get the dust out of my eyes they are quite sore still. The man who came about the chimneys complained that Mr. Bloggs was very rude and would not let him because he did not want him to find out and he says because the chimneys are made crooked and cannot get a brush up to sweep them and perhaps the house will be burnt down. If I had any idea what a trouble it was all going to be I would never have consented, but Leslie will not listen to a word I say and the factory chimney was smoking yesterday and all blowing across and I knew what it would be and if they don't put a proper water-pipe it means the garden hose through the window like we had at Pilchins Drake though I am sure I shall never like the house as much as Pilchins and the fish dying. Really I feel so worried with it all I scarcely know where I am. Phyllis is still away she is always such a comfort.

Yours sincerely,

The poor woman has made herself ill in her anxiety to see matters right, and I feel sorry I have said such savage things about her. She opens her heart to Spinlove in a way that shows she has a friendly liking for him and understands he is on her side, although she does not at all understand that the builder is working under his direction. Spinlove ought to have no difficulty in establishing her peace of mind and guiding her to a wise decision if he relies upon her confidence in his good offices and her obvious liking for him, and avoids any assumption of authority. Apparently, however, the receipt of this letter and Grigblay's by the same post have made him again lose his head.

SPINLOVE TO GRIGBLAY

Dear Sir,   7.9.25.

I cannot accept the position you take in your letter, but agree you had grounds for misunderstanding. Later on I will discuss the question with Mr. Grigblay and come to some arrangement; in the meantime, I will do my best to get a decision from Lady Brash.

I have wired to Sir Leslie Brash, which will, I hope, help matters, and I am writing to him. He is still in Scotland and will, no doubt, pass you a cheque on his return. Your application for certificate has my attention.

Yours faithfully,

SPINLOVE TO TINGE, QUANTITY SURVEYOR

Dear Mr. Tinge,   7.9.25.

I enclose particulars of the state of the work and of certificates granted. Grigblay has asked for a further £2,000. You will see he had £3,000 only four weeks ago.

Will you let me have an estimate of value of work done.

Yours truly,

(TELEGRAM) SPINLOVE TO BRASH

7.9.25.

Brash, Achoe, Glen Taggie, Inverness. Work held up urgent writing Spinlove.

It is difficult to see what purpose Spinlove had in sending such a telegram except to put Brash off his aim for the day.

SPINLOVE TO LADY BRASH

Dear Lady Brash,   8.9.25.

I came down expressly to see you on Saturday, as arranged, and was disappointed to find you out for the day. I have this morning received your letter.

I am very sorry to know you are so worried, but the alterations you want involve all sorts of difficult questions which cannot be settled except at an interview, and your letter makes allusions to matters of which I know nothing. If you will make an appointment, I will gladly come down and settle things with you. Perhaps you could telephone. I rang up and left a message for you this morning, but have heard nothing.

It will not do to delay, as the builder has already had to send away some of the men and the works will be in part stopped if something is not decided at once.

I have received a rather stiff letter from Mr. Grigblay pointing this out and, of course, it all means extra expense.

I could come down to-morrow afternoon if you will telephone before 11, or early on Thursday. I shall not be in town on Wednesday, and have an appointment in London on Thursday afternoon.

With kind regards,
Yours sincerely,

P.S.—As I have already mentioned, you need have no anxiety about the chimney flues. I will see they are all right.

It is difficult to imagine a much more tactless letter. Spinlove asks the poor soul not to worry and then tells her of various causes for worry of which she is happily unaware.

SPINLOVE TO BRASH (INVERNESS)

Dear Sir Leslie Brash,   8.9.25.

I wired to you last night—"Work held up urgent writing" as I am in a quandary, and Grigblay has been obliged to send away some of the men and others will follow them unless I can at once give directions. As perhaps you know, Lady Brash wishes the partition between bedrooms 8 and 9 moved so as to make the dressing-room bigger, and it was taken down without my knowledge, as also partition between 5 and 6, by an error. There are numerous minor alterations and serious displacements involved in the alterations and I feel sure if these were understood you would wish the partition restored. There is also certain other work Lady Brash wants altered but I have not been told what exactly is required. I have, however, stopped part of the work including the drains or this might have to be done all over again.

I feel it is difficult for you to come to any decision from such a distance but think you would wish to know what is happening as, besides extra cost of the alterations, there may be claims for interference with the work and, of course, time allowance will have to be given. The plastering and some other work is going on as well as circumstances will allow.

Yours sincerely,

What sort of an answer Spinlove can expect to this letter it would be difficult to imagine. If he could not set out definite points for Brash to decide—and it is difficult to see how he could do so—it would have been better for him to confine himself to saying that alterations have been ordered which make it important for Brash to be on the spot as soon as possible. However, this letter will give Brash some idea of what is happening.

LADY BRASH TO SPINLOVE

Dear Mr. Spinlove,   *Sunday.*

I really do not know why all this worry with Mr. Blogs not doing what I said and so many questions going on and on and Phyllis away and Leslie and the man about the chimneys again because now is the time and not wait till the house is finished and perhaps have to be pulled down he says. I want the wall moved but not the *wrong one* they have pulled down and the men all smoking and whistling instead of attending and the extra expense which I know Leslie will not pay when he always said the house was for me in case he died first and not for Mr. Grigby to stop the work and do what he likes and make the stairs not wide enough with all the trouble we had at Pilchins over again taking the window out to get it in [? *the wardrobe*] and such small ones [? *windows*] when I wanted them big and not with little squares all over, but Mrs. Spooner says they *will* do it and you can get in quite easily by cutting the squares with a pen-knife and perhaps be murdered so I shall never feel safe in the house when Leslie is away and you cannot have bars in case of fire she says. If I had known that it meant I never never *never* would have agreed with the papers all saying how ugly factory chimneys are and ought to be stopped but I knew what it would be and how am I to get others now the cook and second housemaid have given notice because a new house is damp though I told Leslie all along I could not live in a damp house and the trouble of moving in and the carpets not fitting and things getting broken!!! If Phyllis was here I could get a little sleep and not lie with it all going round and round in my head and how it will all end I really do not know.

Yours v. sincerely,

MISS PHYLLIS BRASH TO SPINLOVE

Dear Jazz,   10.9.25.

I skipped home last night. What *have* you been doing to my poor little Mum? She has made herself ill over this wonderful house of yours. Why cannot the poor thing have clear glass and an Aquarium—she has had one since she was an infant—and the wardrobe that belonged to her grandmother? I know the poor dear is apt to get into states and we have to take care of her, but building without tears is surely poss? Anyhow, come and be nice to her. It's no earthly writing letters and it is very bad for her to be distressed— and what does the dam house matter anyway, you fussy old Architectooralooral Jazz?

Dad jumps in on Thursday week—eight days! Great rejoicings— my sire has slaughtered a nine pointer! *Not* nine pointers, thank goodness. Been staying with Snooty and her lot at St. Austell and doing the Daily Mail dry bathing girl stunt all day. No great larks, but a lovely time.

PUD

P.S.—Be sure and phone train. I will pick you up at station for yap before you see M.

"Pud" is clearly the daughter, Phyllis; not at all the sort of daughter one would expect the Brashes to produce. "Jazz" is perhaps derived from Jas. or the initials J. S.

(TELEGRAM) BRASH TO SPINLOVE

10.9.25.

SPINLOVE, ARCHITECT, RANGER HOUSE, MAYFAIR, LONDON, W.1.
Your telegraphic and written communications received stop desist
from all alterations stop returning next Sunday prox ends BRASH.

Brash seems to be a good customer of the Post Office.

BRASH TO SPINLOVE

Dear Mr. Spinlove,   13.9.25.

I arrived home to-day and am greatly gratified with the considerable advance in progress during the interim of my absence. I shall
be gratified if you will use your best endeavours to come down here
as early as possible to-morrow as the requisite haste brooks no delay. Kindly telephone approximate hour of your probable arrival.

I was so fortunate as to secure a fine trophy, though not a "Royal",
to my rifle while in the Northern Highlands of Scotland. This I
intend shall be affixed over the fireplace in the interior hall and
will augment the embellishments of the apartment, which unless
my apprehensions mislead me, I anticipate may be a little plain in
decorative accessories.

Yours sincerely,

*Nothing much wrong here apparently—nor even with the tautol-
ogy! We do not know what happened at Spinlove's interview with Lady
Brash but we may guess that the buoyant vitality of Pud has made all
sweet and secure.*

SPINLOVE TO BRASH

Dear Sir Leslie Brash,   15.9.25.

I write to confirm instructions you gave me yesterday in conversation, as follows:

Breeze partition between bedrooms 8 and 9 to be restored but
to have door opening between the rooms.

Partition to bedrooms 5 and 6 to be refixed so as to make dressing-room 1' 9" wider and doorway to be closed up.

Leaded glazing to be fixed as already supplied.

Hot and cold service and waste connection for Aquarium to be fixed in front hall window.

I yesterday gave directions to this effect and the work is going ahead. I am grateful to you for giving way on the matter of the glazing, and I am sure that after the house is finished you will have no cause to regret your decision. You would soon gather from the comments of your friends that sheet glass was a great shortcoming in such a house and in time you would be likely to have it taken out and lead glazing fixed.

I enclose receipt for cheque which you handed me on Monday and for which many thanks. I note you are sending cheque to Grigblay. With kind regards to Lady Brash and yourself,

> Believe me,
> Yours sincerely,

In these matters one can never tell how the cat will jump but here is a happy ending indeed! When motives are ingenuous and methods frank, a tough dispute often clears away distrust and establishes a higher mutual respect and a deeper sympathy and liking.

As usual, Spinlove has said more than is necessary. By repeating the adroit argument that appears to have won the day for him he is rubbing in his victory which is the last thing Brash wishes to be reminded of.

TINGE, QUANTITY SURVEYOR, TO SPINLOVE

Dear Sir,   15.9.25.

$$
\begin{array}{lr}
\text{Value of work done to } 12.9.25 \dots\dots\dots\dots & £11250 \\
\text{Retention} \dots\dots\dots\dots\dots\dots\dots\dots\dots\dots\dots & 1844 \\
\hline
 & 9406 \\
\text{Already certified} \dots\dots\dots\dots\dots\dots\dots & 7000 \\
\hline
\text{Balance} \quad & £2406 \\
\hline
\end{array}
$$

> Yours faithfully,

As more than half the work is done the maximum retention of 10 per cent of contract, has accumulated.

A STORM IN A PAINT POT

✳ ✳

BRASH TO SPINLOVE

Dear Mr. Spinlove,   18.9.25.

An influential acquaintance is financially interested in a new novelty super-paint which will shortly, he informs me, replace all other surface coverings now on the market. It is called Riddoppo and is a *super*-paint giving a most dainty and fascinating interior surface to the inside of houses, as it is free from any odoriferous effects, cannot be scratched by the fingernail and is capable of receiving a high polish. It is elastic so that cracks do not permeate through it and it is also *non-inflammable* and *operates as a fire-proofing coat to both joinery and walls*. I should not be doing justice to the merits of Riddoppo if I did not add that it is *acid proof*, is compounded of entirely new secret elements and that a jet of boiling water or super-heated steam may be directed to impinge upon it for some minutes without deleterious effects occurring. The colours obtainable are very exquisite and varied and we have provisionally selected tints which we desire embodied in the decorative embellishments of the apartments of Honeywood Grange—as we anticipate naming the mansion; these will be known as the Pink Room, the Yellow Room, the Blue Room and so forth and the tints available will make it possible for each door to be identified by its independent colour.

Our friend will allow me a special extra discount of ten per cent and we shall have his advice in the choice of tints and decorative embellishments as he promises that our house shall represent the best modern effects possible.

With kind regards,
Yours sincerely,

Silly old man!

175

SPINLOVE TO BRASH

Dear Sir Leslie Brash,   19.9.25.

I know nothing of Riddoppo, I am afraid, except that it is advertised in the Tube lift I daily use as a "new novelty super paint", but this description, I assure you, is no recommendation but rather the opposite. Grigblay is responsible for the painting, and the paint specified is well known and the best results can be obtained from it. I can hardly think that Riddoppo is of any practical value as a fire-proofing, nor that it will hide cracks opening under it. The ability to resist jets of acid and super-heated steam will not count for much at Honeywood, and you will not want it "polished"; and as linseed oil and zinc white have been proved by long years of use to give perfect results it is surely not an advantage, but a *dis*advantage, that Riddoppo does not contain them.

I trust that you will not allow your friend to settle the colours of the rooms. This is a matter which Lady Brash and yourself should alone decide; it should depend entirely on your individual taste and the completion of the design of the house *as a whole*. I do not think your friend can have had any experience in this matter, or he would not make such proposals as you describe; nor would he make any proposals at all before he had seen the house in a state approaching completion.

With kind regards,
Yours sincerely,

P.S.—I am sending Grigblay a further certificate for £2,400, and enclose note of my own fees in respect of that sum.

There is a touch of the East wind in this letter. Its logic is a shade too devastating though we may admire the tact with which Spinlove urges that the Brashes alone should decide the decorative scheme when his intention must be to guide that decision.

BRASH TO SPINLOVE

Dear Mr. Spinlove,   20.9.25.

I have perused your communication with close attention but you must permit me to indicate to you that the confidence with which you asseverate condemnation of Riddoppo super-paint, of which you admit you know nothing, seems to me—if you will permit me to say so—a little wanting in logical reasoning. You also ignore the fact that Riddoppo is free from odoriferous emanations, a charm which makes it peculiarly attractive to Lady Brash, whose gastric equipment is sensitively disposed to olfactory aggression of every description [*i.e. dislikes smells. Excellent!*].

My friend, a most eminent commercial gentleman, would be the last to be misled by deceptive assertions and as the various meritorious desirabilities of Riddoppo make it most suitable to our desires, I request you will direct Mr. Grigblay to apply it throughout.

Certainly it is our intention to decide on the tints selected.

Yours sincerely,

Brash's friend, though the last to be misled, may be the first to mislead.

SPINLOVE TO GRIGBLAY

Dear Sir,   21.9.25.

Sir Leslie Brash wishes Riddoppo super-paint used throughout. Will you please get me full particulars of this paint and the manufacturers' instructions for using, and I will send you revised specification.

I enclose further certificate for £2,400.

Yours faithfully,

Apparently Spinlove is not, as before seemed, fully aware of the danger of experimenting with new kinds of paints.

SPINLOVE TO BRASH

Dear Sir Leslie Brash,   21.9.25.

I have directed Grigblay to use Riddoppo super-paint throughout, as you wish.

I hope you will reconsider painting the rooms out all in different colours. It is, I assure you, a thing which no one with knowledge of house decoration would propose. Your friend's idea seems to be to turn Honeywood into a paint manufacturers' show room. This, I am sure, will be intolerable to you.

With kind regards,

Yours sincerely,

More kind regards! Spinlove has got well home but he hits Brash nearly as hard as he hits Brash's friend, the "influential commercial gentleman".

GRIGBLAY TO SPINLOVE

Dear Sir, 22.9.25.

We know nothing of Riddoppo super-paint, and private inquiries we have made have had no satisfactory result; we therefore have respectfully to state that we cannot accept responsibility for same.

Yours faithfully,

Spinlove should have made inquiries and satisfied himself before calling upon Grigblay to use the paint.

SPINLOVE TO BRASH

Dear Sir Leslie Brash, 23.9.25.

I enclose copy of Grigblay's reply to my instructions to use Riddoppo.

Yours sincerely,

BRASH TO SPINLOVE

Dear Mr. Spinlove, 24.9.25.

I have not been informed of the precise nature of your communication to Mr. Grigblay *anent* Riddoppo paint, but I must protest most vigorously against what I apprehend to have very much the appearance of a conspiracy to resist the performance of my wishes. This is intolerable and beyond bearing. I assume that Mr. Grigblay anticipates that he will benefit financially by the handsome profit he has doubtless credited to himself on the painting, and is desirous to prevent my obtaining the 10% special discount; but Mr. Grigblay should be informed that it is his business to receive orders and not precisely to give them. It is for me, I apprehend, to decide what paint shall be used in my own residence, and for Mr. Grigblay to assume to dictate to me on this or any other matter is—if he will allow me to say so—perfectly monstrous and unendurable.

I do not know what the man means by "responsibility", and if I may be permitted to be perfectly frank, I do not care. I give the order and the responsibility for giving the order is mine. Mr. Grigblay's responsibility is to do what he is told *at once*.

The colours of the various rooms will be eventually decided later, but in that matter also I consider it is for the owner of the house to give orders and not, precisely, to receive them.

Yours faithfully (*sic*),

Liver!

SPINLOVE TO GRIGBLAY

Dear Sir,   25.9.25.

I am instructed by Sir Leslie Brash to order you to paint with Riddoppo, as already directed. Sir Leslie Brash accepts all responsibility.

Yours faithfully,

Does Spinlove understand fully what that responsibility is? Grigblay understands well enough, but the indications are that Spinlove does not.

SPINLOVE TO BRASH

Dear Sir (*sic*),   25.9.25.

I have instructed Mr. Grigblay to use Riddoppo, as you direct.

Mr. Grigblay knows nothing of the discount you speak of and it would make no difference if he did for he is not going to pay it. If profit were his chief concern he would not have tendered for such a house as Honeywood.

I enclose copy of my letter to Mr. Grigblay of to-day and also of my previous letters to him, so that all evidence of our conspiracy may be safely in your hands. These can be attested if you wish. My files are open to your inspection.

I think it is very hard, Sir, that after my unsparing efforts to give you a house which will be entirely satisfactory to you, it should be handed over for a paint manufacturer to celebrate himself by turning it into a colour-cure asylum for lunatics—Red for melancholia, Blue for homicidal frenzy, Yellow for religious mania, etc.—for this exactly describes—if you will permit me to be perfectly frank—the ignorant folly of your friend's proposal; and that because I warned you of the risk of experimenting with an untried paint, utterly discredited by the claims of its lying advertisements, I should be taken heavily to task; and because the builder independently expresses the same distrust I should be charged with conspiracy with him to deceive you.

I have arranged to go abroad for a belated holiday on Friday and expect to be back in three or four weeks. I shall be moving from place to place so that I shall be out of reach of letters, as I am in need of rest.

Yours faithfully,

Nerves! Brash has broken the camel's back. Brash's letter which provokes this spirited answer is in autograph. Had it been typed, the reference to conspiracy comes very near indeed to libel and as it was sent to Spinlove's office where the presumption is that all letters, not marked confidential, are opened by clerks, the question of libel may still stand.

It is clear that Spinlove was bound to protest, and undignified and childish as his letter is, he has probably met the matter in the best kind of way. Since his letter is a spontaneous expression of natural feelings, it may be easy to excuse and forget; whereas a stiff protest and demand for the withdrawal, which cannot be refused, might not readily be either forgiven or forgotten. If Spinlove had written on the same impulse, but without losing self control, he would be likely to have served his own and Brash's interests perfectly. In doing so he might well have said—"I am sure on reconsidering your letter you will feel that it is not only unfair to me and to Mr. Grigblay, but that I am bound to ask for a withdrawal of the word 'conspiracy.'"

In point of fact Spinlove is making far too big an outcry over this rainbowed bedroom idea. When the time comes he will no doubt be able to soften the horrors he dreads, but in any case the Brashes are entitled to have what decorations they want, and the enormity of the proposal depends rather on its application than upon its principle. Spinlove's vanity is more deeply concerned than his aesthetic convictions, I fancy.

BRASH TO SPINLOVE

Dear Spinlove (*sic!*),   26.9.25.

I hasten to immediately respond to your communication. I apprehend that the epistolatory intimation to which you take exception was indited with unduly hurried precipitation for which I desire to proffer profound regrets and tender sincere apologies. I employed the word conspiracy, as I anticipate you will on reflection perceive, terminologically and figuratively and solely in its loose phraseological and allegorical application without ulterior signification. [*Bravo! A bag of nuts to Sir Leslie Brash.*]

Lady Brash and myself design to enter into consultation with you on the subject of the decorations before arriving at definite decisions on variegation of tints and, as you are aware, we greatly appreciate the attentiveness of the care you have expended on the operations, and the excellence of Mr. Grigblay's meritorious performance of the work.

With best wishes from us both for a successfully regenerative holiday.

Always yours sincerely,

P.S.—I shall be gratefully appreciative of occasional messages signifying your whereabouts for telegraphic communication, if necessary. In the interim of your absence I will keep a close inspection on the operations and communicate with your office.

As Spinlove's friend Dalbet said, "a real good sort"! Ridiculous as the old boy is, this is not merely a generous but a sympathetic letter. It is, however, a little surprising, as was that it replies to. There is somehow a lack of reserve—a background of intimacy—which the facts before us do not explain. Perhaps the upheaval when Lady Brash took control is accountable. Anyhow, Spinlove can go away and enjoy his holiday. There is a note "Answered 27.9.25." on the corner of the letter, so that Spinlove appears to have acknowledged it in his own hand.

SIR LESLIE BRASH
TAKES CHARGE

There is a partial hiatus in the file owing to Spinlove's being on holiday abroad. If he has left adequate drawings and instructions behind him, Grigblay will endure his absence with an equanimity Spinlove probably has no idea of and on his return all will be found safe and satisfactory—unless possibly it is not. The chief dangers are Brash's interference and the immovable steadfastness of Bloggs the foreman who is likely to follow what he deems to be his instructions with a devotion which no obstacles will discourage.

SPINLOVE'S ASSISTANT TO BRASH

Dear Sir,   12.10.25.

Regret was not at office when telephoned inquiry received.

Have heard nothing from Mr. Spinlove except one word wirelessed from aeroplane near Barcelona ten days ago. On inquiry ascertain this not code word but given to understand means Mr. Spinlove in good health and enjoying holiday.

At present Mr. Spinlove believed to be Corsica or Athens unless breaking journey Constantinople; therefore difficult to cable, but in any case scarcely possible make your question clear or for Mr. Spinlove to reply without drawings at hand. In circumstances think best hold off work terrace steps until return. Have directed Mr. Grigblay accordingly.

Yours faithfully,

R.S. PINTLE,

for J. SPINLOVE.

Pintle seems to have modelled his style on the penny-a-word diction appropriate to inland telegrams. Spinlove should not allow this.

PINTLE TO BRASH

Dear Sir,   15.10.25.

Your telephone message directing proceed work terrace steps received. Have instructed Mr. Grigblay accordingly.

Yours faithfully,

MISS BRASH TO PINTLE

Dear Sir,   15.10.25.

If you feel at liberty to do so, will you say what the single word was which Mr. Spinlove wirelessed, as there is a great difference of opinion here.

Yours truly,

PHYLLIS BRASH.

PINTLE TO LADY PHYLLIS BRASH (*SIC*)

Madam,

In reply beg state word wirelessed by Mr. Spinlove Oct. 2nd *YOICKS*. This not code word but informed means Mr. Spinlove in good health and enjoying holiday.

Yours respectfully,

Pintle has, it will be seen, made "Pud" a lady in her own right.

He evidently supposed the letter was from Lady Brash and was ignorant of the titular distinction. "Pud" will laugh and her dad's ambitions may be flattered. Pintle is apparently a draughtsman who has taken charge in Spinlove's absence.

(TELEGRAM) BRASH, PENZANCE, TO SPINLOVE, LONDON

On further cogitation decided desist from work terrace steps ends Brash.

PINTLE TO BRASH

Dear Sir,   18.10.25.

Am in receipt your telegram and ordered work terrace steps be abandoned.

Yours faithfully,

BRASH TO PINTLE

Dear Sir,   22.10.25.

My telephonic communication from Penzance was I apprehend too hurriedly precipitate, as on inspecting the work on my return I find I was a little misled in my preventative precautions and I desire that Mr. Grigblay shall now proceed with the steps.

Yours faithfully,

PINTLE TO BRASH

Dear Sir,   23.10.25.

Your instructions regarding terrace noted and have ~~again~~ cancelled previous order, as directed.

Yours faithfully,

The word excised hints that even the purely vicarious duties of Pintle do not save him from an impulse of rebellion.

PINTLE TO GRIGBLAY

Dear Mr. Grigblay,   23.10.25.

Sorry, but old man Brash written now definitely terrace steps *are* to go on. Am doing best keep things straight but O.M.B. not able make up mind.

Yours truly,

Pintle addresses Grigblay personally apparently to propitiate him, and because he is ashamed of writing these contradictory orders. He has, of course, no business to write letters behind the scenes. He is clearly a second-rate fellow deficient in loyalty. We may suppose the copy was made and filed without his cognisance.

GRIGBLAY TO SPINLOVE

Dear Sir,   24.10.25.

We note that work on terrace steps is now to go on and we have given orders accordingly. May we remind you that in eleven days we have laid our men off this work or put them on again no less than *four times*. We must point out that such confusion of orders is not reasonable and is beyond what we are entitled to expect. If there is any question, the work had better stand till Mr. Spinlove can decide what is to be done. This disorganisation of our arrangements is a serious matter for us, and we regret we shall have to make a charge to cover loss of men's time.

Yours faithfully,

As before, Grigblay shows he will not stand nonsense.

PINTLE TO BRASH

Dear Sir,   25.10.25.

Enclosed copy of letter received to-day Mr. Grigblay which perhaps you ought to see.

Yours truly,

BRASH TO PINTLE

Dear Sir,   26.10.25.

I shall be obliged if you will signify to Mr. Grigblay my apologetic regrets that the necessary preventative precautions should have incommoded him. In the circumstances I am greatly pleased to accept the suggestion he makes and I desire him to desist from operations on the terrace steps until Mr. Spinlove's return.

Yours faithfully,

Five times!

GRIGBLAY TO SPINLOVE

Dear Sir,   30.10.25.

We understand you are back and enclose list of extras ordered by Sir Leslie Brash during your absence. They are of a minor character and as Bloggs received the orders when the men were actually at work, he had to do what he was told or stop the work. We have kept time sheets as the work cannot be measured and must be charged day-work.

We understand from Bloggs that the bedrooms are to be papered. As you know, they are being finished with a felt-faced float for distempering. We shall be glad of particulars of papers at once. Bloggs was given orders to dark stain oak, but we await your directions.

Yours faithfully,

Builders are always ready to render day-work accounts—that is accounts based on the cost of the men's time and of materials—instead of accounts based on measurements priced at the contract rates, and it is only fair they should do so when the work involves pulling down or small separate jobs; but the method is unsatisfactory for the owner because, as the builder will be reimbursed for all his outgoings and he receives in addition (usually) 15 per cent on the net cost for establishment charges and profit, there is no inducement to economy; and because, as the workmen and the foreman are aware of the circumstances, there is a tendency for everyone to ease off on day-work. In addition to this, the logging of the men's time is in the foreman's charge and, as he is accountable to the builder for keeping down the cost of labour covered by the tender, the day-work time sheets are apt to record hours which, properly, should be charged against the contract. Day work accounts, unlike measured accounts, always *pay the builder; and from what has been said it will be realized that a dishonest builder can make them pay a great deal too well.*

THE AFFAIR OF
THE COTTAGES

(CONFIDENTIAL) GRIGBLAY TO SPINLOVE

Sir,   30.10.25.

I think I ought to let you know at once that a fortnight ago Sir
Leslie Brash sent me drawings and specification for block of four
cottages he wants erected down at bottom by lower road, and asked
me for a price. The name on the drawings is Mr. Cohen Snitch,
but a young man in our prime costing says they are copied from
published plans by Mr. Sutcliffe Regenstook, A.R.I.B.A., and we have
turned them up in our file of the "Builders' Record" of May 7th,
1923. The specification is a ready-made affair with just a tender-
form without any conditions, and the bricks, chimneys, windows,
and all sorts are to be "same as at Honeywood".

Now, apart from the work being only half described and position on site, drains, roads, and water supply, etc., left out, we don't
do speculative work and don't care to tender without proper particulars and quantities. At the same time we should be quite willing to do the work under our present contract schedule and leave it
to Mr. Tinge to measure and settle the account, but we do not
think this would suit the old gentleman as what he is after is a cut
price and cut fees, without doubt. Not in any case should we agree
to a proposal of the kind without consulting with you, and this was
the reply we made and were then asked to return plans etc.

Since then Bloggs tells me Nibnose & Rasper's manager sneaked
in down at bottom looking for mushrooms Bloggs thought, but
young Rasper turned up after, and had the face to ask questions
about water. Bloggs told him we were managing without any and
saw him off, so it's pretty clear what is going on; but I'm not going

to have Nibnose & Rasper learning how to build from me, and if Sir Leslie Brash brings them on to the ground he will have to pay me for a night watchman and a new lock-up or I shan't be able to keep a plank or a ladder or a drain pipe or a bag of plaster or anything else on the job without a man sits on it. That young Rasper would strip the tiles off the roof, if you so much as turned your head to cough. I don't forget the trick he played me with that old six hundred gallon cast iron tank I loaned them and then they told me they hadn't had it. I happened to go along by, and there was my brave tank set up ten feet in the air on a staging and daubed over so it won't be recognized. Ho says Master Johnny Rasper, all of a surprise; *Is that yours?* Forgot where they had stole it.

Sir Leslie Brash sent me a plan and a picture of a gimcrack garage affair with pink asbestos slates and blue doors and a bit of bargeboard painted yellow and a flag at the gable. He had torn it out of Hutt and Gambols' reach-me-down bungalow catalogue, but had cut off the firm's name and the price for fear I should know too much, and he wanted me to give a price for two of them joined together for his cars to go in at the North West end by trades entrance. It would be a pity to put a thing like that up against his house, as I think you will agree; besides we can't build the stuff H. & G. spew about all over the country nor at their price if we did, and I think the old gentleman should be told so.

With apologies for troubling you but thought you ought to know it.

Yours faithfully,

A very pleasant chatty letter—the letter of a friend! It has apparently occupied Grigblay's evening hours. Brash's intention, no doubt, is to save his pocket by cutting out architects' fees—for no doubt he made a bargain with Mr. Snitch; and he may feel, also, that Grigblay's work is unduly expensive and that this is due to Spinlove's complicated methods and exacting demands. He may also wish to "be his own architect", and believes that by uttering the words "two three- and two five-room cottages" and getting someone to "draw out the plan" and by agreeing a price with the builder, he is being it. Whatever the results are he will be slow to see defects in "my own work", and if the plans do not give him what he wants he will enjoy "making improvements" and take great credit to himself for the ingenious botching and makeshifts by which the shortcomings are made good. He will helplessly protest against the builder's account for extras, whether it is fair or not, and will always believe that he was "swindled".

As for Mr. Cohen Snitch, his kind is common. He has a knowledge of building sufficient to enable him to hold himself out as an architect in those wide fields that public ignorance puts at his disposal; and his many diverse activities bring him commissions which his reputation as an architect would deny him. The obligations of a profession of which he is not a member do not weigh with him; and he enjoys the same advantage over the accredited architect as the man who ignores the rules of a game has over one who observes them.

It is difficult to believe that Brash is not aware that he is treating his architect shabbily; but we have already seen that Brash can outface such consciousness. He perhaps regards the whole affair as a matter of fees. He is paying Spinlove for the house, but sees no reason why he should pay him when he can manage without his services; his instincts, in fact—or let us say his antecedents—do not allow him to distinguish between obligations due to a professional man and the consideration expected by a commercial agent. If Brash is conscious that Spinlove is giving Honeywood a devotion for which he can never be paid except in thanks, he probably merely regards his architect's services as remarkably good value for the money, and is too unaware of any reciprocal obligations to take any pleasure in acknowledging them.

What is the unlucky Spinlove going to do about it all? He first flies for rescue to his friend Wychete, it seems.

SPINLOVE TO WYCHETE

Dear Mr. Wychete,   1.11.25.

I am sorry to bother you again but a most awkward thing has happened. I enclose copy of the builder's letter which gives the facts. I found it on my return from a four weeks' holiday abroad. Mr. Snitch is a house and land agent. I met him once, as he was appointed by the adjoining owner to agree a water course. The cottages will probably be three hundred yards or more from the house, but associated with it as is evidently the owner's intention—note the similar brickwork, chimneys, etc. I should be most grateful for any hints what to do.

With kind regards,
Yours sincerely,

P.S.—Could you possibly send me a line at once? I shall have to meet the owner in a few days, at latest.

SPINLOVE TO BRASH

Dear Sir Leslie Brash, 1.11.25.

I returned to the office yesterday. Mr. Grigblay has sent me a list of variations and extras ordered during my absence, and there is a question you have raised about the terrace steps. I can come on to the site on Friday or Saturday, if you will let me know when I can meet you, so that these and any other matters may be settled on the spot.

I had a delightful time abroad.

With kind regards,
Yours sincerely,

Spinlove has apparently put off meeting Brash until he may hope to have had Wychete's reply.

WYCHETE TO SPINLOVE

My Dear Spinlove, 2.11.25.

Your luck seems out. The position is certainly awkward, as you say, but the probability is that your client does not realize the unfairness to you—though one would imagine he intends a snub. Much depends on your personal relations and upon the kind of man he is. You alone can judge how far expostulation or protest may be made to weigh with him. Mr. Snitch's action seems most unprofessional, but he does not belong to our camp and in any case we do not know what happened; there is nothing to prevent your client employing him if he wishes, and it is no good taking any steps to get Mr. S. to withdraw. Even if you were able to do so it might not persuade your client to entrust the work to you.

Adopting Regenstook's design is, of course, a breach of copyright, and would give him grounds for an action for damages. Copying your details also comes very near to the same thing. Your client's intention is clear, and the wrong is of the same kind though so different in degree that you would scarcely be in a position to claim damages.

I should be interested to know the end of the story. You must not lose time or your client may accept the other builder's tender.

Ever yours,

SPINLOVE TO BRASH

Dear Sir Leslie Brash,   3.11.25.

I confirm telephone message fixing Friday at 10 a.m. for our meeting on site.

Mr. Grigblay has mentioned to me that you asked him to tender for a block of cottages which, for certain reasons, he felt unable to do without first conferring with me. I am, naturally, so much interested in Honeywood that I should be indeed grieved not to be allowed to design the accessory buildings, particularly as you mentioned these cottages to me as matters in which you would want my advice.

However, we can speak of this on Friday, but I write to warn you, before you commit yourself in any way, that the plans you sent Mr. Grigblay are not an original design at all, but have been copied from plans by another architect which were published a short time ago in one of the building papers. The designer holds the copyright in his plans and you will be liable to action for damages if you proceed. In the same way my detail drawings of Honeywood are my copyright and cannot be used for the proposed cottages without my consent.

Yours sincerely,

Spinlove is quite right in his statement of the fact of the copyright ownership, but he manages to suggest a masterfulness in architects which exceeds the life.

SPINLOVE TO WYCHETE

Dear Mr. Wychete,   6.11.25.

I am most grateful to you for your letter. Directly I got it I wrote to my client and warned him of the breach of copyright, but when I saw him two days later he told me he had "provisionally accepted" (as he termed it) tender for the cottages from a local firm, Nibnose & Rasper. He had, however, accepted the tender in fact; by "provisionally" he meant that he was at liberty to accept, or not, a supplementary estimate for outbuildings.

Well, there was a great to do. He was most indignant with Snitch for fobbing him off with someone else's design and charging thirty-five guineas for it as an "inclusive fee", and he means to make him disgorge, for he has already paid the fellow.

He was quite nice to me—in fact particularly so, for he is a self-important man and rather obstinate in favouring his own ideas [*ahem!*], and I really do not think it occurred to him that he was injuring me. He thought he would save fees and get a cheaper building, and that it was entirely his own affair.

The tender he has accepted is for £1,350 for the block of four cottages—an impossible price. A great deal of the work is left out of the specification, to say nothing of drains, paths and water supply, and though the specification calls for the building to be completed in all details etc., Nibnose & Rasper attach to their tender a letter which, rather slyly, excludes work not described. There are no conditions of contract.

I had to point all this out to Brash and insist that the cottages will cost at least £1,700 before he has finished, and perhaps nearly £2,000, and that there was nothing in the contract to prevent the builder putting in the cheapest and most shoddy work, and that he would have a huge bill for extras and be at the builders' mercy—in fact Brash began at last to understand what an architect is for.

The next difficulty was how to get Nibnose & Rasper to withdraw with merely nominal compensation or none at all. Owing to a previous muddle they have a quite unfounded grievance against me; however, Brash wrote and told them he had discharged Snitch and appointed me his architect, and I got Nibnose to my office and, after cross-examining him on what he had included for and what not, he was obliged to agree that, as a basis for a contract, his tender was a farce. He was quite reasonable; said he had done his best with the particulars supplied, that there were big risks—and so on. Finally it was agreed that he and Grigblay should tender to a new design and that the lowest tender should be accepted. So that's that, and I am enormously obliged for your hints, without which I do not know what would have happened; and Brash, if he only knew it, is still more deeply indebted to you.

I am putting up a temporary shed of larch slabs as garage, which will look quite inoffensive pushed back among the trees.

With many thanks and best wishes,

Yours very sincerely,

Spinlove seems in fine fettle. His recent holiday has done him good. He has evidently carried Brash quite off the ground upon which he had taken so formidable a position and won his surrender.

LADY BRASH
CAUSES A DIVERSION

SPINLOVE TO GRIGBLAY

Dear Sir,   10.11.25.

I had to call your foreman's attention to boarding on flats over bays, which is specified to run with the fall, but has been laid across it to suit the joists which run the wrong way. I must ask you to nail ⅝ boarding over present boarding with feather-edged border so as to get neat finish of lead on to brick cornice. [*Boards are apt to curl up at edges under lead, and prevent free drainage of water if laid across the fall.*]

The trefoil piercings in skirtings of panelled rooms have been omitted. This makes the broken battening and openings in top of capping useless. Please put stout cop-bronze wire mesh behind piercings. [*The purpose of this arrangement is to give free ventilation behind the panelling, for if air is bottled up between panelling and damp walls the warmth of the house will favour dry-rot. The wire gauge is against mice.*]

The eaves gutter at N. of kitchen wing stops short of the gable verge. I am aware that the verge is tilted but the finish is unworkmanlike. The stopped end should be 1" in front of line of verge. [*The tilting of the tiles at gable verge throws the water back so that the eaves gutter probably is effective in catching all of it. It is the rigid exactness of modern building that makes this immaterial deviation an offence.*]

Now that the heating service is working will you please see that the windows are *kept open*. I have called your foreman's attention to this before. [*The heating is put on to dry out the house, but if the windows are kept shut the steam-laden air, which can take up no more moisture, cannot escape, condensation takes place and the object of having heat on is in great part defeated. The windows are kept shut because of the blinking draught, and in pursuit of snug comfort. Even at the best of times the luxury of shutting oneself up for a day with a mate and a radiator in an unventilated bathroom with a few cans of paint, a plumber's furnace, two clay pipes, a quart of boiling tea and a pound of putty, is rarely enjoyed.*]

The lead tacks of soil pipes, as well as of waste pipes, are to be wiped on the front angle. This has not been done. The service pipes carrying taps are to be *vertical*. The double tacks above and below taps are as specified, but in the pantry the pipes are *horizontal*. They must be carried along under sink and then taken up vertically to match scullery taps.

[*The nozzle of a tap fixed on a horizontal pipe tends to sag down after a time. A vertical pipe, properly fixed, resists the leverage of the hand screwing down the tap.*]

Please give these matters your attention.

Yours faithfully,

Spinlove has been away from the works for some weeks and, if these are the only matters he has to complain of, Grigblay is doing well.

SPINLOVE TO GRIGBLAY

Dear Sir,   15.11.25.

Sir Leslie Brash rang me up to-day to tell me Lady Brash is complaining of a *smell* in the house. Will you find out what is the matter? I could get no description of it except that it is an unpleasant smell.

Yours faithfully,

Most of them are so or they would not be smells; and it is difficult to describe a smell even when it will bear description, which is rare. Lady Brash's famous "olfactory sensitiveness" has claimed tribute.

BRASH TO SPINLOVE

Dear Mr. Spinlove,   17.11.25.

Would it be practicably feasible to insert french windows in the drawing-room, and what would be the amount of the probable anticipated estimate? A friend has pointed out that it will not be

practicably possible for a person seated in the middle of the drawing room to get a view of the gardens owing to the excessive height
of the bottoms of the windows. This is disturbing. Alternatively,
and as a different proposition, could not the windows be lowered a
foot or two? What would be the probably approximate estimate
for doing so, including, of course, the bay windows? I comprehend
the necessary desirability of disposing the windows of the bedroom chambers in a lofty situation in view of the danger of a fall,
but this desirability scarcely obtains in the downstair apartments.

Lady Brash informs me the smell is much worse. It is desired
that the necessary steps towards eradication may be *at once* put in
active operation, as Lady Brash spends several hours of each day in
the house.

Yours sincerely,

SPINLOVE TO GRIGBLAY

Dear Sir,   19.11.25.

Have you done anything about the *smell?* Sir Leslie Brash referred to it again in a letter I received on Saturday and he has rung
up to-day to say that Lady Brash was in the house on Sunday and
that the smell was "dreadful". Please take steps to have the nui-
sance ended at once, as it is causing great annoyance. I wish you
had not allowed the plumbers to use the den as a shop. They have
made the place in a disgusting state—litter of all kinds, bacon rind,
banana peel thrown about, crusts and bones and tea leaves—your
foreman ought to be told to look after things better.

Yours faithfully,

*Spinlove is evidently getting rattled; but until Lady Brash is ap-
peased there will be no peace for anyone.*

LADY BRASH TO SPINLOVE

Dear Mr. Spinlove,   19.11.25.

I really think I ought to write to you about the smell! It was
quite dreadful on Sunday they all noticed it and Mrs. Bingham said
it made her eyes water she is so subject to hay fever like my dear
mother was and I take after them *both*!!! I could never consent to

live in a house with a smell like that which goes on and on even after I get home like the monkey house in the Zoo especially the drawing-room. Whatever Sir Leslie may say something will have to be done or none of our friends will ever come to see us!!!

How fast the leaves are falling!

Yours v. sincerely,

SPINLOVE TO LADY BRASH

Dear Lady Brash,   20.11.25.

I do not know what the particular smell is that you do not like. I have asked Mr. Grigblay to try and find out. Of course many of the materials used by the workmen have strange smells, but that is unavoidable and they will all disappear, I can assure you, before the work is finished. If you find the atmosphere of the house so unpleasant it would perhaps be wiser *not to go into it* just at present, or why not ask Mr. Bloggs to *open the windows;* have you thought of that I wonder?

Yes, I noticed the leaves were beginning to fall.

Yours sincerely,

Spinlove's solicitude leads him to ascribe to the lady a degree of imbecility which is scarcely flattering.

GRIGBLAY TO SPINLOVE

Dear Sir,   20.11.25.

We have noted the various instructions you gave our foreman, which are receiving attention. He has searched for the smell complained of but has not succeeded in discovering it. His report is as follows:

"About her Ladyship's smell there is not anything to complain about as I can see. The paint is nothing at all scarcely. There was a bit of a hum in the kitchen but that was just a coat the gasfitter's mate had there. He said it was fish and I reckon like enough it was. I told him take it outside. The plumber's shop is swept out."

We do not know what more we can do in the matter.

Yours faithfully,

SPINLOVE TO BRASH

Dear Sir Leslie Brash,   21.11.25.

I have twice written to Grigblay about the unpleasant smell, and I have to-day heard from him that they cannot detect anything which is not as it should be. In writing to Lady Brash yesterday I suggested that she might perhaps see that the windows are opened.

In answer to your question, french windows are impossible. They could not be fitted to the existing openings, could not be made to match the other windows and would be disastrous architecturally, as you would at once realize if I made you a sketch of the altered elevation. If you had said originally that you wanted french windows I could have designed them suitably, but the style of the house would have been entirely different.

It would be possible to lower the windows, but if you did so the transom—that is the intermediate horizontal member of the frame—would come right across the line of vision of anyone standing. The top of cills is 2' 9½" from the floor and this is as low as can be managed. I may point out to you that the reason you cannot see the ground outside when seated away from the window is that the ground slopes away. In any case the top of the terrace wall will appear above the line of the window cill to anyone seated in the room, so that even if you lowered the windows you would have no better view of the garden.

I had intended to suggest to you, when the subject was allowed to drop, that instead of painting the doors pink, yellow, blue—for I am sure you would dislike the array of differently coloured doors—the name "Pink Room", "Yellow Room", etc. might be lettered on each door. I could design a scutcheon upon which the words might appear, and this might be of the appropriate colour if you wish, or the coloured scutcheon without the words might serve. Personally I would recommend the words without the scutcheon.

I hope you will not think me unduly persistent, but I am sure you would regret a parti-coloured corridor.

With kind regards,

Yours sincerely,

Apparently the conversations grew heated when the rainbowed bed-room proposals were discussed, and Spinlove had to change the subject. It is a torturing effort for the designer to get the heads —or transoms— of casement windows above the eye, and the cills duly low, while at the same time keeping the proportions of windows satisfactory.

BRASH TO SPINLOVE

Dear Mr. Spinlove,   22.11.25.

I have considered your remarks *anent* the windows and suggest you will raise the floor of the room which will, I apprehend, give the same equivalent effect as the lowering of the windows to which you demur, and prevent the terrace wall obstructing the view. There will be no objection to going up two steps into the drawing-room— in fact most pleasing effects may be obtained in this manner, and we can postpone using the apartment until the operations are completed. What will the cost of this work be? I recall that £300 is included in the contract amount to meet contingencies of this kind.

I am not at all averse to your proposal for identification of bed-room doors. If you will have a door painted and appropriately lettered as you propose, I will give you an ultimate final decision.

We are contemplating moving into the house for Xmas day. Do you think that a feasible proposition?

I have seized the opportune occasion to purchase certain cottages and shall in consequence not now find the necessity to erect those conveniences. Will you please advise Messrs. Nibnose & Rasper with the appropriate intimation.

Yours sincerely,

PHYLLIS BRASH TO SPINLOVE

Dear Jazz,   24.11.25.

You ought to hop down as soon as poss. Mum is worrying dreadfully over the smell in the house. She spent most of this morning and part of the afternoon listening for it; it did not squeak to-day but was apparently known to be in hiding. I have not been in the house myself on a good hunting morning when the scent was lying well, but two people besides M. found on Sunday, so something must be wrong.

Dad started an innocent little frolic with a dentist ten days ago; it became a serious game and poor Dad is now seventeen down with nine to play. He is staying up in town till after the final round, which is why I write. Will you phone to-morrow, please?

PUD.

SPINLOVE TO GRIGBLAY

Dear Sir,   25.11.25.

I am directed by Sir Leslie Brash to say that he does not now intend to build any cottages.

Will you please tell your foreman to see that all windows are securely *shut* before the men leave on Saturday, so that I may satisfy myself about this reported smell.

Yours faithfully,

SPINLOVE USES TACT

SPINLOVE TO BRASH

Dear Sir Leslie Brash,   28.11.25.

I am sorry to know you are having such a bad time of it.

As you will no doubt have heard, the smell Lady Brash complained of is that of the *new oak*. It is a penetrating smell certainly, but most people like it. It will entirely disappear in a short time, in fact I do not think it will be noticed after the oak has been waxed.

I am afraid it will not be possible for you to get into the house for Xmas. There is much more to be done than appears. In six weeks' time it might be possible, but it would be better for you to wait. The house is drying out well, and I do not think there would then be any actual objection to its being lived in, but if you waited, say, till March you could be certain of no ill consequences.

As regards raising the floor of the drawing-room, there are grave difficulties and objections which I think you have not realized. Ten or twelve inches off the height of the room would make it appear very low. This is a big room and the height to ceiling is no more than is necessary, for it fixes the height of the first floor throughout. To raise the floor would mean raising the panelling to about 10 in. from the ceiling which would look very ugly, and also rebuilding the brick chimney, for the opening of the fireplace would be much too low. The transom of the window would also come very awkwardly; people looking out would have to stoop or stand on tip toe. It would be dangerous to have the steps close up to the door; a landing outside would be necessary which would stand out, with the steps, four or five feet into the hall, and, of course, the new floor would have to be carried on joists. The concrete floor is prepared for nailing the floorboards to it, and the only reason this has not been done is that I told Grigblay to hold off so that the concrete should be thoroughly dry. The cost of the alteration would, as you may judge, be a considerable sum—£200 very likely.

The £300 contingencies you mention, is not available for extra work of this kind. It is to cover the contract work—that is to say to pay for work which may be found necessary but which is not described in the contract because it may not be. Part, at least, of this sum has been spent. If there is any left unexpended, it will, of course, be credited in the final statement of account.

I have written a tactful letter to Nibnose & Rasper letting them know you do not now intend to go on with the cottages. As you remember, they agreed to cancel their previous contract on the understanding they should tender, against Grigblay only, to the new design I was preparing; but I hope they will not make any trouble.

With kind regards,
Yours sincerely,

SPINLOVE TO NIBNOSE & RASPER

Dear Sirs,   28.11.25.

My client desires me to present you with his best compliments and inform you with his profound regrets that he has now decided not to build the cottages for which you were so obliging as to consent to submit a tender. Sir Leslie Brash asks me to tell you that he looks forward on some future occasion to the pleasure of availing himself of your services.

Yours faithfully,

If this suave and buttery letter is Spinlove's idea of a tactful one, he has much to learn. It not only reeks of insincerity, but is intolerably condescending in tone and would be likely to give offence to anyone and under any circumstances. "Nibrasp" will perfectly understand that the purpose of it is to disarm their claim to compensation, and as the firm has already, in its own opinion, been unfairly deprived of the contract for the house, anything more provocative and inflaming could scarcely be devised. Spinlove ought to have written somewhat as follows: "An unfortunate thing has happened. My client has an opportunity of buying cottages close at hand so that there is now no reason for him to build. I am afraid you have been put to a good deal of trouble and Sir Leslie

Brash is sorry for this and will bear it in mind, and hopes to be able to make use of your services on a future occasion".

BRASH TO SPINLOVE

Dear Mr. Spinlove,   29.11.25.

I am glad to be in a condition to intimate that I am now emancipated to freedom from the dental surgeon's sanctum—though still unable to make spectacular public appearances.

I am naturally disappointed to be apprised that our occupation of the house at Christmas is not practicably feasible. Christmas Day eventuates precisely fourteen days subsequently to the contract date of completion. I advisedly apprehended that certain extra days would be allowed to Mr. Grigblay to perform his undertaking, but six weeks is surely a very excessive apportionment of latitude? It is, of course, in your hands to see that Mr. Grigblay is kept informed of his obligations, but I desire that you will intimate to him that I consider his procrastination beyond what is reasonably to be anticipated, and that I shall certainly not feel inclined to remit any proportion of the sums which may become due to me as penalties for delay.

I note your remarks *anent* the lifting of the drawing-room floor. I do not precisely apprehend the full interpretation of your remarks as I am not in a condition to immediately make the public appearance involved by the journey to the site, but I am prepared to accept your views, although they do not favour my ideas, as the amount of the anticipated estimate is altogether more than I can contemplate.

As regards the "contingencies", I apprehend that the money is mine and that I am, therefore, at liberty to spend it as I choose—however it is not necessary to deviate upon that eventuality. The mansion certainly more than satisfies our anticipations. I look forward shortly to viewing the experimental lettering on doors.

With kind regards,

Yours sincerely,

"NIBRASP" ASKS COMPENSATION

NIBNOSE & RASPER TO SPINLOVE

Dear Sir,   29.11.25.

We were just a little surprised at your letter—but nothing to worry about—as this is the second time we have been passed over by you and we are getting used to same.

We shall be glad if you will present our respects to Sir Leslie Brash and inform that gentleman that we shall be glad to serve him at any time that he may honour us with his orders and abide by them, but we do not much care for the way he has served us so far, for what we expected is not compliments but compensation.

We may remind you that when Mr. Nibnose saw you at your office on this matter it was clearly understood that we would agree to cancel our contract if we were given a fair chance to tender to a new design against Mr. John Grigblay only. As Sir Leslie has chosen to disregard his side of the bargain and break your word to us, we must respectfully ask a sum representing our reasonable profits in compensation, viz: 7½% on the amount of our tender.

Yours faithfully,

"Nibrasp" are entitled to compensation for the cancellation of their contract, since the acceptance of a tender constitutes a contract binding on both parties, each of whom is entitled to compensation for breach by the other. The sum that would be allowed by the Courts in compensation would depend on the circumstances. It might happen that a contractor or a building owner would, by a breach by the other, be involved in losses far in excess of the direct loss of profits or loss of the bargain.

SPINLOVE TO TINGE, QUANTITY SURVEYOR

Dear Mr. Tinge,   1.12.25.

While I was away on a holiday my client obtained tender for £1,350 for a block of cottages from a new builder, Nibnose & Rasper, which he accepted. He has now decided not to build and the contractors ask 7½% on the tendered price as compensation for breach. Is this a fair claim? The firm states that 7½% represents their expected profits. Is this right?

Yours truly,

TINGE TO SPINLOVE

Dear Sir,   2.12.25.

7½% is about right for profits.

Yours faithfully,

Tinge, as usual, keeps strictly to facts. It is for Spinlove, and not Tinge, to decide whether the claim is a fair one. All Tinge will say is that 7½% is a reasonable estimate of profits.

SPINLOVE TO BRASH

Dear Sir Leslie Brash,   3.12.25.

I enclose copies of my letters to Nibnose & Rasper and of their replies. The amount they claim is about right. I will make an appointment with Mr. Nibnose and agree the best terms I can get.

Yours sincerely,

We must suppose that Spinlove explained to Brash, when he decided not to build the cottages, that "Nibrasp" could claim compensation; but he does not appear to have any authority to agree the amount, and although 7½% may represent expected profits it does not follow that "Nibrasp" could make good a claim for that amount.

SPINLOVE TO NIBNOSE & RASPER

Dear Sir,   3.12.25.

Sir Leslie Brash could not foresee the circumstances which now make it impossible for him to build, and he is aware that he is liable to you for compensation; but there are special circumstances which have to be considered in settling the sum to be paid and I think it would be satisfactory if Mr. Nibnose could call at my office to agree the figure. If you will ring up I shall be glad to make an early appointment.

Yours faithfully,

Spinlove, as agent, here pledges Brash to pay compensation. Even if Brash had agreed to pay—and it does not appear he has ever done so— it was a serious error in diplomacy on Spinlove's part to tell "Nibrasp" this. He should have opened negotiations by saying that his client resented paying compensation and that unless "Nibrasp" substantially reduced the amount of the claim they would get nothing.

SPINLOVE TO BRASH

Dear Sir Leslie Brash, 4.12.25.

On my return to the office this evening I found your telephone message telling me to come to no understanding with Nibnose & Rasper until I had seen you. I am sorry to say that I wrote to them last night in the sense of my letter to you. I enclose copy of the letter. You will see that the amount of compensation is left open, so that this may be merely a nominal figure.

Yours sincerely,

We have here another example of the ineptitude which overtakes Spinlove when he gets away from the actual business of building. How can "Nibrasp" be put off with nominal compensation—nominal standing for "in name only"—when the payment of actual compensation has been promised?

BRASH TO SPINLOVE

Dear Mr. Spinlove, 5.12.25.

I was astounded to peruse your communication to Messrs. Nibnose & Rasper, in which you take it upon yourself to engage me to disburse compensation without any kind of authority from me to do so, and in face of my emphatic objection, expressed to you in verbal conversation some weeks ago, to do anything of the kind. If anyone is to pay compensation I apprehend it is Mr. Snitch for selling me sham bogus plans and preparing documents which you tell me are incomplete and which Messrs. Nibnose & Rasper knew to be incomplete.

It is obvious that I am being robbed and swindled by a pack of extortionate rogues and that so far from doing anything to protect me you are—if you will permit me to say so—actually playing into their hands. However, one thing is definitely certain; I will not pay Nibnose & Rasper, or Snitch, or any jack one of these scoundrels a halfpenny, and you can tell them so with my compliments. Mr. Snitch has now very obligingly offered to charge only ten guineas "to cover expenses" for cheating me, and if Nibnose talks any more about compensation I request you to refer him to Russ & Co., for I will fight these thieving rogues if I have to sell everything I possess to do it, before I will pay them a farthing.

Yours sincerely,

Ease off on the kidney omelettes, my good sir, and walk to the station of a morning! It is true that Spinlove was at fault in pledging his client without written authority, or without a written note of oral instructions the wording of which his client has approved and which he has confirmed to his client; but he seems to have no doubt that he was correctly representing his client's views, and in any case Brash's claim against Snitch for fees paid and "Nibrasp's" against Brash for compensation are entirely due to Brash's acting without his architect's advice or knowledge. Spinlove has, indeed, rescued his client from a much worse disaster.

SPINLOVE TO BRASH

Dear Sir Leslie Brash,   6.12.25.

I much regret that I should have wrongly interpreted your wishes, but when some weeks ago I told you that Nibnose & Rasper were entitled to compensation you made no comment, and I clearly understood you accepted the situation. I have to-day written to the firm repudiating their claim; at the same time there is no doubt they can enforce it. Mr. Nibnose is coming to see me and I will get the best proposals for settlement I can.

May I remind you that I had nothing to do with your contract with Mr. Snitch, nor with your contract with Nibnose & Rasper, but that I have spent a good deal of time in trying to get matters arranged in your best interests.

Yours faithfully,

Spinlove's nerves are not this time involved.

SPINLOVE TO NIBNOSE & RASPER

Dear Sirs,   6.12.25.

I confirm appointment with Mr. Nibnose at this office at 11 on Thursday.

I regret to have to say that in conveying that Sir Leslie Brash was willing to compensate you I misinterpreted what I understood to be my client's views. I am now directed by Sir Leslie Brash to inform you that he does not agree you have a claim for compensation against him.

Yours faithfully,

But they have! All Brash has done is to roar "I won't pay."

SPINLOVE TO GRIGBLAY

Dear Sir,   7.12.25.

May I ask you whether you are aware of what is going on at Honeywood? When I was in one of the bedrooms yesterday with your foreman, there was a sudden uproar downstairs and, while I was asking Bloggs what all the noise was, a rat with a terrier after it ran into the room and bolted into the floor-space where the electricians had a trap open, and men came rioting up the stairs before they could be stopped. I had noticed several dogs tied up and Bloggs said the men brought them "for a bit of a rat hunt in the dinner hour", but I never supposed there were *rats in the house.*

It is really disgraceful and I should certainly have to ask you to replace your foreman if the work were not so nearly finished. Suppose Sir Leslie learnt what was going on, or that Lady Brash saw a rat! The rats have no doubt been attracted by the litter of bits of food in the den which the plumbers used as a shop, but the men have no business to bring food into the house at all. It must be stopped and the rats cleared out, at once. Bloggs says they will go when they cannot get water, but I have heard of them gnawing through lead pipes for it, and with all these spaces under the floors on the South side, the house will become rat-ridden before it is finished. I shall want to see those spaces thoroughly cleaned out. There are shavings and rubbish there. The main thing is to get rid of the rats at once. Poison must not be used or we shall have more *smells*. I am astonished you should allow such a state of affairs.

Yours faithfully,

P.S.—We put the terrier into the floor and got the rat.

From the postscript we learn that the august architect pocketed his indignation and joined the hunt.

GRIGBLAY TO SPINLOVE

Dear Sir,   9.12.25.

We regret the occasion for your letter which we were quite un-aware of. We are sending down an expert who will fume out rats, and have given our foreman strict orders, and trust you will have no further grounds for complaints.

We should like to call your attention to the Riddoppo paint next time you are on the site, as our foreman painter is not alto-gether satisfied.

Yours faithfully,

BRASH TO SPINLOVE

Dear Mr. Spinlove,   8.12.25.

I have to solicit your condolences and ask you to make excuses for the somewhat rough asperity of my last communication, as I was at the time suffering from a dental relapse in a molar which has proved unexpectedly refractory and you will be sorry to hear me say that the distress was extremely chronic. [*It is to be hoped he will be very sorry indeed to hear Brash say it, but then—why say it?*]

Messrs. Russ & Co. are dealing with Mr. Snitch. With refer-ence to Messrs. Nibnose & Rasper, I apprehend that you have noted my asseveration that I have given you no authority to agree any sum in disbursement for compensation. At the same time I desire you to proceed with negotiations directed to determining what amount will satisfy these people's demands. The proposal must then be submitted for consideration to Mr. Russ.

Yours sincerely,

Here is a return to sanity!

SPINLOVE TO BRASH

Dear Sir Leslie Brash,   10.12.25.

I am very sorry to know you have been so poorly and hope you are all right again now.

I saw Mr. Nibnose to-day. He is hurt at the way he has been treated and was inclined to be stiff, but he is a fair-dealing man and, of course, I had plenty to say of the irregularity of the contract arrangement. Finally he agreed to accept £25, in full settlement as a "friendly compromise", on the understanding that if the money is not paid within seven days his offer is to be deemed to have been refused.

I did full justice to your views, but was only able to lead Mr. Nibnose to make this offer by telling him that if he did so I thought he might regard the matter as settled. This was the best I could do and I think you will be wise to accept, for I believe it is your only chance of an amicable settlement.

Yours sincerely,

Spinlove seems to have managed well and his letter is, for a change, strictly to the point.

Christmas is approaching and on the morning of the contract date for completion Spinlove receives missives twain of good cheer from Grigblay. The first is as follows:

DIFFICULTIES AND DELAYS

GRIGBLAY TO SPINLOVE

Dear Sir,   10.12.25.

We have received notice from Mr. Potch, District Surveyor, refusing certificate of occupation on ground that window in bedroom No. 5 is not of area required by by-laws. This is the room which was made larger by moving partition to the orders of her Ladyship.

Yours faithfully,

It seems we have not yet heard the last of Lady Brash's famous big wardrobe. By enlarging the room to receive it, the floor area has been increased to more than ten times the window area, which is the maximum allowed by the by-laws, and it seems Spinlove overlooked this.

The second message of good tidings is more diffuse, but it does not lack sap.

(CONFIDENTIAL) GRIGBLAY TO SPINLOVE

Sir,   10.12.25.

I think best to send you a private word that we are going to have a serious trouble with this paint of the old gentleman's. If you ask me I should say that this new novelty super-paint is a bit too new, a lot too much of a novelty and, if you will pardon me, a damned sight too super, and I think that Sir Leslie Brash who ordered it ought to put on his best spectacles and have a good look to see how he likes it before we go on and finish. As you know I refused responsibility, and I also kept the men's time from the start, and lucky for me for this job is going to cost someone a bit of money.

The painters say the stuff is treacly and don't smell natural, though it flows nicely after the brush and no complaints; but from what our painter told Bloggs I had a good look into things to-day and it's like this. A coat goes on and dries hard and quick, but when the next follows it seems to soften the coat below, and the more coats the worse it gets, at least that's the best I can make of it. As you know, we have four coats on most parts and the finish on one or two doors, and on kitchen and lavatory walls. It seems fairly hard and has a nice oily gloss and a good surface, but if you look closely there is a rim of paint hanging along the bottom edge of doors and bulging out along top of skirtings of painted walls, and where the light is reflected you can make out a kind of a drag and ripple in the surface, in places. In my belief the paint is beginning to creep; it may be hard, but so is bitumen hard and bitumen will flow out like honey give it time. This is only beginning and it isn't going to stop and we shall have R.N.N.S.P. creeping out over the carpets in a few months or I'm mistaken.

It would suit me best to finish and leave Sir Leslie Brash to settle with the manufacturer, but that would be just so much waste, for when you go down you will see what I say is right. I haven't squirted any boiling acids at it nor yet french polished, but if that is to be done it had ought to be soon before Riddoppo super crawls out of the front door and off home, which is about what it's aiming for.

Perhaps Sir, you will let me know what you would wish me to do, as there is no call to have more trouble than can be helped and I gather the paint is no concern of yours any more than mine.

You will pardon me troubling you but thought it might help to keep things straight.

Yours faithfully,

This letter is an autograph, as were the other friendly messages that have engaged Grigblay's evenings with such advantage to Spinlove.

SPINLOVE TO POTCH, DISTRICT SURVEYOR

Sir,   12.12.25.

I am informed by the builder that you have refused certificate of occupation for house at Honeywood on the ground that the window in bedroom No. 5 is not the minimum size required by by-laws. It is true that this room has been increased in size since the plans were approved, but I must point out that the glass area is still more than one-tenth of floor area: viz: glass— three times 3' 6" x 1' 4"= 15 feet; area of floor 10' 9" x 12'= 129 ft.

Yours faithfully,

BRASH TO SPINLOVE

Dear Mr. Spinlove, 13.12.25.

I have desired Messrs. Russ & Co. to transmit cheque for £25 to Messrs Nibnose & Rasper as a "friendly compromise" in ultimate liquidation and final settlement of their iniquitously monstrous and fraudulent claim. I never so resentfully grudged disbursing a remunerative payment more than in this instance, but as Mr. Russ, after his interview with you, confirms endorsement of your opinion, I have no other alternative course but to stand and deliver.

Yours sincerely,

GRIGBLAY TO SPINLOVE

Dear Sir, 13.12.25.

I write to call your attention to the Riddoppo paint which was ordered by Sir Leslie Brash. This is showing signs of creeping and we are afraid the trouble is only beginning. We are going on with the painting, as ordered, until we receive other directions.

Yours faithfully,

Appearances are that Spinlove has had a talk with Grigblay and arranged that he shall write this formal notification. It is to be observed that in this matter Spinlove is not responsible to Brash, who ordered the paint himself contrary to his architect's advice. Grigblay, as we see, takes the position of being a disinterested person, and Spinlove will be wise to do the same or he may, before he knows it, fasten responsibility upon himself by one of those redundancies which are so characteristic of his letters.

SPINLOVE TO BRASH

Dear Sir Leslie Brash, 16.12.25.

I enclose copy of letter I have received from Mr. Grigblay, and await your instructions. I understand that by "creeping" is meant that the paint is slowly flowing down the walls, doors, etc.

Yours sincerely,

Spinlove is justly entitled to disclaim responsibility, but if he had any sense of humour—and we know he has none—he could not blandly have passed the matter over to Brash without full explanation. Spinlove's original objection was rather to the scheme of decorations than to the risk of the paint's failure, as paint: and Brash has good cause for grievance that he was not particularly warned of that risk. It is true he would probably, in giving rein to his temper, have scorned the advice, but he can none the less complain that he was never given a chance of doing so. Spinlove's excuse, of course, is ignorance: he has not had the experience which would have made unnecessary the experience he is now getting.

BRASH TO SPINLOVE

Dear Mr. Spinlove,   18.12.25.

I do not precisely apprehend why you refer Mr. Grigblay's objection to the super-paint to me. That is a matter of technical craftsmanship upon which I anticipate you are competent to adjudicate. I am aware that Mr. Grigblay has all along evinced a protracted resistance opposed to Riddoppo, but after viewing the edifice to-day I can only asseverate—with my respects to Mr. Grigblay and acknowledgments to yourself—that I never viewed a more smooth or glossy or delightfully-tinted surface colouring. I desire that you will direct Mr. Grigblay to proceed with the work, and oblige me by desisting from making these obstructive representations.

Yours sincerely,

SPINLOVE TO POTCH

Sir,   20.12.25.

Permit me to remind you that I have received no reply to my letter of eight days ago. The builder informs me that no certificate has been received by him. As the owner intends to occupy the house very shortly I shall be obliged by your attention to the matter.

Yours faithfully,

POTCH TO SPINLOVE

Sir,   18.12.25.

I duly received your favour informing me that three times 3' 6" into 1' 4" makes 15 feet, but did not understand you wanted me to check same for you. Unfortunately my Council does not allow me to use up their time teaching London architects to square dimensions, but to oblige you my office boy has kindly gone over and makes it 14.

I am, sir,
Yours faithfully,

As Potch's principle is always to hit below the belt, he will feel he has fetched Spinlove a walloper—and even Spinlove must admit a touch.

SPINLOVE TO POTCH

Sir,   19.12.25.

The slip was perfectly obvious and whether 14 or 15 feet is of no kind of consequence. You admit the window area is 14 ft. and floor area 129, and I must ask for certificate without more delay or I shall apply to your Council's Clerk.

Yours faithfully,

POTCH TO SPINLOVE

Sir,   29.12.25.

I have received your letter stating I agree your measurements of floor and window at Honeywood, but can find no record of agreement in this office and shall be glad of reference and date as my assistant says nothing on files.

I am, Sir,
Yours faithfully,

This is a mere quibble intended to obstruct and annoy.

SPINLOVE TO POTCH

Sir,   31.12.25.

I understood you accepted the figures I gave—namely, 14 ft. super for the window and 129 ft. for the floor of bedroom. I must ask you either to forward certificate without delay or appoint someone to agree dimensions on the spot.

Yours faithfully,

SPINLOVE TO BRASH

Dear Sir Leslie Brash,   31.12.25.

The holiday has prevented my replying sooner to your letter.

It is well understood by Mr. Grigblay and myself that the Riddoppo paint is being used by your orders and under your responsibility, and it would suit Mr. Grigblay to finish the painting and have done with it. He pointed out to me what he thinks to be a serious defect and I considered it my duty to report his views, which are quite disinterested, to you. I agree that, superficially, the finished painting looks well; the work has been carefully and skilfully done. It requires a practised eye to notice the defect, but apparently a creeping action has begun. If you look at the bottoms of doors and along tops of skirtings below painted walls you will see rims of paint, and a drag or ripple in the surface can also be discerned in places. Mr. Grigblay thinks the defect will increase. The painting is being proceeded with, as you ask.

With best wishes to Lady Brash and yourself for the New Year.

Yours sincerely,

This is an adequate and wary letter. Spinlove does well to make no recommendation. To do so would associate him with future difficulties and, in fact, no one except the manufacturers of the paint can advise Brash.

POTCH TO SPINLOVE

Sir,   31.12.25.

I do not know what sort of foot rule you use but I go by English Standard (Pinchlocks' Double Folding Pocket 4s. 3d.); and suggest you get a new tape as yours is stretched.

My inspector notes glass—three times 3' 5" into 1' 3"= 12' 10"; floor 10' 11" x 12' 2"=132.'

I am, Sir,
Yours faithfully,

The measure 12 ft. 10 in., by the system employed in building operations, represents 12 feet superficial and $\frac{10}{12}$ of a superficial foot or $12\frac{5}{6}$ feet super; actually, 12 square feet and 120 square inches.

SPINLOVE TO GRIGBLAY

Dear Sir,   1.1.26.

I enclose copies of letter to the District Surveyor and his reply.
My measures are taken from the half inch joinery detail, and from
brick dimensions of room, allowing 2" on each wall for plaster and
skirting. Will you ask your foreman to check my figures against
Mr. Potch's and let me know where the discrepancy is. *Urgent.*

Yours faithfully,

BRASH TO SPINLOVE

Dear Mr. Spinlove,   2.1.26.

I must request to be permitted to reiterate over again that I am
not equipped to adjudicate in a technical matter appertaining to
craftsmanship and which I apprehend belongs to the province of
my professional adviser—by which term I designate yourself—to
see that the painters perform their functions in an efficient manner.

I again inspected the mansion yesterday and Mr. Bloggs indicated what he deemed irregularities but which are, I apprehend, of
quite immaterial significance.

With reciprocations of your seasonable good wishes from Lady
Brash and myself,

Yours sincerely,

*Most lordly and most melancholy! Brash's self-sufficiency will not
allow him to "apprehend" the facts.*

SPINLOVE TO BRASH

Dear Sir Leslie Brash,   4.1.26.

My services are, of course, entirely at your disposal but I am
unable to tell Mr. Grigblay how to deal with the defective paint for
I know nothing of Riddoppo, which as you are aware, is a "new
novelty super-paint compounded of new secret ingredients". You
will recall that I advised against its use and that neither Mr. Grigblay
nor myself were able to accept responsibility for it. The blemish is,
so far, inconspicuous, but it may be a symptom of inherent defects.

Yours sincerely,

Spinlove here is "reiterating over again" the very thing Brash has asked him to "desist from intimating", but his tenacity is here very much to the point. When Riddoppo begins to "crawl out of the front door and off home"—as Grigblay expects it one day will—this letter will safeguard Spinlove from being involved in the catastrophe. The very long head James wears through these interchanges he owes, no doubt, to Grigblay having "put him wise", as they say in America.

BRASH TO SPINLOVE

Dear Mr. Spinlove,   7.1.26.

I have received your further communication *anent* Riddoppo. I can only once again asseverate that the blemishes indicated by Mr. Bloggs are of insignificant importance and that the painting satisfies the anticipations of the person most vitally concerned who is paying for it, and who I apprehend to be not precisely Mr. Grigblay nor my architect, but, to be brief, myself alone.

The lettering on the doors is esteemed by us as a distinct advance in the improvement of the house, and you will be gratified when I intimate to you that we agree that the parti-coloured variegations of tints originally proposed would not have provided the refined appearance now obtaining. Will you be so obliging as to have the door of the chamber apartment now lettered "Salmon" altered to "Strawberry", as the connected association is unpleasantly distasteful to Lady Brash.

We are proposing to arrange to move in our furniture on the 22nd inst. prox.

Believe me,
Yours sincerely,

Brash is evidently pleased with the house. We may detect in his letter a note of bland, proprietary self-congratulation.

SPINLOVE TO GRIGBLAY

Dear Mr. Grigblay,   8.1.26.

Sir Leslie Brash wishes the painting with Riddoppo completed as he does not consider the defects of any importance. He proposes to move in furniture on the 22nd. Will that be possible? I enclose a list of matters which need attention.

Will you please have the door now lettered "Salmon" altered to "Raspberry".

Yours faithfully,

Spinlove has made a slip here.

GRIGBLAY TO SPINLOVE

Dear Sir,   8.1.26.

Our foreman has checked measurements and says Mr. Potch is right for glass area. Your figures are correct clear of window-frames. The iron casements stand in $\frac{9}{16}$ in. full. Mr. Potch's dimensions are also right for area of room but he has measured above skirtings. Our foreman suggests why not fill in recess with cupboard fixture so as to reduce floor area.

Yours faithfully,

It is to be noted that in most right designs—if not entirely in all— the size of casements is a unit of the elevations which cannot be varied, and that the minimum of one-tenth of floor area for windows gives an excessive amount of light to some rooms with some aspects, if aesthetic judgment rather than hygienic theory is the guide. The consequences are that to obtain a good disposition of windows in the elevation and an adequate, but not excessive, window area to rooms is a matter which particularly exercises the ingenuity of the designer. The bedroom in question was properly lighted by a range of three casements, but the moving of the partition has increased the floor area up to, or over, the maximum size allowed by the by-laws in respect of these three casements. If a fourth casement is added it will be likely to play "Old Harry" with the elevation and to over-light the room, and as the only way of arranging four casements will probably be to take the window out, remake it with new head and cill and recentre it in the elevation, the breaking down and making good of brickwork is likely to show up on the elevation for some time. Though everyone else may soon forget the ungainly room and never notice the botched elevation, Spinlove will remember his regrets to the end of his life. Potch does not know this and would not understand if it were explained to him; the annoyance, humiliation and cost to his rival and the man who employs him, is his aim.

SPINLOVE TO POTCH

Dear Sir,   9.1.26.

I find that your measures of windows are taken to the glass line, and of floors to walls above skirtings.

My measures are taken to the line of the frames as this, in my experience, is customary, and I claim that the floor area is properly measured up to skirtings and not above them.

Even if you insist on the window area being estimated as the area of actual glass, the floor area, measured to skirtings, is still only two-thirds of one square foot more than ten times that of windows and, I submit, so small a discrepancy depending on an unusually exacting computation of window area, does not justify the withholding of the certificate. The addition of another casement is an extremely awkward matter and will ruin the elevation and is surely a scarcely reasonable demand?

The owner wishes to move in on the 22nd, so time is short. I hope, therefore, that with these explanations before you, you will feel able to draw the certificate.

Yours faithfully,

This is a quite foolish letter. Spinlove seems to be so distressed at the prospect of having to mutilate his elevation and spoil the room that he is reduced to begging for mercy, which, as he must know, is perfectly useless. A man like Potch reacts only to impulses of greed or funk and, as Spinlove is incapable of "working it", he must fight.

Spinlove's measure of window area is 14 ft.: Potch's 12. The difference represents only $\frac{1}{2}$ in. on face of each frame, but involves a floor area of $11\frac{2}{3}$ ft.

SPINLOVE TO BRASH

Dear Sir Leslie Brash,   11.1.26.

I was speaking to Mr. Grigblay on the telephone to-day and I fear it will not be possible for you to move in on the 22nd nor, indeed, this month. As you know, there are a good many odds and ends remaining to be done and the painting of various cupboard fittings Lady Brash has ordered have yet to be finished, and I do not think you ought to fix a date much before February 12. I am also sorry to say that the Local Authority has refused certificate of occupation on the grounds that the window in bedroom No. 5 is not big enough, but I am hoping to get this matter settled quite shortly.

Yours faithfully,

POTCH TO SPINLOVE

Sir,   12.1.26.

You should not have made the window too small if you did not care for the trouble of altering it larger. My Council cannot change its by-laws to suit A.R.I.B.A.s and if time is short you would be better correcting your mistakes than wasting more of it writing letters instead.

I am obliged to you for pointing out what my duties are, but it would be better if you spent your time some other way as it happens I have had more chance of learning it than what young London office architects have.

I am, Sir,
Yours faithfully,

Spinlove's letter produces an insult from the Potch mechanism as surely as his penny would a bit of chocolate out of an automatic machine.

The Model By-laws which Local Authorities are at liberty to select from and "adopt" at will speak of "floor area" and "area of windows clear of frames". Spinlove has either been misled by a bluff on the part of Potch and overlooked this last definition, or the words "clear of frames" may possibly have been omitted from the Marlford District Council's version. In the latter event Spinlove would get his measurements upheld by appeal to the local Government Board.

SPINLOVE TO GRIGBLAY

Dear Sir,   15.1.26.

I cannot reduce floor area by putting cupboard fixture in recess as this is wanted to take Lady Brash's wardrobe.

I enclose detail of a small casement window. This, as you will see, is to go over the lavatory basin and will come very nearly central between the ranges of adjoining casements. I am sorry to have to order the work, but the Surveyor insists.

Yours faithfully,

BRASH TO SPINLOVE

Dear Mr. Spinlove,   14.1.26.

I really must asseverate my protestation at the successive procrastinations *anent* completion. Permit me to remind you that the
builders contracted for eventual occupation on or before Decem-
ber 11th last year; I was then informed I might arrange to take up
residence shortly after Xmas, and subsequently the 22nd was the
extended date fixed. I am now informed that the middle of next
February prox. is the anticipated day, and am given to apprehend
that this date may eventually be eliminated and so on infinitum
(*sic*), which is, as you will agree—if you will permit me to express
myself so—a most preposterous succession of prevarications and
procrastinations.

In addition to these delays and postponements, for which I apprehend the contractor is responsible, you now inform me that the
necessary certificate entitling me to occupy the house is not forth-
coming because, forsooth, you have made one of the windows too
small! Are we ever going to get into the house at all?—that I apprehend to be a question to which it is now incumbent on me to
request a definite assurance. Why is the window not large enough?
I apprehend that to be a matter on which I was entitled to rely
upon your judicial discretion.

Yours sincerely,

*Our sympathies may well be with Brash's impatience, though not
with his grievance, which is unreasonable. He and Lady Brash have, in
fact, been accountable for greater delays than they complain of; but for
one reason or another there always are delays, and Grigblay, all circumstances considered, has done well not to be more behindhand than he is.*

(CONFIDENTIAL) GRIGBLAY TO SPINLOVE

Sir,   17.1.26.

I noticed your correspondence with Mr. Potch in the office and
have seen your detail of little port-hole makeweight. I fancy it goes
against the grain for I know something of the way architects feel,
so I take the liberty to let you know that Mr. Potch is not so particular with his own building nor yet with that of some others, and

I can drop him a hint that will make that certificate come by special messenger. If you do not care for that—and I would rather not start any mix up with Mr. Potch—why not brad a bit of ovolo down on the floor against the skirting just to make it easy for the poor housemaid to sweep the dust out of the corners and not tire her pretty self? $\frac{1}{2}$ in. wide would bring the floor area down to limit and leave a bit over for good manners. No trouble to take up again before the family move in.

With apologies for troubling you but thought you might like to do it.

Yours faithfully,

SPINLOVE TO BRASH

Dear Sir Leslie Brash,   19.1.26.

The 22nd was named by *you*. I said "before the end of the month", and were it not for the many fittings which have been ordered only after the house is on the point of completion, there would be no reason why you should not move in this month.

You must permit me to excuse myself. The window of bedroom No. 5 was big enough for the room as I planned it, but the room was made too big for the window when, by your orders, the partition was moved. The grounds for the Council's objection are trivial and since I last wrote I have succeeded, I think, in arranging matters and there will be no delay on this account .

Yours sincerely,

Spinlove has certainly advanced in discretion and force; his early diffidence and shyness, and consequent indecision and impulse to be plausible and to explain and justify himself, have in great part disappeared. The reason is, no doubt, that he now knows the person he has to deal with and feels himself master of the position now that his knowledge of past history, rather than his judgment in making new, is involved.

SPINLOVE TO GRIGBLAY

Dear Mr. Grigblay,   18.1.26.

I am much obliged for your letter. Will you please have the skirting fillet fixed as you suggest and return my detail No. 49.

Yours very truly,

SPINLOVE TO POTCH

Sir,   22.1.26.

I write to notify you that lighting of bedroom No. 5 at
Honeywood has now been amended to comply with the by-laws,
and to apply for certificate of occupation.

Yours faithfully,

SIR LESLIE BRASH MOVES IN

(CONFIDENTIAL) GRIGBLAY TO SPINLOVE

Sir,   28.1.26.

I went down to Honeywood to-day to have a look round and you may tell Sir Leslie Brash the house will be ready for him on February 10th, unless he orders other work to keep himself out of it. The road etc. will take a couple of weeks to finish and had better stand till the old gentleman has got his furniture in. I've seen something of the mess these heavy lorries can make of a new road and this one is none too heavily bottomed. Bloggs will be clearing up next week.

While I was down there Mr. Potch paid us a friendly call. He ran to bedroom No. 5 as if he'd buried a bone there, and I followed and found him huffing and blowing his nose; but I soon stopped his nonsense and we shall get the certificate in a day or two.

Riddoppo super is beginning to act up and I shall be glad to be out. Potch went away with a bit of it on his behind end, but I don't know where he got it for the surface is dry and firm though it does not look to be so underneath, for in places it is beginning to ride up over itself, and it is hanging from the bottoms of doors again for all it was cut away once, and a bead of it laying along top of skirtings. There is one place where furnace flue goes up kitchen wall, where it is beginning to craze like a really fine old picture. In my opinion it will all have to come off again, unless it's kept on to prevent the house catching fire, but it can't be burnt off, because it's fireproof, and it can't be pickled off because it's acid proof, so there you are! It is a pity the makers, who had such a lot to say about laying it on, didn't spare a word or two about getting it off. Apologizing for troubling you but thought best to tell you.

Yours truly,

GRIGBLAY TO SPINLOVE

Dear Sir,   31.1.26.

We have received certificate of occupation from the District Council's Surveyor.

We note that your client wishes to move in on the 8th, instead of the 10th as arranged, and we think there will be no objection to this.

We enclose rough approximate statement of account and shall be glad of your final certificate. The detailed statement will follow in due course.

Yours faithfully,

Grigblay is entitled to a certificate for the whole value of the work less 5 per cent, on completion.

HONEYWOOD GRANGE,
MARLFORD,
KENT

Tel.: FORGETMENOT 178.
Postal Address: THADDINGTON.
Station: WEDGFIELD JUNC.: 4 *m.*
         (Taxi 5s.)

My dear Mr. Spinlove,   13.2.26.

Here we are eventually! We commenced to take up residence at Honeywood Grange on Thursday and occupied the sleeping apartments last night for the first occasion. Although there still remain a vast number of dispositions of furniture to adjust I desire, on behalf of Lady Brash and myself, to intimate that we are completely charmed and delighted with the mansion. We consider it to be most elegant in every respect and anticipate that we shall esteem the convenience and appropriateness of the various different arrangements still more as time progresses, and we already have had occasion to appreciate the recommendations you have suggested and your forethought in providing beforehand many excellent devices. We shall anticipate seeing you here when we have settled down. Believe me with best regards from Lady Brash and myself,

Yours very sincerely,

So that's that; and a handsome letter for even a grateful client to write.

SPINLOVE TO BRASH

Dear Sir Leslie,   14.2.26.

Very many thanks to you and to Lady Brash for your most kind letter, which, I can assure you, gave me great pleasure. I shall look forward to seeing the house when you have settled down. One cannot really see a house properly until it has been furnished.

I am sure that Mr. Grigblay would very much appreciate a line from you telling him you are pleased with his work. He has taken great pains to make it a success.

With kind regards and good wishes to Lady Brash and yourself,

Yours sincerely,

And so the file ends; but it ends at the point where the folder will hold no more papers: the last score of letters have, in fact, been packed under the clip to bring the chapter to a close—for a chapter, only, it is. There must somewhere in Spinlove's office be another chapter enshrined in another folder. That second chapter* may be a short and uneventful chapter, or it may be neither short nor uneventful nor even the last. The Honeywood account has to be settled, and the numerous items of that account may raise many questions of fact and lead to a review of events gone almost out of memory. Question of extras may arise in which the architect, although involved by his own acts of omission or commission, has to keep the scales balanced between builder and client, and gild for the latter, as best he may, the often bitter pill called "final balance due". Last, this second chapter will contain the history, be it long or short, of the inevitable small defects and the possible big ones, which reveal themselves after a house has been occupied and which, should they appear within nine months—or more or less—and so far as they are due to improper workmanship or materials, the builder is engaged under the terms of his contract to make good. Yet a third chapter clipped, perhaps, within another folder may lie upon Spinlove's shelves; but we, who have come to know him, may hope that it does not exist. It could only be a record of pains and miseries—a chapter of bitter memories; for while the builder's liabilities end when he has redeemed those of his faults which reveal themselves within the limit of nine, or other, months fixed by the *contract, the architect's liabilities are for all defects due to his negligence, whether faults of himself, of manufacturers, of specialists or of builders, which may appear within the limit of six years fixed by the law. We know, however, nothing of what other files may lie in Spinlove's office. The last page of* The Honeywood File *is the front cover, and that we now close.*

*This second chapter will be published under the title *The Honeywood Settlement.*

X